MaF 08
2015

Imaginary Brightness
A Novel

Sheila Myers

Map: 1899 Raquette Lake Quad USGS
Source: Old Book Art
http://www.gallery.oldbookart.com/

Cover Design
Brendan Cox Design Studio
http://www.brendancox.co.uk

Owl sketch by Melissa Johnson

This is a work of fiction. Although some of the characters in this story are historical figures and some events are based on facts, the story is a product of the author's imagination.

Library of Congress Control Number: 2015902294
CreateSpace Independent Publishing Platform, North Charleston, SC

ISBN-13: 978-1506181325
ISBN-10: 1506181325

DEDICATION

To librarians everywhere, because they never stop searching.

Many Love
+ Jerry –
Enjoy the story!
Sheila Myers

"History, like love, is so apt to surround her heroes with an atmosphere of imaginary brightness."
— James Fenimore Cooper, The Last of the Mohicans

List of Places

Binstead – Locock Country Estate, Isle of Wight, England

Bluff Point - Stott Family Camp, Raquette Lake, NY

Camp Kirby - Raquette Lake, NY

Camp Huntington (Pine Knot) - Durant Family Camp, Raquette Lake, NY

Camp Uncas – William West Durant's second great camp

Eighth Lake, NY - home of Lawrence Family

North Creek, NY – Durant family home

Osborne House – country estate of Queen Victoria, Isle of Wight, England

Osprey Island – Alvah Dunning's cabin, Raquette Lake, NY

Prospect House – Frederick Durant's Hotel, Blue Mountain Lake, NY

Sagamore – William West Durant's third great camp

Saratoga, NY – location of Adirondack Railroad offices

Thirlestane – Napier family estate, Scotland

Under the Hemlocks /Antlers, Bennett's hotels, Raquette Lake, NY

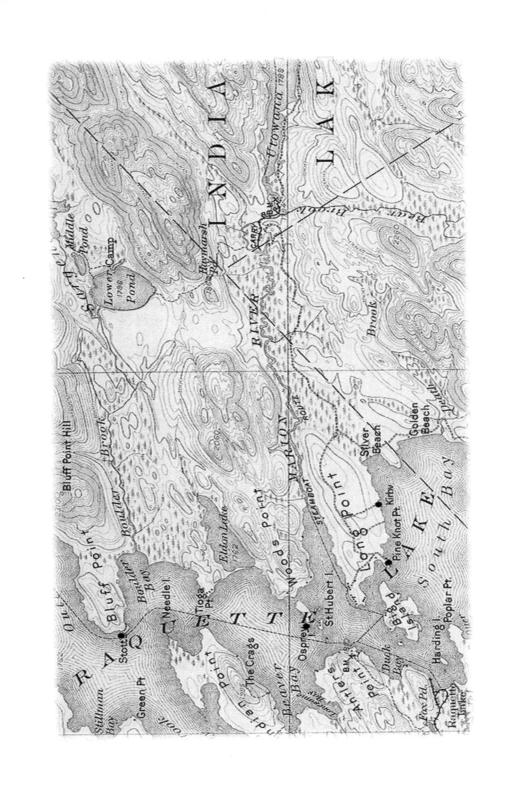

Part One

LONDON
DECEMBER 1873

On the rare occasions that Dr. Durant came to visit, William always found his habit of pacing the floor while talking unnerving. This time however, it wasn't his father wearing down the carpet that unsettled William. It was what he was telling them.

"You're all coming home to America. I've invested in land in the Adirondacks," Dr. Durant told his family as they gathered around the fireplace in the parlor of their apartment on Hertford Street.

"Where are on earth is that? And how do you pronounce it again? Add der rawn dax?'" Ella said.

"Where is Margaret with my tea?" Dr. Durant stopped to scout for his wife's companion, who had gone into the kitchen to make it. The clock on the mantel chimed two pm and he reached for his pocket watch.

"We're going to build another railroad," he said, glancing at his watch. Satisfied it was accurate, he clicked the case shut and put it back in his waistcoat pocket.

William stood leaning against the mantel, observing his father. Checking the time regularly was another habit Dr. Durant must have picked up while he was building the transcontinental line. It was the third time within the hour he had consulted his timepiece.

"William will assist in the enterprise. I envision a full transportation system from New York City that will eventually take passengers through the Adirondacks all the way to Canada."

He directed his entrepreneurial enthusiasm at William, gesticulating wildly and in the process almost sideswiping Margaret when she came up behind him with the tray of tea.

"I planned it all out. We are going to live in North Creek where I've purchased a lumber mill. All of us, except William, who will need to work in New York City," he said.

This was unexpected news. Indeed, William had returned only days before from his trip down the Nile and couldn't wait to brag about it to his friends at the clubs on Piccadilly. He and Charlie Arkwright had pitched tents at various sites along the river where they bagged a crocodile, hippo, several exotic birds and a monkey— even had the head to prove it. He had been planning another expedition, this time to India, until now. Because according to his father, there wouldn't be another one.

Dr. Durant was summoning his family home to New York State. "I am optimistic about our future. But we will need to economize," he said, leveling his gaze at William.

William wondered if this meant that the family finances were under duress but didn't dare ask.

"Where is North Creek?" Ella asked. When she failed to capture her father's attention she turned to William. *"Qu'est-ce qu'il dit?"*

William was about to respond in French that he had no idea what their father was talking about either but thought better of it when he saw him glare at Ella for speaking in 'code'.

"Pet, why are we in such a hurry? Can't we stay here through the year? We have the apartment let until October. And I would like time to say goodbye to our family and friends," Hannah said.

"No. I've already begun to look for someone to take over our lease," he said, neglecting the tea Margaret poured. He turned to face his wife who was sitting dumbstruck on the divan.

"I see." Hannah bit her lower lip and looked around the room at their scattered belongings.

Dr. Durant hadn't anticipated the family's stunned reaction.

"You knew this day would come eventually," he said sternly. "Here, maybe this will help."

He pulled a map out of his frock coat, unfolded it, and placed it on Hannah's lap. Ella quickly rose from her seat to hover over her mother's shoulder as her father pointed to North Creek on the map.

It was a tiny speck lodged next to a mountain named Gore, surrounded by forests, the nearest community miles away. It took a few minutes for them to take it all in, but once they did, Ella and Hannah were confronted with the reality of being shipped off to some outpost town in the foothills of the Adirondack wilderness.

William didn't move. He stood watching his sister and mother fuss over the map, murmuring about how far away New York City was from North Creek. Ella let out a heavy sigh and sank back in her seat.

"I suppose we need to consider what we can bring with us. What's the climate like?" Hannah said.

"Of course, of course, we will figure all of that out soon enough. Now if you'll excuse me, I have business to attend to," Dr. Durant said. Hastily, he retreated to the library, shutting the door firmly behind him.

Hannah and Ella turned their gaze beseechingly to William. He was as shocked as they were by his father's news and unwillingness to discuss it further. How dare the man treat his family this way!

"I'll talk to him," he said. He left his spot by the mantel and entered the library without knocking.

"Father, what is the meaning of this? You ask us to uproot ourselves so quickly without any explanation of what to expect."

"Sit down son," Dr. Durant said. He poured himself a snifter of brandy and pointed his glass at William. "Have a drink with me?"

William took a seat. His heart was beating so hard in his chest he wondered if his father could hear it.

Dr. Durant passed William a drink and sat down himself.

"Son, you've had the best upbringing I could provide. Private tutors, hunting and riding lessons, travel. But the extravagance has to end. Now. Your mother showed me the bill from the Shepheard's Hotel in Cairo. What were you doing there?

Lavishing everyone you met with wine and food?" He shook his head in dismay. "It's time you start earning money instead of spending it."

William took a sip of his drink and assessed his options. He wanted to stay in London. He just had to convince his father this would benefit the family. "Let me stay in London and find investors for your railroad. After all, it was here you found your first investors for the Union Pacific."

The doctor downed most of his drink in one swallow and shook his head. "No. I need you to attract investors in New York. And I need you to help us plan the building of our family vacation home in the Adirondacks. That is where we will entertain and entice them. It is already a popular vacation destination. The *New York Times* calls it the Central Park for the World."

His father rose to refill his glass and walked about the room holding his snifter in the air, waving it around.

"You should see it, Will, the forests — they are virgin — just ripe for cutting. And the iron ore, we have mines. This railroad will bring people in to work, we can build them homes. We can build whole communities!"

"I have plans for this year's deer stalking season at Thirlestane with Bill Napier and well, I still don't see why I can't stay and—"

Dr. Durant scowled, his face darkening. "It's time you grew up and earned your keep. You're twenty-four. A man now. You need to consider your future, in America. The decision is made," he said. "You and your mother and sister are coming home, and that's the end of it."

"But Father—"

"Enough! This is not a debate. I am done talking." Dr. Durant slammed his glass down on the small table, breaking the delicate stem. The sound startled them both.

"I see." William cleared his throat uncomfortably.

"Son, look here." Dr. Durant softened. He left the broken glass to search through his leather satchel on the floor. He pulled out a small book and gave it to William. "It's a gift. The Adirondack forests are wonderful hunting grounds. The best you've ever witnessed. There are deer, pheasant, grouse, bear, catamounts."

"Catamounts? Really? Are the forests that ancient?" William took the book from his father and examined it. It was entitled: *Adventures in the Wilderness* by W.H. Murray.

"This book you see," his father said, planting his finger on the cover, "is all about the opportunities for hunting, camping, and taking in the beauty of the Adirondacks, and it's causing everyone to take notice of the area."

Dr. Durant continued, his voice growing louder and faster. "People are gobbling up the stories, Will. Everyone is looking for adventure in the woods, thanks to this genius." He paused and poured himself a drink, then turned and raised it to William. "And best of all — we are one of the largest land owners in the region. Think about that!" he said triumphantly, throwing back his head and emptying the brandy glass in one swallow.

William felt he was in a battle that he had no way of winning. He half-heartedly leafed through the pages of *Adventures in the Wilderness*. He couldn't help but be in awe of the man and his positive outlook. Yet underlying his public persona William sensed a suppressed agitation he hadn't experienced with his father before.

Why was he dragging them back to the States? It was ruining everything, all of William's plans. And why not allow him to stay behind to conduct his father's business from England? What, exactly, was his father hiding from him, from all of them?

BINSTEAD, ISLE OF WIGHT
BOXING DAY 1873

The air smelled like damp earth and wet dog. William's horse was jittering, its clomping hooves echoed off the flagstones in front of the Lococks' stable. He looked round at the other riders who, like him, were eager for the courtiers to arrive from Osborne House, Queen Victoria's holiday home, so the foxhunt could begin.

William glanced at his sister, sitting proudly on her horse across from the men, casting furtive glances at Basil Napier.

Dear God, he thought, try not to make a fool of yourself Ella.

Basil, however, didn't seem to mind: William watched as he maneuvered his horse away from his brothers and discreetly guided it next to hers.

"That is a fine mare," Basil said, resting his hands on the mane of Ella's horse. She blushed and glanced at the sea.

"I can see you know how to manage her."

Ella sat upright at the compliment. "I ride her as often as possible, when the weather permits us to come visit."

Basil moved his eyes over her long figure, taking in her slim riding skirt, her right leg hoisted up on the leaping horn. "Ready for an adventure in that saddle are you?"

"The saddle was a gift from my father for my twentieth birthday. He wants me to feel secure while riding." She neglected to mention how she had argued with her mother and father about the necessity of the specially made and expensive saddle that was fitted with an extra pommel so she could jump.

"Very good. I can't imagine sitting sidesaddle during a hunt; it is a wonder women can enjoy hunting at all," Basil said. Ella smiled at his small gesture of approval.

Jack Napier's horse trotted up alongside William's and he slapped William lightly on his sleeve. "Seems my brother has found his way to your sister again," he said, nodding over at the lovestruck couple.

"Yes, and for once my sister seems to be at a loss for words."

The horses' ears flickered at a distant sound, and the riders turned their heads in unison to see the rest of the hunt party trotting up the path. Florence Jones was among them, sauntering into the circle of riders on her grey mare. She appeared especially festive in a bright green riding habit, her blonde curls escaping from under her velveteen hat. William was giddy at the sight of her, and as anxious as the horses and hounds for the hunt to begin so he could show off his riding prowess.

While the fox hunting party commenced with merry-making — complimenting each other on their attire, flirting with members of the opposite sex, wishing each other Merry Christmas — the Lococks' servants carefully weaved between their horses, passing around stirrup cups filled with wassail. William lifted his glass to his lips, and winked at Florence. She batted her eyes at him, and tossed her head back, laughing at something someone next to her said while they waited for the command from the Master of the Hunt.

Once the hounds and hunt terrier were let loose, William's horse, along with the others, wasted no time following in chase. The terrier rooted a red fox out of a covert and into the open fields within minutes, and the horses leapt into full gallop after the hounds, tailing the small canine. William could see flashes of red fur bounding up and down in the tall grass of the meadow.

It was a breathless run for the riders. The hounds bayed excitedly, while the wind whipped William's face. His ears were ringing from the men's cries, the blare of the horn and the thunderous pounding of the horses' hooves. He turned his head to view the ladies' progress. Ella was laughing, the wind had blown her hat off and her cheeks were pink from the excitement, but Florence was trailing cautiously behind. When William looked forward he saw why: a high hedge about 20 rods ahead meant they would have to jump to follow the fox and hounds crawling under it to the other side.

William fell back and pulled up alongside his sister, motioning for her to stop before trying to make the jump. He knew she could make it, but he also knew Florence couldn't, and he didn't want his sister to show her up. Ella scowled at him. He motioned again and took hold of her reins to slow down the mare. By then Florence had reached them.

"You two ladies take the path around the hedge farther down field," he instructed, pointing to the right. He was off before Ella could protest.

Catching up to the others, he jumped the hedgerow in time to see the hounds heading toward a field house where they would surely corner the fox. When the riders pulled up, the pack was tearing it apart. The Master of the Hunt presented the tail to Jack Napier for his superb horsemanship.

"How dare you make me stop at full gallop. I could have made that jump without any trouble at all and you know it," Ella said to William as they were being driven later that evening back to Binstead for a gala.

William sighed. "I didn't want Florence to feel that she had to make the jump as well and she may have attempted it just because you had."

"Pffft. If she rode properly and had the right saddle she could have made that jump," Ella said.

"For once try not to think only of yourself. You would never have considered that jump if father hadn't given in to your constant nagging for that custom-made saddle. And I was the one that intervened for you remember?"

Ella smiled mischievously, "We both know why you stopped me from making the jump."

"If my gallantry lands me on Florence's dance card more than once this evening, then yes, all the better for me," William said, slapping her knee lightly with his gloves.

"All the better for you, yes, but I had to endure the indignity of reining in my horse so you could appear chivalrous."

William raised a brow. "Better to rein in your horse than to show off for Basil Napier."

"I wasn't showing off for anyone. Unlike you with Florence," Ella retorted.

"Oh yes you were," William said with a smile and gazed out the window at the growing dark.

Ella opened her mouth to protest but before she could speak the driver called back to the siblings, "Mr. Durant, we have arrived at the Locock residence."

Charles Locock, the Durants' lawyer in England, and his wife, Fanny, greeted them at the grand entrance hall in Binstead.

"How are you enjoying your stay in Cowes?" Fanny asked them.

"We have a wonderful cottage overlooking the sea," William said.

"How lovely. Your parents arrived about an hour ago," Fanny said. She turned to Ella. "Your mother is waiting for you, Ella, in the ladies' drawing room. Nell will show you the way." Fanny took hold of Ella's arm and handed her over to the servant waiting to take her coat and hat and guide her to the ladies' drawing room.

After preparing himself in the drawing room set aside for the men, William went to the ballroom floor.

"Champagne sir?" A servant held a tray up to him.

He took a crystal glass from the tray, and scanned the room until he saw his father. Dr. Durant was occupying a corner with Thomas Brassey, whose family were investors in the Union Pacific

Railroad. William knew Brassey, had raced him at Cowes, and started toward them to find out if the conversation was one of business or pleasure, although he guessed it was not about yachting. His father looked as if he was chewing Brassey's ear off.

"Willie, there you are old boy." Charlie Arkwright sallied from nowhere to William's side, preventing him from crossing the room.

"Charlie, I was just looking for you," William lied.

Jack Napier came out of the men's drawing room and approached them. Arkwright turned to William, "Say, did I tell you that man Lorenzo asked if he could photograph the two of us with our trophies from our trip up the Nile?"

Jack laughed. "I can see it now, Charlie, you and the monkey-head. There'd be quite a resemblance."

"Bahhhh." Arkwright playfully punched Jack in the arm. He turned his attention to William. "Willie, we must plan our next expedition to Egypt soon."

"It will have to wait, Charlie. My father has informed us we are to return to America," William said.

"You're leaving England?"

"Hopefully I won't be away long. It's probably just temporary; I imagine my main task will be here in England, finding investors for his newest company." As soon as the words were out of his mouth William knew it was largely wishful thinking, but as he watched his father out of the corner of his eye, he sensed that maybe there still was a chance for him to do his father's business in London.

"Where are your lovely sister and mother?" Jack asked.

Dr. Durant signaled to William after Brassey left to talk to someone else.

"They are waiting for us. If you'll excuse me." William turned from his friends to join his father so they could escort the ladies from the drawing room to the ballroom seating area.

The ballroom was humming with the sounds of voices and tuning violins. Sprigs of holly were tied with red ribbons to candelabras and banisters. Ladies in flouncing dresses with diamond-studded aigrettes fastened to their heads found their seats against the wall. They sipped champagne on the opposite side of the room from the men, eyeing them coyly, waiting for the first dance set of the evening.

William stood next to his father, chatting with a group of men about yacht racing, when he noticed Florence being escorted by her brother to the floor. He waited patiently for her to sit, and when he thought a reasonable amount of time had passed, excused himself and walked calmly across the floor to where she was seated.

Bill Napier stopped him mid-way. "That was quite a hunt today wasn't it?"

"Brilliant." William scowled, his eyes focused beyond Napier. Bill turned to see the object of his irritation. Charlie Arkwright, pencil in hand, was scrawling on Florence's dance card.

"Did I prevent you from reaching my cousin in time to get on her dance card before Arkwright?" Napier chuckled.

They watched as Charlie flirted with Florence.

"Go, quickly. Before her card is full. She'd prefer to dance with you all night if she could. And I see I need to move quickly as well if I'm to have a dance with my maiden." Bill Napier clapped him on the back and headed off in the direction of his own quarry.

William bowed slightly in front of Florence.

"May I have the honor of your hand for the first set?" he said.

Florence blushed and handed William her card as the ladies around her giggled.

"Perhaps the second?" one of her companions said.

William took the small pencil to write his name in for at least two sets, realizing more might raise a brow. His jaw tightened slightly when he saw that Arkwright had already penciled in for the waltz, William's favorite dance. He put his signature next to the Quadrille and Saratoga.

Florence watched him sign with his perfectly smooth, long fingers.

"I am earnestly anticipating our dance." William bowed again and nodded to the tittering ladies. Although he knew it was rude not to sign one of their cards as well, he had no interest in dancing with any of the foolish girls.

After watching from the sidelines as Arkwright waltzed Florence around the dance floor, William had his turn. He approached the pair as Arkwright whispered something in her ear. Whatever it was, it must have been amusing because it caused Florence to blush and let out a pretty laugh that jingled in the air like small ringing bells.

"Excuse me, I believe it is my turn?" William interrupted them before Arkwright went any further with his flirtations. Florence stopped laughing and looked at William as if she had forgotten he was next in line for a dance. Her eyes, which matched the pale blue gown she was wearing, were sparkling from all the attention she was receiving.

"Yes of course," she said, recovering herself. She tapped Arkwright's arm with her small fan.

Arkwright smiled, bowed slightly in front of Florence and left them, grinning as if he had just won at a game of dice.

William took Florence more firmly than he was planning and guided her to the dance floor as the musicians started playing the next dance. He held her in his arms as she fluttered around the floor. It took every ounce of restraint he had in him not to grasp her small waist too firmly while they danced.

"William, you are rather quiet tonight. Not your jovial self." Florence locked eyes with his while they danced.

"I'm preoccupied by your beauty," he said.

"Aren't you charming." She threw her head back, revealing her long, slender, neck and the wisps of perspiration dampening her skin, giving off a delicious fragrance of lavender. When the dance was over he reluctantly led her to her seat.

"I haven't been able to speak with you since our visit in London. When can we talk privately?" he asked.

"Don't worry, William, we'll have the chance to catch up over supper. Mrs. Locock has you escorting me to the table. I'm sure she's put us near each other," Florence whispered in his ear.

"That would be wonderful," he said.

Ella was well aware her friends were gossiping behind their fans, irritated by the fact that she was monopolizing Basil Napier. She didn't care. The Royal Navy was sending him to the Bay of Biscay in a few days and she had no idea when she would see him again.

During one of their last dances he steered her across the floor toward the terrace. They looked around to see who was watching and then dashed outside to sit on one of the benches overlooking the sea.

"Basil, there is something I must tell you," Ella said.

"You have my full attention," Basil said. "You're shivering. Here, take my coat." He took off his coat and placed it around her shoulders. They gazed at the full moon casting a sheen on the sea.

"My father told us that we are to return to America." Ella searched his eyes to see what kind of reaction this would provoke. She wasn't disappointed — he was crestfallen.

"So we're both being sent off to sea?" he said.

"You know I would wait for you if I could. But he's insisting we leave sometime this year. I don't have all the details yet. With the holiday, we have not yet had time to discuss the particulars."

"You'll be back? It's only temporary? Your home is here."

Ella shook her head and then rested it on his shoulder. She didn't care who might find them in this compromising position. "My home is with you, Basil. No matter where I go."

Basil moved to take her hand in his just as his brother came out to the terrace and found them. Ella quickly lifted her head off his shoulders.

"Basil, Doctor Durant is looking for Ella. He saw the two of you leave the dance floor. You should be more circumspect."

"Thanks for the warning." Basil sighed and gently lifted his coat off Ella's shoulders.

***

As the family was riding back to their cottage from the ball Dr. Durant made his opinion of Basil Napier known. "He's making advances because he believes you're heir to a fortune. All the aristocrats here think they can lure an American heiress with their titles," Dr. Durant said.

"Papa, please understand! Basil Napier isn't luring me for my wealth. He has a position with the Royal Navy. Why would he need my money?"

"They all do around here. Don't scoff at me young lady. I see the advertisements in the *Daily Telegraph*: English peer looking for marriage to wealthy American lady who may purchase the rank of peeress for £40,000."

"I hardly believe Basil is looking to sell anything in return for Ella's wealth. He's the youngest of the four brothers and last in line for the title. That goes to Bill," William said.

"I don't care, he's after her money," Dr. Durant said.

"I'm twenty years old. I think it's time I consider a suitable marriage, and Basil Napier would suit me well."

"I have to agree with Ella, Pet. The Napiers are a fine family," Hannah said.

"Once Ella is back in the States we will find her a suitable *American* match, one that might benefit *our* family as well. No more discussion about it," Dr. Durant said.

LONDON
JANUARY 1874

William glanced up from his newspaper just in time to watch her make an entrance into the tea parlor. Everyone else seemed to be doing the same thing: observing the golden beauty in the swishing pink tea dress, her dainty white kid boots peeking out from under the folds. She stopped to chat at a table, and otherwise gave tiny polite nods to people she knew as she glided across the floor. He stood up when she approached the table.

"Florence," he greeted her warmly and pulled out the chair for her to sit.

"William, so nice to see you again."

"Of course. You must thank your brother Henry for escorting you here to meet me. How was the rest of your holiday?"

She smiled weakly as she took her seat. "Eventful. But then things always are at Osborne House."

William followed suit and sat down after her.

"Tea sir?" A waiter approached the table.

"Yes, tea and sandwiches."

The waiter bowed slightly and left them.

William locked eyes with Florence; she blushed and concentrated on removing her gloves, pulling at the cotton fabric, slowly revealing soft, white fingers and perfectly manicured nails. When she was done she placed the gloves on her lap and met William's gaze.

"William I—"

"Florence, I have—"

They stopped and smiled at each other.

"It's lovely here isn't it?" Florence said, casting her eyes about the room. Someone in the corner caught her eye and she nodded. Finding nothing more to distract her, she turned her attention back to William. "You first," she said.

William lifted a box out from under the table and placed it next to her just as the waiter came with tea. Swiftly, William moved the box out of the way and met her eyes. His gesture obviously startled her.

"It can wait," he said.

"I will bring your tray of sandwiches shortly," the waiter said as he poured their tea into the cups. William and Florence waited patiently for him to finish and move on.

"The service is very good here," Florence said as she lifted the teacup to her lips.

William nodded. "How long will you be visiting your sister in London?"

She set her cup on its saucer. "The Princess has released me from my duties for the next few days."

"Good." William paused for a moment and leaned toward her smiling. "I am so glad to see you again." He brought the box back out from under the table and was about to place it in front of her when the waiter approached with the tray. He quickly removed it once again.

"I guess kismet will not allow me to hand you this gift." William tried to catch her eyes. *Why wouldn't they meet his?*

Florence removed a sandwich from the tray and nibbled on it, looking into her teacup.

William produced the package and slid it across to her. "For you," he said.

"Really William, you shouldn't have." She looked pained by the idea of having to open it.

"I found it while in Dorf Gastein."

Florence's hands, now visibly shaking, opened the box. She peeked inside. It was a music box, a model of a Swiss chalet.

"Oh my, William," she gasped as she took it out and turned the box around to see it from all angles. She lifted the lid and heard the tinkling sound of Brahms.

"These music boxes are all the rage now since Prince Albert built the Swiss cottage at Osborne House. It reminded me of you. I know you have fond memories of times spent there painting and drawing with the Princess."

"It's beautiful." Again, the pained look in her eyes took William aback.

"But I mustn't—" She faltered for a minute and then set the music box back in its container.

"You mustn't. Why?"

"William," she said, "It's lovely, really it is. But I cannot accept it. I don't want to lead you astray. You're a close friend of my cousin, and a dear friend to me and I just cannot accept this gift." She shook her head, tears welling in her eyes.

"Florence, what is it?"

"Must we do this now?" She pulled a tiny handkerchief out of her clutch and dabbed at her eyes. William noticed people were watching them. The room suddenly seemed to become silent, almost stifling, as if the air had been sucked out by a strong force and was pulling him with it. He leaned in.

"Florence, you at least owe me an explanation. Surely a small gift like this isn't too bold of me? I hope that once I'm finished with this business in America I will come back to you."

"Sir, is there anything else I might bring you?" The waiter arrived at the worst possible moment. Or maybe he had planned it that way. William glanced around again and saw that other patrons were engrossed in their own conversations, ignoring him and Florence. Perhaps he had only imagined them staring.

"No, not now." William waved the waiter away.

Florence regained her composure, brushing a crumb off the table. "William, you know how much you mean to me. But my father has forbidden me from encouraging any more of your advances," she sniffed, staring into her teacup.

"For heaven's sake why?" William said.

Florence's eyes never left her teacup. "Well, you see, there have been certain rumors concerning your father's business affairs." She paused. "And, well, my mother saw your mother's companion, Miss Molineaux, in the jewelry store last week." She let out a large sigh and leveled her eyes on his. "She was selling your mother's jewels."

William clenched his jaw and fervently hoped she didn't see his anger or astonishment. He knew his father's finances had taken a turn for the worse, but he had no idea of the severity of the situation. So his mother had sent her companion Margaret to sell the family heirlooms? This was an outrage and a humiliation.

"As a matter of fact, I took a risk coming here," Florence continued, "My father only allowed me to come when my brother offered to escort me. But I wanted to tell you in person we cannot see each other again. And I didn't want you to hold out hopes that one day we would be together. My father has other plans for me." She hesitated for a moment and then met his wondering eyes. "Another suitor." She saw his look of dismay but it couldn't be helped. Her family could not afford the scent of a scandal and the Durants were aromatic.

She rose to leave and William stood up. He took her hand in his but she quickly pulled it away.

"I am so sorry. Good-bye, William," she said as she held back tears, and carried herself with dignity out of the Queen's Hotel tea parlor.

William left the hotel, choosing to walk back to the apartment on Hertford Street instead of hiring a cab. He barely noticed the cold rain pelting his silk hat as he clutched the package holding the music box he had hoped Florence would treasure. The streets were littered with people and coaches trying to navigate the puddles forming in the wet afternoon gloom. As he was about to turn the corner a man approached him.

"If it isn't Durant!" Charlie Arkwright slapped his back. "My God man, you look like you just lost a high stakes dice game."

William greeted his friend with a wan smile. "Sorry old chap, you took me by surprise. I didn't know you were in London."

"Business as usual. Say, why not join me? I'm meeting Jack at the club to get screwed on whiskey after a long day of bad news. I'm sure he'd be so glad to see you. And maybe we can win back your money over cards." He took William's arm and without waiting for a response, led him toward Piccadilly and the St. James's Club.

Unlike the city streets, the club was warm and welcoming, the walls and chairs wrapped in velvet and damask. William and Arkwright shed their wet coats, handed them to the doorman, and looked for an empty table. Within moments Jack Napier appeared and the men found a small table to sit at together.

"How's the duck hunting been?" Arkwright asked Jack as he lifted the decanter and poured a round of drinks.

"It was fine until that spell of cold weather caused the fowl to move out to open water," Jack said, helping himself to a tumbler of whiskey. "While we are on the subject of hunting, Will, I was hoping you'd join me on that excursion to India. What's the news on America old boy? Will you be back in time?"

William shook his head. The warm amber liquid was beginning to work its magic and calm his nerves. "It's hard to say. My father has left instructions for us to start preparations for departure and he's given me no indication as to when I might be able to return here. He wants me to visit our land holdings in the Adirondacks." He put his glass down on the table.

"Where the devil are the Adirondacks? Did I pronounce that correctly? Sounds like it's right out of an adventure book," Arkwright said.

"It is," William and Jack said in unison.

"It's a vast wilderness area in the northern part of New York State. If I had a map I'd show you. Nothing much there apart from trees. My father has a grand idea of developing a rail line that will transport passengers from New York City all the way to Canada."

21

"Sounds like good hunting grounds," Arkwright said filling his glass again. "Will, I think it fair for me to tell you that your father has been making the rounds looking for investors for this scheme of his."

William remembered the Boxing Day Ball, and the way his father was badgering Thomas Brassey like a hunt terrier trying to flush a fox out of hiding. Charlie Arkwright would be another potential target. His family's textile business had left him very wealthy indeed.

"I see." William contemplated what to say next. He knew his father's brash American tactics would not go over well at the clubs on Piccadilly. Although it hardly mattered, London businessmen were loath to take risks in this economy, and the Durant name was now tainted.

"Poor sap Carlyle. Bloody snookered," Jack said, ignoring the direction the conversation was moving and saving William from having to discuss his father's business.

The men turned their attention to the man Jack was talking about. He was sitting alone by the fireside wallowing in an alcoholic stupor, mumbling greetings to anyone passing his way.

"He's been kicked out of his London flat," Jack explained. "His father needs to let it out, and Carlyle can't pay the rent. No prospects for an income either. Failed the Foreign Service exams, his older brother will inherit the land holdings and title, and his younger brother is already in the Seminary."

Charlie snorted. "Yes, and it doesn't help that he bedded down with a betrothed lady-in-waiting from the Queen's entourage."

"Why would his father evict him from his own London apartment?" William said.

"Lord Carlyle needs the money. He owes taxes on his country estate and is not about to sell family land so his son can continue to live a scandalous lifestyle in London," Jack said.

It was Charlie's turn to change the subject. "See those gentlemen over there?" He nodded his head in the direction of another table where three men sat talking in hushed tones.

"I knew them at Harrow. They like cards, let's ask them for a hand. I'm in the mood to win some money and Durant needs to brighten his spirits," he said, slapping William on the back so hard that it caused William to spill some of his drink. He then flew off to ask if the trio were up for a game.

"Are you sure you're ready for this?" Jack said.

William cocked his head in question, unsure if Jack was referring to the card game or something else.

"Not that interested in America are you, old boy?"

"Not in the slightest," William said.

"My brother asked me if you plan to visit Thirlestane before you leave."

"Tell him I'll send word about my plans as soon as possible," William said.

"How is your sister?"

"The same, writing her poetry. She writes at least once a week to Basil. I imagine the Royal Navy is wondering who is sending him so many letters."

"Those two are smitten," Jack said. "What does Ella think about leaving?"

"She's very unhappy about it. She implored my father to stay. She even suggested she stay as a companion to Mrs. Locock since Charles is quite often absent on business. I suppose she thought my father might agree as long as he didn't need to keep the Hertford street apartment. He's all about economy now."

"Who isn't these days? This economic downturn has everyone in a quandary."

William instinctively glanced over at Carlyle, a grim reminder of how his own luck might change for the worse. He felt a wave of anger toward his father for putting the family in this predicament and was anxious to get back to the apartment to question his mother about the pawned jewels. He was suddenly irritated that Arkwright had roped him into coming to the club. Although good at it, he was in no mood for forced joviality.

Jack leaned closer to William so no one would overhear what he had to say next. "William, my brother told me what happened to your father's Union Pacific and the Credit Mobilier investigation. He wants you to know he has full confidence in you, and if there's anything we Napiers can do—"

"Don't worry Jack, although you're very kind to offer assistance. I know what people are saying but I also know my father. Whatever business dealings are causing him trouble now will probably end up in his favor."

"That's the attitude." Jack raised his drink in a salute to William's optimism.

It was quiet as William stumbled into the dark hallway of the apartment later that evening. He was glad Ella and his mother weren't awake. His father had returned to America the previous week. The quiet gave him the reprieve he needed to think.

William knew the depression staggering the economy in Europe and Great Britain was also affecting business interests in the United States.

He had read about the run on a major bank in New York City the previous fall. The Panic, as they were calling the financial failure, was due to a number of factors, but from what William knew, much of his father's undoing derived from heavy investments in the Union Pacific Company and transcontinental railroad.

And worse, the political buy-offs his father so cleverly maneuvered through the Credit Mobilier Company to get the railroad built were putting what sound financial investments the Durants had under scrutiny.

Credit Mobilier was Dr. Durant's brainchild: a front company for the Union Pacific that managed the construction of the railroad across the western frontier. A corporation in name only, from what William surmised, that imploded when a cracker-jack reporter for the *New York Sun* discovered some prominent American politicians, including backers of President Grant, were also major stock holders, purchasing their stock of Credit Mobilier at greatly reduced rates and in return, ignoring the fact that the company was billing the government for millions in false construction claims.

Is this how his father financed William's expeditions in Egypt? By bribery and scandalous business dealings? He was appalled and disgusted by the thought. Every glass of wine he drank, every fowl he ate while staying at the Shepheards Hotel in Cairo, was financed by his father. He had never been allowed, or instructed to make plans for his future. Now he was told to return to America to help rebuild his father's reputation and fortune. When, he pondered, would he be allowed to become his own man?

Upset by his own feelings of inadequacy, William decided self-pity was not helping. He got up from the chair and went over to his mother's desk to find stationery. Someone must know this was not the end for the Durants. He planned to write Florence and tell her exactly what he thought of her rejection.

One afternoon when his mother's companion Margaret and sister Ella were out shopping William found the courage to confront his mother about their finances.

"If we are so low on funds how is he managing it?" William asked her.

Hannah looked up from her knitting to answer. "William, you need to understand, your father wants the best for all of us, he really does. But he has made some unwise decisions with the Union Pacific railroad and well, over the past few years we've been relying on the sale of the land in Brooklyn."

The park commission in New York City had given Hannah over $200,000 for the land her father had so astutely purchased years before his death. The commission needed the land to annex as part of the new Prospect Park.

"And?" He wanted her to reveal why she pawned her jewels.

"And, we need to support him as best we can."

"Is that all, Mother?"

"Yes," she turned her attention to her knitting.

He persisted. "What about the passage home? How are we paying for that?"

Hannah sighed, wrapped the yarn around her knitting needles and stowed them away in a basket next to her seat. She put her hands on her lap and studied her son for a moment before speaking. "We borrowed it."

"Borrowed it? From whom?" William wasn't sure if it was embarrassment or anger that made the blood rush to his head.

"Charles Locock," she said. "Now don't worry about all of this. We will not sully our reputations with the Lococks. I plan to repay the money as soon as we return to the States. Your father's credit ran dry here. That is all."

"Mother, I don't understand. What has father done with your $200,000?"

"He invested the money in the Adirondack Railroad Company, a lumber mill in North Creek, and the family's new home," Hannah said. She looked up at William and he could see that tears were welling in her eyes.

"My God, what has he done?" He moved a foot stool up close to her and sat down on it so he could be closer to her.

"Oh, I don't know, William. He has always provided for us. But now everything is going wrong. I'm feeling so desperate! I've been through this all before. I know we will never live down the shame of it all."

"What are you talking about?"

"My own father." Hannah reached for her handkerchief in the pocket of her dress to control her sniffling. "He went bankrupt here in England when I was a little girl."

"Is that why he moved your family to America?"

Hannah nodded.

"Well it worked out for the best didn't it?"

She smiled up at him and wiped her tears away.

William was upset to see her this way. His mother always held her composure, even in the most trying of times. She was their stability while Dr. Durant worked in the States. She remained resolute in times of trouble or when one of them was sick. He put his hand on her shoulder to console her.

"I don't know what that was like for you. But I can promise you this. I won't let you live through that shame again," he said.

THIRLESTANE, SCOTLAND
FEBRUARY 1874

The birds flurried out of the box as soon as the gamekeeper opened the hatch and winged over the mist-covered moors. William raised his Henry gun and fired. Two birds landed with a thud and the setters gave out a howl as they raced to retrieve them.

"I've always admired how well trained your dogs are." William cocked his gun and loaded it again.

"Richards knows his dogs," Bill Napier said as he aimed his gun in the air and shot at the next batch of birds that flew from their cages. "We pay him handsomely for the knowledge." He smiled at William. "Had enough yet?"

"Never." William lifted his gun and took aim. The dogs were barking in the distance at the plethora of birds. He wished they were hunting for grouse but the season was over.

"What's the game hunting like in… how do you pronounce it again? Add der Ron Dax?" Napier asked as he loaded his gun.

William shrugged. "From what I've read there's plenty. Deer, fowl, wolf, bear. Even catamounts."

"Wild cats and wolves? Still? How about Indians? Are there Indians in this wilderness?"

"Doubtful," William said. "It's not like the wild west. The colonists killed off any tribes that got in their way. The wars and Revolution did the rest. Haven't you ever read *The Last of the Mohicans*?"

Napier laughed. "As I recall, Jack loved that story and made a game of playing Magua while you played Uncas."

"Yes, hiding a forbidden love for Cora Munro, I remember." William said glumly.

"I always preferred Hawkeye," Napier said.

William silently admired the view of the river Yarrow meandering through the vale. He would miss this place. "I always thought I would have an estate like this one. Delusional I know."

"Not really old boy," Napier said. "It's still plausible. Your father's fortunes could take another turn. And besides, from what you've told me your father owns large tracts of land in the Adirondack forests. Maybe you could develop your country home there."

"Hmmm." William walked to where his horse was resting by a small fire they had built to keep them warm and took a flask out of the saddle holster. He took a swig of scotch.

"Not exactly as I imagined though, an estate on the downs of the Isle of Wight. I thought I would be able to stay in London and act as father's liaison for the railroad. If he'd only let me in on his business dealings instead of closing me out when he was speaking with the London investors. I can't imagine what he'll have me doing in America. I hardly know the man."

Napier followed William to the fire, took the flask out of his hand and helped himself to the scotch. "You'll win him over soon enough with that famous charm of yours."

"Then maybe I can win over your cousin again," William said.

"I would advise you against trying to win back Florence. She's a charmer, I know, but she's also in a most precarious position at court. Her brother Henry has had a few questionable business dealings of late too. It's not just your family's scandal that has thrown her off your scent. She's been instructed by my uncle to watch her back. Besides, I understand that Charlie Arkwright is now courting her." Napier moved to put his gun in its holster on his horse's back and did not register the momentary anger in William's eyes.

"Let's go in and dine, shall we?" he turned back to William. "It may be the last time for quite a while."

"I'll follow along after you. I'd like a few moments to enjoy the scenery one last time," William said.

"Of course, you know the way. Don't take too long with your musings, we have quite the dinner planned and cards afterwards. My mother is anxious to see you."

William watched him gallop away and then pulled a letter out of his breast pocket. It was addressed to Florence. He had planned to ask Napier to give it secretly to her. William scanned the words he had written one night while ruminating on his plight.

Dear Florence,

After your abrupt departure from the tearoom I feel it necessary to explain my situation. I expect that my prospects in America will improve my family's finances considerably and your father will not object to our union. I promise that if you would wait for me I will return to England in the hopes that you might consider a proposal of marriage.

Please don't cast me off just yet. I know this is not of your choosing and that your feelings for me are as strong and steadfast as mine for you. We still have a future together if you would allow it.

Yours affectionately, William

William crumpled the letter into a ball.

"Yes, I will be back," he said to the wind that was coursing over the moors, "and when I do Florence, it will be to prove your father wrong." He pitched the letter into the burning logs, mounted his horse and rode back to Napier's manor home.

LONDON
MARCH 1874

Ella and Margaret were arguing again.

"You can't possibly stuff another gown in that chest! Besides you won't need as many where we're going," Margaret said.

"What a welcome reminder that we are being exiled to the outskirts of the wilderness," Ella said as she tried to slam the trunk shut. Margaret pushed her aside, opened the trunk and started re-folding her dresses into submission so that they could fit.

Ella left the room to sulk in the parlor. She was too tired to argue with Margaret. She flung herself down on the loveseat and took inventory of their furnishings, suddenly realizing that they had never owned any of it. All of her life they had lived in places that never belonged to them. Except for the few things her mother dragged around wherever they went such as their tea service, a few portraits, and William's bust they had commissioned in Italy, they rented everything. The only real connections to England were Hannah's extended family, otherwise they were a ship without an anchor, she thought sullenly.

Her mother bustled into the room, breaking up her thoughts. "Ella, stop brooding and finish packing. The coach will be here soon enough and we can't be late."

They had lingered as long as they could over preparations for their journey to America and now had no excuse to stay. It was time to move on.

For Ella however, it was just a tragic mistake she hoped would correct itself. Each day that had passed after her father broke the terrible news of their imminent return to the States, she had waited for some word, some note from Basil Napier, instructing her, imploring her, not to leave, to stay behind for him. A proposal of marriage. And each day was like another tear at her heart until she thought there would be nothing left of it to take to America. He still hadn't replied to the poem she sent him:

Thou to the East dear love, I to the West;
Dense forest nooks, rose-tinted sky, all varied space between us lie.
In all we find the other, Love-apart?
Not while each are blessed with faithful heart.

She wondered if he had received it yet, or was he not willing to respond? Exactly what were his intentions? He had been whisked off to the Bay of Biscay before ever revealing them. Disgusted with her situation, she decided action was the best remedy and rose to finish packing but was stopped by the knock at the door. Her mother heard the knock and looked frantic. William opened the door to find a messenger with a note addressed to him. Ella's heart leapt out of her chest; maybe it was word from Basil. *Was this it? Permission for her hand in marriage?*

William thanked the messenger, paid him and opened the note while Ella stood, waiting, stopping herself from accosting him to grab it out of his hand. She watched his face fall and knew it was not the news she had hoped for.

"William, what is it?" Hannah said. "It's not your father is it? Is he ill?"

William walked over to Ella and stood next to her. "No it's not father," he said taking Ella's hand and letting the note float to the floor. "It's Basil Napier. He was killed in service."

Part Two

CAMP KIRBY
MAY 2010

She raised the maul over her head with both hands. Trying not to sway from the weight of it, Avery brought her arms down over the piece of wood stationed on the stump waiting to be split. The maul missed its mark, again, and buried itself in the stump with a loud thunk.

"Damn it!" She had to figure this out or it would be a miserable summer. The lighting in the cabin was dim at best in the evenings and the small kitchen appliances worked on propane. Cooking over a fire pit out by the lake was much easier and more aesthetic anyway.

She wished she had paid more attention all of those years when her brother split wood at the family's summer camp. It was always so much easier to watch him sweat it out while she whittled away at a twig. Besides, she didn't want splitting wood, like everything else they did, to turn into a competition.

She struggled with the maul, twisting and wrenching it until it came free of the stump so suddenly she stumbled backwards. Lifting it in the air, she brought it down again with angry force and hit the corner of the piece of wood. The log went flying off the stump and left her a few splintered pieces. This wouldn't do; she was going to throw out her back if she wasn't careful.

"What idiot left me with un-split logs?" she said to herself. There was no one else to talk to here.

Avery was red-faced and sweating and still had split no more than three pieces of wood when she saw a small motorboat with a man at the helm maneuvering it up to the dock. Leaning on the maul, she waited to see who was disrupting her solitude. He was about her age, late twenties. He got out of the boat carrying a duffel and waved at her.

"Hi," he shouted. "You ordered some stuff from the store in town?"

She had ordered some supplies from the Raquette Lake store but hadn't known they delivered.

"Yes, I did."

"Well, sorry to startle you," he said as he came up the hill toward her. "My mother asked me to drop these off while I was delivering some things for the College at Camp Huntington."

Avery looked over at his small boat and wondered why he didn't just drive the supplies to Huntington from town. The staff at Huntington would have kept them for her; it was only a mile hike through the woods. *And who was his mother?*

As if reading her thoughts he said, "I like getting out on the boat when I can, and there are other people on the islands that can always use a delivery of milk or coffee or something."

He had on typical Adirondack attire: jeans, a flannel shirt and baseball cap. He was medium height, dark skinned – she couldn't tell if it was his natural glow or from too much sun – and brown eyes.

He noticed her eyeing him up and down, smiled, and nodded at the pile of wood, her maul, and the splintered pieces at her feet. "Splitting some wood?"

She looked around her, and at the paltry pile of split wood she had accumulated after an hour's worth of work and sweat. "Just got started," she said as she pulled a wisp of brown hair away from her eyes.

He nodded. "Yeah – I dropped that load of wood off last week. The director at Huntington told me somebody was staying out here for the summer and would need it. I didn't know it would be a girl though – if he had told me that I would have split it for you."

Avery bristled. Very few people called her a 'girl' anymore. At age twenty-eight she wouldn't expect it. "Great, thanks," Avery managed, even though it was not the first reply that came to mind. *Who the hell is this clown?*

He dropped her duffel onto the ground. "I'm Jake," he said, putting his hand out to shake hers.

She returned the handshake. "I'm Avery."

"Mind if I ask what you're doing out at Camp Kirby all by yourself this summer?"

"I'm doing research on the saw-whet owl."

"That little bird? Why you hardly ever see them in the woods. You sure there are any?"

"That's what I intend to find out. I plan to survey as much of the property around Long Point as I can."

"Why?" It was a fair question. These owls were not endangered nor were they threatened in the Adirondacks by any particular predator except the occasional great horned owl or raven. But that was the point for her really. They were not much studied, especially during nesting season. It was a wide-open field.

"Because I like to study things that I find mysterious," she said.

"Well, that sounds like as good an explanation as any. Not sure it's such a good idea for a girl to be out here by herself all summer though," he added as he picked up a twig off the ground and chucked it toward the woodpile — kindling. Avery watched it sail through the sky and land neatly on top of the large pile of un-split logs.

Avery frowned. It was hard enough without him telling her.

"Do you know the story behind the cabin here?" He glanced over her head at the cabin.

Avery turned her head in the direction of the cabin. "What story? Oh wait, I know, you're gonna tell me there are ghosts that particularly like to taunt *girls* that decide to stay alone in the woods."

"No, nothing like that," he laughed. "Just a mistress."

"A mistress? Whose mistress?"

"Why the owner of Huntington of course."

"Collis Huntington kept a mistress here?" Avery said.

"No, not that owner, the original owner, the one who built all of these cabins, William West Durant."

Avery studied the cabin, seeing it in a completely new light. A mistress? William Durant, the famous architect of the Great Camps in the Adirondacks kept a mistress in the woods? How rich, she thought.

"How do people know this?" Her analytical mind needed answers before she could believe.

Jake shrugged. "Not exactly sure, but people around here say it's so. They named this cabin after her, Minnie Everette Kirby – Camp Kirby."

The two stood staring at the cabin.

"The folklore says that every room of the cabin has an exit door so William could skedaddle if his wife ever came looking for him," Jake said with a grin.

For some reason Avery didn't find Jake's comment amusing, and wondered who she had last heard say that word skedaddle – her grandfather maybe? She stared at him blankly. Jake stared back. Realizing he had nothing else to contribute to the folklore, and since she didn't ask any more questions, he decided to leave.

"Enjoy your time here, it's got a lot of history," he said as he tipped his hat and headed back to his boat. "I'm sure we'll run into each other again."

"Oh." He thought of something and turned around. "It helps to drive the maul straight down in front of your body with your strong hand on top of the weaker one." He mimicked the position on a pretend handle in the air. "Don't swing it in an arc, hurts your back."

"Thanks," Avery said. "I think I'm getting the hang of it!"

He smiled and gave her a backhand wave as he walked to his boat.

"Smartass," Avery said to herself. She waited until he was out of sight before trying his approach. Putting her right hand closest to the head of the maul on the handle, she lifted her arms in the air and brought it down in front of her body. Immediately, her left hand slid to meet the right.

With a satisfying thwack, the log split neatly in two.

After unloading the contents of the duffel on the front porch, Avery went into the kitchen to fix herself something to eat. Annoyed by how much time she'd wasted on splitting wood, she made a quick sandwich out of bread and cheese. She then filled her water bottle with the filtered water she stored in the refrigerator, grabbed her backpack with the gear she needed for the day, and headed out the kitchen door to use the composting toilet in the outhouse before venturing into the woods.

The cabin was situated on a small hill overlooking the lake. There were a front porch and four rooms downstairs: a master bedroom, a parlor, another bedroom with bunks, and a small kitchen. There was an upstairs loft as well that was blocked off and not used. Cortland College inherited the cabin when they took ownership of Camp Huntington in 1947. All of Long Point came with it — some 200 acres of land. Camp Huntington was more like a compound, a mixture of cottages and halls, now used as dorms and classrooms by the College. It was named after the previous owner — Collis Huntington — a railroad tycoon from the 19th century who had bought the buildings and land from William West Durant in 1895.

Camp Kirby was a small outpost cabin the College rented out to Alumni. It was probably used at one time as a hunting cabin and not, as Jake said, a hideaway for a mistress. Avery had to laugh at the idea. Although she didn't care what it was used for then, for now she felt lucky to be granted permission to rent it for a whole summer to do her research. She arrived during black fly season — a time when no one else would have wanted to rent it anyway — and was here until the end of September.

A grant was paying the rent and with her being the only tenant, it allowed the College to do some much needed repair work to the cabin. She had been here a few days so far and the work crew was due soon. She wasn't looking forward to it; she didn't mind being alone and didn't want anyone disrupting her research.

Avery knew there were saw-whets in the area. She checked the bird census carefully to make sure. Besides, the habitat around Long Point was ideal for the owl, with coniferous forests all around, White, Red and Jack pines, and places to roost during the day under cover from predators. There were also holes left by woodpeckers in some of the trees, perfect nesting sites for the saw-whets, and enough prey to keep them satiated. They were small, seven to ten centimeters in height, and weighed only a few ounces.

Avery had been looking for signs of the owl since she arrived and believed she had found them about half a mile from the camp. While exploring the trails around the cabin the first day she arrived she heard a group of boisterous chickadees, clearly agitated, as if chasing away a predator. The saw-whet would be a perfect candidate. Given the opportunity, the owl would eat a chickadee for dinner. She planned to go back there today.

Tracking this species of owl was particularly difficult. Like many owls, saw-whets are crepuscular, mostly active at twilight and early dawn, making them hard to sight in the woods. And their brown feathers were good camouflage.

It was still chilly in the woods, so Avery put on her sweatshirt and started down the trail. The forest always allured her. As she walked silently to her destination, she could feel the soft cushion of duff beneath her feet, built up over the years from leaves and pine needles that fell to the ground and decomposed. Stopping briefly to take it all in, she inhaled a big dose of balsam-laden oxygen into her lungs, a tonic for her soul.

Before too long she reached the small grove of pines in the forest where she had heard the chatter of the chickadees. Looking around, she found several tall White pines and guessed they were at least 150 years old. She looked for signs of the saw-whet — pellets of their regurgitated food and markings of their fecal whitewash on the tree trunks. Her eyes lit upon a pine, standing taller than the others in the grove. It was in its last stages of death. Two-thirds of its branches were bare. The only needles still photosynthesizing were at the very top of the tree. Even more telling were the pine knots that were forming where the dead limbs met the trunk. Over time, resin from the tree settled in the crooks of the limb's base creating a deadwood that repelled water absorption and, if cut off the tree, made a great fire starter. Even more interesting though were the designs the resin-collecting process left behind: sculptured ornaments for a mantel.

The tree trunk hosted a hole about five feet off the ground. She peered into it. No owl. There were however some small brown feathers — possibly from a saw-whet. Her heart pounded, could it be a roosting site for the little raptor?

Avery knelt to examine the base of the trunk. There was a crevice, just the right size for a chipmunk or squirrel. She reached for the flashlight in her backpack and shone it into the hole.

She could just make out several items and saw what looked like regurgitated owl pellets, but also a strange, square, solid-looking object.

Her curiosity got the best of her. She tried to reach for the square item but to no avail, it was too deep in the trunk and her hand was too big for the crack. She pulled a small folding saw from her pack and carved a bigger opening.

The decaying bark gave way easily. Avery pulled at the decaying matter. It was like sawdust in her hand. She placed several pellets into small plastic baggies, to dissect later (that was the purpose of her visit to the tree after all) and then reached for the small square item that had piqued her interest.

It was tightly wound up in canvas – the type used to make sails. Avery carefully unraveled the material and discovered a small black leather book, about six inches tall and four inches wide. It was a diary from 1893. Intrigued, Avery re-wrapped it, put it in her pack and hiked back to the cabin. This was too interesting a find. The saw-whet search could wait.

RAQUETTE LAKE
WINTER 1876

William used his last ounce of energy to shake the snow off his collar before entering the tent. He hoped they were in the right place. Last summer he had visited the Adirondacks with his father, and they eventually stopped at this piece of land jutting out into Raquette Lake. They were staking out a spot for the Durant family compound. Charlie Bennett, his father's guide, had hosted them in one of his crude cabins in the woods. However, William couldn't find Bennett's cabin in the blaze of snow that had been falling on them since dawn. It was now dusk and they didn't have time to find Charlie or his cabin, they needed to get warm and stay warm. His feet were frozen and so were his hands. He had ventured as far as he dared to gather some wood so they could start a fire while Jem Stone put up their tent on the frozen ground under a huge hemlock. The branches, laden with snow, offered protection from the relentless winds.

"Stone, come help me make a fire before we freeze to death out here," William said. Stone had emptied out his pack to find an extra pair of wool socks but stopped his search to help his employer.

They went to work with the kindling and flint in front of their tent. Both men stamped their feet in unison, trying desperately to bring back some blood to their extremities.

"You think they'll find us?" Stone asked.

William nodded. "The fire will alert them we're here."

***

Stone looked at the small crackling fire and wished he hadn't come. Though loyal to the Durants, he didn't fully comprehend William's sense of adventure, and this was proving to be too much. They had left the Durants' North Creek home five days earlier, William insisting they travel to survey in the winter. "It's the only time when most of the trees are bare and I can get a good feel for the layout of the land," he had said.

What choice did he have? Stone packed up the gear, tent, and whatever provisions they could carry between them and took off with William by horse and sled. They took what roads were cleared of snow by horse and plow and worked their way to Blue Mountain where they stabled the horse at an inn.

After one night of rest on a soft warm bed, they crammed their packs with whatever provisions they could, and took off on skis for the eight-mile trek to Raquette Lake. The trip should only have taken a day but as the day progressed the weather turned on them. The small flakes of snow floating in the air aimlessly when they took off in the morning became a vengeful deluge as the day wore on. The blizzard was relentless. They stopped and slept in the tent to gain their strength for a night before starting out again that morning. They were supposed to meet up with Charlie Bennett and stay in one of his cabins, but in the blinding snow it was hard to see one foot in front of them. And now it was too dark to look. They were going to have to spend another night in a cold, dreary tent. To make matters worse, they were running out of food. Although they had plenty of ammunition and guns, and William was a good marksman, finding game was impossible in the current conditions.

"I'm hoping the weather clears by tomorrow so I can scout for some meat," William said as if reading Stone's mind. Stone grunted agreement.

"For now, its beans and salt pork," Stone said. He went back into the tent to collect the food and implements needed to cook.

William took off one of his leather gloves to check for

symptoms of frostbite. Although the gloves were lined with wool they did not provide enough warmth for this climate. His hands were a bright red, his fingers were numb, but so far had not turned white. He clenched his fists, winced in pain, and then splayed his hands over the fire. The heat prickled his skin. Satisfied he wasn't going to lose any digits, he left the warmth of the fire to find more firewood.

They ate by the fire as the clouds and snow slowly gave way to a clear starry evening. It was too cold to admire; as soon as they finished cleaning up from dinner they retreated to the tent to bury themselves under wool blankets and listen to the icy winds whistling across the frozen lake.

"Allo there!"

William was relieving himself outside of the tent when he heard someone calling. He hurried about his business, dreading frostbite. It was early dawn, and the skies had cleared considerably, making it feel even colder than the day before.

He walked to the front of the tent to find Stone with Charlie Bennett and a tall man with beady, penetrating eyes, a grayish beard and a nose the shape of an eagle's beak. He had on a big cap made of fur and gloves. William wished he was wearing something like it. On both men's feet was a type of snowshoe William had never encountered. They were contrived of similar material as the pack baskets they carried. The frame was constructed from bent wood and the netting was an intricate lacing of rawhide that kept them from sinking into the snow. They were round at the foot and had a tail of wood that met at the base of the heel. Perfect symmetry for tracking game in two feet of snow. William recalled hunting for hare in Norway using skis for traveling long distances. These shoes were far superior for navigating the forests and staying afloat.

"Bennett, so glad to see you. I thought we might be lost," William said as he shook his hand.

"We saw smoke last night but figured we'd wait til morning. I knew you'd be all right for the night. It's too cold even for the wildcats to be roaming," Bennett said. The man to his side said nothing, but William could feel his disapproving glare.

Bennett said, "This is Alvah. Alvah Dunning. Best trapper, nimrod, and guide you can find in all of the Adirondacks."

"Good to meet you." William extended his hand.

Alvah returned the greeting and said, "You mighta come better prepared for the turn of weather round here." Then he turned his head slightly and spit a stream of brown liquid. The men watched as the gob of tobacco juice crystallized in the frozen snow.

"Don't mind him. We's glad you made it," Bennett said.

"And so are we. It was a more treacherous journey from Blue Mountain than I expected, especially on skis."

"Skied eh? Yeah that would tack on a few days," Bennett said. "Eaten yet?"

William shook his head.

"Follow us then." He led Stone and William back to his cabin in the woods.

They followed a path along the shore. On their right the dark mountains framed the frozen lake. The sky, so threatening the day before, was an intense sparkling blue in the morning sun.

When they reached the small cabin William was taken aback. It was no longer the small shanty he and his father stayed in the summer before. This building was constructed with logs, the bark left intact, each piled one on top of the other and joined at the ends, and the roof was shingled with bark.

"We upgraded a bit this fall," Bennett remarked.

When he entered William could see that Bennett had added a potbelly stove with a pipe extended up and out of a hole in the ceiling. There were a few small wooden chairs cast about the room. The men gathered the chairs and sat by the fire drinking coffee from tin cups. William explained their mission.

"I told my father I would stake out the best place to start construction for our camp compound. I think I like the point of land where we set our tent down last night. It gets both the morning and afternoon sun," he said.

43

Bennett and Alvah nodded in agreement. "It's called Long Point," Alvah said.

There was rustling at the front door and Bennett walked over to open it. A slight man with two young people by his side stood at the entrance.

"Isaac," he said to the man, "come on in."

Bennett introduced Isaac Lawrence who was accompanied by his young son Ike and daughter Louise. William guessed she was older than Ike by a few years. They removed their snowshoes, stamped their feet at the entrance and walked into the cabin. They were dressed in unusual outfits, which William recognized as the Iroquois attire he had read about and seen pictures of in the books his father sent him while living abroad.

They had on deerskin moccasins that covered their calves and were lined with some type of fur, possibly rabbit. They also wore rabbit fur hats and deerskin pants. Ike's looked well worn, a hand-me-down, William imagined. All in all, it suited this landscape, and the need to be light on your feet for hunting in the terrain. Each carried a rifle. Ike's large hunting knife swung from a belt at his waist.

William couldn't take his eyes off the young woman. He had seen many exotic women when he traveled the Nile, but she was different. He had never witnessed anyone so beautiful. Her complexion was flawless, in a tint that reminded him of copper, and her eyes were as dark and deep as a doe's. Her black hair was plaited and ran down the length of her back. As the men talked quietly, she barely spoke, signaling instead to her father or brother when she needed something or if they asked her a question in their native tongue.

"You left the bark on the logs," Isaac said.

"Yeah, Alvah told me. Said to use cedar," Bennett responded.

"Cedar lasts longer than hemlock, but if you can find elm, it lasts longest," Isaac said.

The men shook their heads in agreement and William thought how he wouldn't know the difference. He left to use the outhouse. When he came back he said to Bennett, "I see you put an entranceway in this room and the one in the back."

"Makes it easier when the cabin is full and the men have to excuse themselves. No one is disturbed that way."

Isaac, who was sitting cross-legged on the floor, rose to his feet. "We are following the trail of a wolf. I left traps before coming here to rest. Louise insisted on coming to prepare our food." Ike followed his father's lead and got up as well.

"Of course, and I have enough to feed all of us. Why don't we join you on your hunt and Louise can stay behind and cook?"

Isaac shot a questioning glance at his daughter. She smiled and quickly moved to open their packs and bring out the venison and vegetables they had wrapped to make stew.

Alvah grabbed his gun and loaded it. "If there's a wolf, there's a pack."

William and Stone picked up their guns as well. Bennett handed them snowshoes. "You'll need these."

Isaac, William learned, was an expert trapper. He had followed the urine trail of the wolf from his own homestead and laid a trap. Before he arrived at Bennett's cabin he had baited the trap with fresh deer meat. When they came upon it, they found one wolf crying in agony, his leg clamped by the heavy steel jaws, and another circling, howling in fear. Alvah raised his gun and shot the frantic animal. The shot echoed in the forest, and the trapped wolf whimpered.

"I can't stand to see an animal suffer, and I'm a better shot than you Isaac," Alvah said.

Isaac said nothing, just walked up to the trapped animal and shot him in the chest, ending his suffering as well.

William was astounded by the size of the beasts. They loaded them on a sledge Isaac had brought and walked back in the snow to the cabin.

"You keep the bounty Isaac, me and the Warden don't get on too well," Alvah said.

"How much will these two skins bring you?" William asked.

"Thirty," Isaac said.

"I'll give you that and more if you can make fur accouterments for me and Stone," William said.

Isaac stopped and looked up at William. "You'll have to negotiate that with Louise. She and my wife make our clothes." He continued walking.

William's height had always been his advantage, but speaking to Louise, who was at least a foot shorter, made him feel awkward, like a ponderous giant. Further adding to his humility was the fact that he didn't have the currency he needed to pay her to make the garments, just a few coins. What little money he had brought with him to the wilderness he spent mostly on boarding his horse and sled at the inn at Blue Mountain.

He fumbled to get the coins out of his pack and held them out to her in his outstretched hands, promising more when he saw her next. Louise shook her head.

"No need to give me those now. I will make the clothing for you. You can pay me when we see each other again." Her faith in his sincerity took him by surprise. She smiled at him as if they shared a secret.

"You are worried about paying me yet you hardly know of my abilities to prepare the skin and sew," she said.

"Your father told me you make his garments. That is proof enough I think," William said. "How can you trust that we will see each other again?"

"These woods are big but unlike animals, people are easy to track. Most men do nothing to hide any sign of their existence," she said. William found her warm smile endearing.

The Lawrence party was in no hurry to move on. Ike skinned the wolves and Louise prepared the hides for sewing. Ike gave her the brains to soften the hides. She boiled these in water and after scraping away the fat layer on the hide with Ike's hunting knife, she brushed the brain mixture over the skin, the oils from the brain absorbing into the flesh. She then soaked the hides in water and repeated the procedure. After a couple of days of this she stretched out and hung the skins from two oars over a fire outside the cabin. "The smoke will keep them soft while they dry," she told William who watched her with fascination as she processed the skins. Once the skins were prepared she used sinew to sew the clothes.

Each day the men went out to hunt and each day they came back to eat at the cabin with Louise.

She could feel William watching her while she cooked. When she reached for tools or items in the shelves above, he would leap up from where he was sitting and reach them for her. She sensed he was a bit shy with her, as if he were handling a clay pot that might break if he wasn't careful. She was pleased by this. Unlike the other men she knew, she noticed that his hands were not calloused. His skin did not see much sun. He had long fingers, long arms, everything about him was long. Why, if he wanted to, he could wrap himself around the trunk of a pine.

William never wanted to leave. Then he remembered why he came. Early one dawn he hiked the mile to the point where he and Stone had set up their tent. He stood along the beach, his back to the lake, and surveyed the forest. The trees here were mature, they had never been cut. There was little undergrowth; no small saplings to contend with. He envisioned situating the cabins to take advantage of the sun all day, and the lake views. Satisfied with his decision, he retreated back to the path to Bennett's cabin and heard a small sound. He stood motionless, hoping to hear or catch a glimpse of game. And then he saw her, a doe, on her hind legs, browsing a cedar tree along the shoreline. Carefully, he lifted his gun and took aim. She must have caught his scent because she got back down on her front legs and stared directly through the muzzle of his gun. Her intense stare rattled him. He hesitated. She shuddered, and bounded back into the woods. The moment to shoot was lost. William solemnly walked back in the snow. If they didn't already own it, he knew he would talk his father into buying this point of land.

CAMP KIRBY
MAY 2010

Avery sat on one of the Adirondack chairs on the front porch of the cabin, for once unaware of the stunning vista in front of her. Her attention was entirely focused on the small book in her hands. The inside pages were yellowed by time, but the tree and canvas had protected it from the elements. There were small initials embossed in gold on the front, MEK. The writing inside was done with black ink that had spotted and faded in places. The first few pages contained sketches of the cabin and the lake and poetic descriptions of the local scenery. Although she knew she should be dissecting owl pellets, she couldn't help herself; she read the first few passages.

June 1, 1893

William arrived today to ensure that I am settling in. It was glorious to see him again! He is so handsome, so smart, and so kind to me. He stayed with me until late in the evening. We sat by a fire he made for us on the grounds down by the waterfront.

He informed me of his plans to build Camp Uncas. I imagine this will be our new home once he divorces Janet. I am not sure why it has taken so long but he promises me that it should be all settled by the end of this summer. My father will be very disappointed in me for not completing my schooling, but I don't care. All that I care about is William.

Minnie

"Holy shit!" Avery stared at the page in stunned disbelief. She had the proof that Minnie actually was Durant's mistress.

The sound of human voices caused her to look up from the diary. Three men were heading her way from the trail that led to Huntington. She quickly stowed the diary in her pack.

"Hey Avery!" Tom, the director of Camp Huntington, called to her. He had two men with him, one was that Jake fellow she recognized from earlier that morning, and the other, she guessed, was about thirty years his senior.

"Avery, I wanted you to meet the men who will be working at the cabin this summer." The three men stood at the base of the porch steps.

"This is Jake, I heard you two met this morning? And this is Frank. They will be doing the bulk of the rehab on the loft. Every once in awhile there may be others coming, but for the most part these two are going to handle it."

"Nice to meet you," Frank said as he worked his way up the steps to greet Avery with a handshake.

Avery rose to greet Frank. "Nice to meet you as well."

"So Jake here tells me you're studying saw-whets?"

"That's the plan if I can track any down, I think I may have had some luck today."

"Yeah, well they're elusive little guys. I've only seen one once, while hunting in the woods. Came upon him sitting quietly in a tree. He looked like a pinecone, still as a mouse, with his eyes closed. I waited to see if he would open 'em. Sure enough, he did, and when he saw that I was still standing there, well wouldn't you know it, instead of flying off like a smart bird should, he just closed his eyes again." Frank let out a laugh.

Avery liked him immediately.

"If you don't mind, we'd like to take a look around," Jake said, bringing the focus back to their work, not hers.

"Sure, go ahead," she said.

The men entered, Frank giving her a quick wink as he walked through the door of the cabin.

RAQUETTE LAKE
SUMMER 1877

Ella and Hannah were exhausted from the thirty-eight mile, seven-hour trek by stagecoach from their North Creek home to Blue Mountain Lake. Ella held her tongue so as not to upset her mother more than she already was by the journey, but she was irritated that William failed to warn them how rough the roads would be. They both had to strap themselves to their seats in the carriage so as not to fall onto the floor during the ride. Yet they, along with the rest of the crew Dr. Durant had hired to carry their belongings, still had a way to go before reaching Raquette. They stayed overnight at Holland House, a small establishment overlooking Blue Mountain Lake. It was not up to Ella's standards, yet any luxury at this point was better than none.

In the morning Ella woke up early to explore outside. She left her mother sleeping peacefully in the room and quietly walked out through the front door.

Blue Mountain Lake shimmered in the background as she wound her way around the lodge and found a trail left behind by loggers that led into the woods. She buttoned her collar all the way up her neck and wrapped her shawl closely about her chest to keep out the chill of the morning air. The forest was foreboding as well as enchanting. The smell of pine greeted her as she followed the swath of cleared land that led away from the hotel and the lake. The pines that lined the path towered above her, carpeting the floor of the forest with their needles. The cacophony of birdsong added a lyrical symphony to the sylvan setting. After walking a short distance Ella came upon a clearing in the woods, a burnt out area left by the lumbermen.

Pioneering White birch were breaking through the log slash, sparsely interspersed with fireweed. Ella picked some for the caretakers' table. If the place they were going to was half as beautiful as these woods, maybe this wilderness her father was staking their future on wasn't going to be so God-forsaken after all.

After a breakfast of fried bread and fresh raspberries and cream served with hot tea, Ella and Hannah were summoned by Dr. Durant's trusted guides Jerome Wood, Charlie Bennett and their helper, young Ike Lawrence. They gathered their belongings for the next leg of the journey which started by loading the guideboats with luggage and supplies.

"Planning on a social?" Bennett muttered as he lifted the ladies' trunks. Ella and Hannah overheard but chose to ignore the comment.

The men then loaded the food supplies: five tins of caviar, biscuits, ten bottles of Riesling wine from the Rhine Valley in Germany, two bottles of port, two boxes of Havana cigars and two pounds of cheese.

"How quaint," Hannah said, as she touched one of the woven packs Ike used to carry supplies.

"My sister Louise makes these," Ike said. He hoisted his pack over his shoulders and put his arms through the leather straps.

"Look at these interesting boats. Are we riding in these or is another boat picking us up?" Ella said.

"Well, Miss Doo'rant, these guideboats are the only transport around. Your father had these built special for the trips to Raquette," Wood answered her. "Made of White pine and able to carry up to thous' pounds I'd say, easy. Special order from Long Lake."

Leaving Blue Mountain, the crew and passengers had to take a waterway journey through Eagle and Utowana Lakes before they reached the Marion River and finally, Raquette. Wood and Bennett faced the stern as they handled the eight-foot oars of the boats, gliding them over the tannin-stained water, which reminded Ella of steeping tea. The men landed the boats on shore at the mouth of the Marion where a small, bark-enveloped lean-to sat, providing shelter for weary travelers.

"We must stop here for a carry," Wood said. The strong, burly guides first helped the ladies climb on shore, then took the trunk and Adirondack packs out one by one and laid them on the ground to organize for the carry. Ike pulled out the horsehair blanket and put it down on the raised floor of the lean-to for Ella and Hannah to sit on.

"As much as I appreciate the rest, tell me, why on earth can't we keep going? Must you portage through here? We can't navigate?" Hannah said.

"There's rapids we must go 'round. We'll come back for you and the boats 'fore too long," Bennett said. He and Wood left the ladies with young Ike Lawrence and his loaded musket.

Ella gazed longingly over at the boy's musket and wished she could take off in the woods for a hunt. Realizing this wasn't appropriate, she filled her time making herself more comfortable. She lifted her wide-brimmed felt hat off of her head and took out the piece of sheer Swiss cotton mull that William had instructed his mother to purchase specifically for the woods. It was fashioned into a veil that, when draped over the head, covered both the nape of the neck and the face — protection from the biting insects.

Ella let the veil fall over the nape of her neck but folded back the cotton that would otherwise cover her face and placed the hat back on her head. She didn't want anything coming between her and the smell that lingered in the air. She watched as her mother fussed with her own veil.

"Can I help you with that?" she offered.

"Yes, these flies are a nuisance," Hannah grumbled. She waved away the insects that were starting to hover around her face and neck, the only skin she revealed to the sun.

"I hope it's better at the camp. Thankfully Margaret isn't with us, she'd be pestered to no end by these bugs."

Ella frowned at the idea of dragging Margaret along. She placed the veil around her mother's face and sat back to enjoy the view and sounds of the forest. To Ella, the shade of the lean-to was a haven from the afternoon sun, but to Hannah, impatient to move on, it was a prison. This being Hannah's first visit to the area, and, as usual, uninformed by her husband about what to expect, she was growing increasingly irritated, so she turned her attention to Ike.

"Ike, you're rather dark-skinned, too much sun perhaps or are you part Indian?" Hannah inquired of Ike.

"Yes ma'am, I'm part Injun. My father is a Mohawk," Ike answered.

"Are you educated?"

"Mother, really, is this the Inquisition? Why not look around you at the woods and enjoy the quiet?"

Hannah would not be deterred. "Well?" She looked at Ike for an answer.

"Yes, Mrs. Doo'rant, we're all educated in the Lawrence house."

"And who taught you? The Jesuits?" Hannah kept up the inquiry.

"No ma'am, I don't know a Jez-oowet. My Ma taught me to read and write, and my Pa taught me how to hunt, fish and trap."

Hannah raised her eyebrow. "So you like sport then?"

"Sport ma'am?" Ike said. "I don't know about sporting but I do know I like to eat."

"I think that hunting to stave off hunger would make anyone a good sportsman," Ella said. "Tell me Ike, what does Adirondack mean?

Ike pulled a small jar out of his dark brown flannel shirt pocket. "Yes ma'am, it means, the people that eat bark. My Mémé told me they were here first."

"Who were here first?" Ella said.

"The people that eat bark. The Algonquins. Want to try some of this?" Ike handed the jar to Ella. Inside was a semi-solid concoction that resembled black oil and appeared toxic. He put a lump of the stuff on his own hand and lathered it on his neck and face.

Ella sniffed it quickly and declined. "No, thank you, though."

"My goodness, what is that horrible looking substance?" Hannah said.

"It's what saves you from the bites, Mrs. Doo'rant. I make it myself from a recipe my father gave me."

"What in the world is in it then?"

"Bit a caster oil and tar all boiled together." Ike rubbed some on his hands.

Ella decided to try a dab, to assure the boy he might be on to something. "Here Ike, let me try a bit of it," she said. She took a small amount of the oil, which was not all that bad smelling, and rubbed it on her own exposed hands. She didn't put any on her neck or face, that would be too daring, even for her. Just as she was about to ask who the Algonquins were, Wood and Bennett came back to retrieve them.

"Why that took a long time, these flies are getting the best of me," Hannah said.

"It's about a mile there and back, Mrs. Doo'rant," Bennett said. He grabbed another pack and put it on his back, then hoisted the one hundred pound boat into the air with the help of Wood. Wood placed the built-in yoke onto his neck for the carry.

Ike assisted Wood in doing the same with the other boat. Ike carried a pack and the oars, and the women followed in step behind as they portaged around the rapids. Ella was glad she was wearing the walking dress her seamstress had sewn for the woods. Her sturdy Balmoral boots with cordovan leather were perfect for walking the dirt pathway. Hannah had already told her the dress was too short and the boots were manly. But then, Hannah was also tripping over her too long hem at every step and almost twisted her poorly-supported ankle on a rock.

Ella refused to let her mother's complaining bother her as they stumbled along the trail. As much as it was tiring, this trip was a reprieve from the Durant North Creek home. Since coming to the States from Europe three years earlier, Ella's only escape from North Creek was the monthly visit to William's rented apartment in New York City. Otherwise she was left with her dull acquaintances, mothers and daughters of the local upstart businessmen who invited her and Hannah to their tea parlors where she had to hold her contemptuous tongue against their gabble and gossip. Besides these trying social events, she had her books, and her writing, which lately had become her passion. She also shared correspondence with friends back in London and an acquaintance she had made in New York City through William— Poultney Bigelow.

He was the son of a prominent politician and journalist. Her father didn't approve of him or his family connections and she wasn't exactly sure why. But although she was entertained by her literary tête-à-tête with Poultney, at age twenty-three Ella felt like a caged cat, just waiting for her chance to escape from the confines of a stifling household and overbearing father.

Her father had threatened more than once to cut off Ella's allowance if she didn't settle down and find 'reasonable' friends. Dr. Durant invited what he deemed were prospective husbands to visit the family home. They were the newly established North Creek elite, if there could be such a thing. Young bankers, lawyers, industrialists trying to make a living off the timber and minerals found in the Adirondack forests. Out of courtesy, and a show of submission to her father, Ella would act the gracious host to the gentleman callers, never planning on following up with their requests to enjoy each other's company again.

The few times she did she regretted it. The would-be courters, dull as dishwater, would pick her up in a coach and bring her to a local dance or affair at some upstart's home or local hall. She'd endure their banter about how much money they planned to make and how they planned to spend it. They would ask asinine questions about her time in England and Europe and tell her how much they envied her upbringing.

She was usually bored and suppressing a yawn within an hour. This did nothing to improve her reputation with the locals. At an afternoon tea one day she overheard the neighborhood ladies titter that she was becoming known as a quencher by the eligible North Creek bachelors. She told Poultney the story during one of her visits to New York City. They met for a stroll in Central Park and after relaying the story she thought he'd take pity on her.

Instead he suggested, "Why not ask the would-be suitors to bring an umbrella as a caution?"

As much as she wanted to laugh, she realized how pathetic her plight was and only found his humor degrading.

The walk and her thoughts came to an end when the guides pointed to the river, where the rapids were faltering. They put the boats back into the water for the ladies to get in again and then loaded the packs and trunk for the final leg of the journey downriver.

"Good heavens, there is more to this journey?" Hannah said.

Winding down the Marion, the entire party was quiet. The place commanded it. They were enveloped by the woods, which lined the still-water pathway. Maples, pines and beech intermingled along the banks. Squirrels, birds and chipmunks flitted from tree to tree.

When they finally reached Raquette Lake, the mood of the party changed. The open waters caught the wind and put more strain on the oars. The guides earned their wage forcing the boats to comply. As they rounded Long Point the wind picked up speed and the men were struggling with the weight of the passengers and luggage. Ella's hat blew off. Waves sprayed up against the gunwales and soaked the women's clothing. Ella cast a sympathetic glance at Hannah. Although her hat was still on her head, her thick mass of hair was whipping around her face, giving her a slatternly appearance.

"Can't we do something about these waves?" Hannah pleaded as she tried to pull a clump of hair back into place under her bonnet.

Bennett ignored her. He was too busy keeping the boat upright. Everything was rocking and it didn't help that they were loaded down with a trunk of clothes that he knew the women would never wear here.

Ike, in the boat with Wood, was working his way from the front of the craft to the middle, trying to keep the food supplies from being swept up by the waves, which were now coming full force over the gunwales. He secured a flapping cover to one of the packs carrying the food before the contents were lost to the lake but lost his balance in the struggle and fell overboard.

Ella screamed. Ike flailed in the water. Wood held out the oar. Ike grabbed the end of it and kicked like a madman to the side of the boat. Coughing and heaving, he hoisted himself over the gunwale, tipping the boat enough that one of the packs carrying the wine, precariously situated due to the rocking and rolling of the boat, fell over the side and immediately started to sink. Ella and Hannah watched in despair as the waves swallowed the pack.

Ella disembarked first when they reached the Durant compound. Having lost all patience, and fatigued by the drama and length of the tiresome journey, she left Ike in charge of helping assist her mother out of the boat. She spotted William coming toward them and ran to embrace him.

"William, for heaven's sake, help me out of this boat!" Hannah was waving away Ike's outstretched hand and glaring at William from her position in the boat.

"Ella, you left mother!" William scolded his sister. He untwined himself from her arms and went to assist Hannah. Dr. Durant, walking several paces behind William, came up to Ella and brushed her cheek with his.

"How was the trip?" he asked, casting an apprehensive stare past her toward Hannah.

"Eventful. Good to see you again, Papa," Ella said.

"You're wet."

"Yes, we had a bit of a mishap on the boat."

"Louise here will help you with your things and show you and your mother where you're staying." He did not wait for an explanation. He pointed Ella in the direction of the small young woman standing quietly to the side. She came to Ella, touched her elbow lightly, and guided her toward the cabins.

Hannah came upon them and immediately complained to her husband about the inconvenience of the trip and the near drowning of his servant.

"My dear, but you've arrived safely, haven't you? And Ike here looks no worse for the excitement," Dr. Durant said.

"No sir, I know how to swim, that's why," Ike said.

"My word boy, I am astonished by your composure!" Hannah said to him. The boy was not ruffled at all.

"The wine went overboard," she said, gathering her dress up to wring out the water. William and his father stopped walking.

"No wine?" Dr. Durant said.

"Exactly," Hannah said pertly. She lifted up her skirt and followed Ella and Louise past her tongue-tied husband.

When they reached the ladies' cabin, Hannah sighed at the state of her new sleeping quarters. "So this is your father's idea of a country manor?" she said.

"At least it has walls and a roof mother, and look, the floor is lined with deer skin and the windows have curtains! Some type of red-stained linen I would guess." Ella said. She walked over to the windows and took hold of the fabric.

"Humph," Hannah scoffed.

Louise observed the exchange between mother and daughter.

"I dyed them," she said.

Ella and Hannah stared at her and then the curtains.

William came into the cabin and assisted his mother to a chair.

"You should rest, Mother," he said. Then he went over to where Ella was standing by the window and whispered, "Stay in your walking attire. I want to show you around before father barks another order at me and we're both doomed to listen to some long-winded plan of his to rape the Adirondack Wilderness and bring crystal and fine china to the woods."

Ella let out a laugh. Hannah glared at the two of them.

"What are you two giggling on about?" Hannah turned to Louise. "What's your name? I missed it in the commotion while getting out of that sad substitute for a yacht."

"Her name is Louise mother, Louise Lawrence, Ike is her younger brother," William answered for Louise. He glanced at her and smiled warmly.

"Where may I take care of some personal affairs?" Hannah asked Louise.

"Mother, your impatience is showing. We have to go to the lake to take care of personal hygiene," William teased.

"William, you may excuse yourself now, I've had enough of your impertinent humor," Hannah said.

William winked at Ella and left them for Louise to manage.

It didn't take Ella long to shake her mother and seek out William. Louise knew where he would be waiting. When she walked Ella to the lean-to, Ella thought that Louise might know more than where William liked to spend his leisure time. She dismissed the idea when she saw her brother.

"What's father thinking, bringing us all to this deep forest?" Ella asked once Louise had left them.

"From what I've learned, he's been buying up land in and around Raquette Lake for the past fifteen years. Speculators buy the land and extract iron ore or clear-cut timber. Once they're done getting what they want, they abandon it and hand it back to the state for unpaid taxes. Father's lawyers for the Adirondack Railroad Company attend the tax sales and buy the land at a pittance; he even ordered me to go once to see how it's done. We now own about a half million acres. And the State Land Office has granted tax exemption on lands to any entrepreneur willing to invest in rail — father's favorite endeavor. He wants to bring people to this place and have them experience the luxury at Raquette Lake that we have at home."

"That's ludicrous! Even if he can bring rail to the interior, people will still have to contend with all of these inlets and outlets and meandering rapids to access the lake. Who besides men looking for a good hunting and fishing expedition will be prepared to make that journey we just finished, waiting amongst the biting flies to camp out in the open?" Ella said.

"You don't understand. This land is all he has left," William said with gravity. "We need to support him if we ever want an inheritance."

Ella lingered on this news for a moment. "But what do you know about building anything?" Ella said finally.

"I have ideas. I envision a grand country estate."

"Here? Hah! I don't see it. This isn't Binstead or Thirlestane."

"Don't be such a naysayer, this is America, anything's possible. Besides that's not exactly what I was thinking anyway. But I can picture it, a country estate in the Adirondack wilderness." He swept his hands in the air. "And the natives that live here year round are great carpenters and woodsmen. Just look around you," he said, "there's plenty of material to work with."

Ella and William left the lean-to and walked into the woods. William knew the trails well. They went deep into the forest. While walking Ella came upon a branch that had broken off from a pine tree.

"Look at this, William," she said lifting it off the ground, "it looks like a dagger."

William examined the piece. "I'd say it looks more like a woman. Either way, it's very intricate. They call those pine knots. The resin collects here you see." He pointed to the design that the resin-collecting process had shaped into the wood. "They make great fire starters."

"William, here's an idea! We'll call the Durant family compound Pine Knot."

Ella and William returned to the camp for a dinner of mutton and potatoes, served in a rudimentary dining cabin with open walls, no more refined than the lean-to Hannah and Ella had rested in earlier in the day. Afterward, when everything was cleaned up and the food secured from bears and raccoons, Dr. and Mrs. Durant retired to their cabins with an order for Ella and William do so as well.

"A photographer is coming tomorrow to take pictures of us in our cabins and other bucolic settings around the compound. We need to be on top of our game, look our best. These pictures will appear in the brochures and promotional material the Adirondack Railroad Company is using to 'sell' the experience," Dr. Durant said.

Ella and William ignored their father's orders so they could sit up with the 'natives', as William liked to call the locals, to hear tales around the campfire. It was well past nine pm when they all settled on logs around the fire.

"We had a group come meet us at Blue Mountain, last summer. Showed up late at our meeting destination, came in from New Yerk City, all of them. Came ill-prepared." Wood started in as he stuffed a wad of tobacco in the bowl of his pipe and paused to light it. "They's paying $2.50 a day for our services and they's just taking their time about it all morning, like there's no tomorrow. I keep saying to them, we best be moving along before the flies start in and it gits unbearable, but they's lingering over breakfast like they're not in any hurry to get going."

Ella and William looked around for their father. Neither he, nor their mother would approve of this conversation, or the late hour, especially for Ella to be socializing.

But the campfire was too inviting and the stories too interesting to pass up. Louise Lawrence was glowing in the firelight. Ella noticed William catch her eye on several occasions.

"They're finally ready to leave and we have a long day ahead to reach the Raquette, then Fulton Chain. And the carries would slow us down tremendous with all the gear they brought. They's got butter, bread, whiskey, tea, sugar, canned goods, that's besides their clothes. I told them, you won't need all that gear, we be eaten what we hunt and fish. But keep the whiskey!" Wood laughed at his own joke.

"But they insisted on bringing it all with them in the pack

basket. About seventy pounds of it I'd guess." He stopped, took a long toke of his pipe, removed the stem from his mouth and let the smoke curl into the night air.

"So off we go. An when we get to the rapids at the Marion, I tell them, can you carry those packs of yers for the next mile or so? Cause I have my own hands full with the boat and the packs of gear for cooking and eating, plus blankets. And then there's the hunting rifle. I must've had at least twenty-five pounds plus the boat on me alone. The other guide, he has another hundred or so and he's rolling his eyes at the New Yerkers."

"What'd they carrying for weapons?" Ike asked.

"Oh, yes, that too. They got the latest breechloaders and six shot repeaters, no muskets for them folks. And the nicest rods alright. They're all set to shoot the first deer they see and catch the first trout they lay their eyes on. It's a good thing many of the New Yerkers can't aim, no reference to you, Mr. Doo'rant." Wood nodded in William's direction. "Because if they were able, there'd be no deer left in the woods for every New Yerker that comes here looking for them."

"We guides go by the rule, never hunt for more than you can eat," Bennett added to the conversation even though he had not taken part in the expedition. "But not all these city folks think that way. No they want to get that trophy deer even if they don't plan to eat the meat."

"What did they end up doing for the portage then? Were they able to carry their loads?" Ella asked.

"Well, they started to, but soon enough they knew they'd brought too much, just as I told them. An so they had to abandon some of the load, an me and the other guide had to make two trips to come back an git all them packs. It took us twice the time, mind you not just on Marion, but the whole week we traveled with them. That was twice the time spent carrying and twice less the time hunting." Wood let out a hearty laugh, which the rest of the party joined in.

"I know these men you speak of," William said. "Not by name, but I see them everyday in the social clubs of New York City. The effete lifestyle they lead and the tedious jobs that got them there are why they come here to escape, if only for a week."

Wood put his hand to his mouth and cleared his throat. The group was silenced by William's somber statement.

The mood was broken by a loud 'clang', coming from the kitchen area.

"He's back," Bennett said. "The bear."

The men grabbed their guns and headed in the direction of the sound, taking the oil lanterns with them. The women followed behind.

The party moved in unison to where the racket was coming from. They had been expecting this nocturnal visitor; he had tried to steal a hind end of venison from the smokehouse the night before. Ike had set up a bear trap in anticipation of his return. When they came closer to the noise they noticed he was limping. Although injured, he had somehow got loose from the leg irons and was making the most of his freedom by turning over pots and pans looking for scraps of food in the dining area, finding the smokehouse was locked tight. Wood and Ike held their lanterns high.

"How'd he escape those irons?" Wood asked Bennett.

"Damfino," Bennett said.

The bear was a good six rods from where they stood. Wood and Bennett loaded buckshot into their rifles while Ike snuck as close to the bear as he dared and placed a lantern on a tree stump to illuminate the area. William held his hand up to stop the guides from taking action.

"Wait," he said handing his breechloader to Ella. "The bruin is yours, Ella. Do you have enough light to see the mark?"

Ella lifted the rifle to her eye, nodded her head at William, pulled the trigger, and hit the bear in the chest with one shot. There would be bear meat for the camp and a new rug for Ella and Hannah's cabin floor. Even more important to Ella however was that the guides were gawking at her with admiration.

The next day the staff were abuzz with Ella's daring. Dr. and Mrs. Durant were not as impressed. After breakfast they pulled her aside to speak about it away from the staff.

"Ella, if you put as much effort into finding a husband as into your marksmanship you might actually be successful," her father said.

"For heaven's sake, Ella, what were you doing up with the men anyway, sitting around a campfire talking about who knows what?" Hannah said.

"William was with me, Mother. And I wasn't the only woman present, Louise was there with her brother Ike."

"I hardly think you should be comparing your manners with that of Indians. And William or not, you must comport yourself like a dignified lady," Dr. Durant said.

"Really? Or else what? Who of our society is here to report back to the papers any scandal I may bring to the family name?"

"Mind how you speak to me," Dr. Durant said, fixing her with an icy stare. Ella heeded the tone and went to look for William who usually saved her from these encounters.

"You really should try harder not to antagonize father," William chided Ella as she sat on the other end of the boat he was rowing across the lake. The two of them had snuck away from the camp to explore Osprey Island after the picture-taking that morning.

Ella gave a most unladylike snort. "It doesn't take much to antagonize him. And aren't you being somewhat hypocritical? After all, you handed me the gun. You know as well as I do I'm as good at hitting my mark as any man."

William scowled. "Yes I know. We all know, but that isn't the point. When he scolds you, you should say you are sorry meekly and move along. Instead you stand your ground and fight him and you know how much he hates it. It has always surprised me that he never disciplined you with force the way most fathers would to make you obey."

Ella scowled back. "If he wanted me to be obedient he should've been around more often to teach me to be so."

"Well said, but believe me, if you're not more careful, he'll find other ways to make you comply with his wishes. And you know as well as I do that isn't what you want."

Ella put her hand into the water and let it skim the surface as William rowed. The water felt cool and lovely. Blue Mountain stood like a majestic guard in the background. At once dark, then light, the sun's rays cast shadows on the forest range as it peeked in and out of the white cumulus clouds in the sky.

All morning long they had been forced to pose while the photographer, Stoddard, took pictures of them and their rustic lodgings as Papa shouted out orders.

"We need to portray the family enjoying themselves: reading on the porch, eating in the open air dining cabin, strolling along the paths," he had said.

After modeling for what seemed like hours, she jumped at the chance to join William and get away from the Durant camp — now called Pine Knot, as William had talked their father into the name, acting like it was his find, his idea. William knew Papa would never agree if he thought Ella was the mastermind behind it.

"A bit of a farce this morning wasn't it?" Ella turned her attention away from the clouds toward William.

"Anything to drum up more investors in his grand Adirondack Company Railroad scheme," William said. He strained at the oars for a moment as a swift wind picked up and riffled the water.

"You seem enamored by the young Indian woman," she said.

William was visibly flustered by her directness. "Who I may find attractive is none of your damn business, Ella."

"Well, you and I both know it will eventually become father's," Ella said.

William thought for a moment and then said, "Which reminds *me*, how is your Muse of Malden-on-the-Hudson?"

Ella flashed an angry look at William. He was trying to rile her she knew, but she was not going to fall into the trap.

"You know better than I do. Poultney only communicates with me through you. I haven't seen him since my last visit to New York City."

William remained silent.

"Have you seen him lately?" she asked.

Picking up on Ella's eagerness for news of Poultney Bigelow despite her attempt to sound casual, William relented. "I haven't seen him at the clubs in New York in awhile. I'm sure he'll send news, or a letter as soon as he's able to do so. You know he cares about your writing."

"Who's this Murray fellow we're going to visit?"

"Henry Murray? He's a clergyman and writer from Boston I think you might enjoy meeting. He's written several articles and a book called *Adventures in the Wilderness*. They call him 'Adirondack Murray' around here. The guides claim it's because of him their trade has doubled these past few years. People from all over are coming to the Adirondacks to experience the 'spiritual cleansing the woods provide'," William said.

"You say that with a note of sarcasm. How, after all, do you expect to make the family's fortune if people don't long to experience this?" Ella waved her hands in the air to encompass the clear blue sky, the lake and forested mountains that were their backdrop.

"I have no problem with people coming here as long as they know why they're here. Father's idea is for the masses to bring all the trappings of city life with them that they feign trying to escape."

Ella smiled. "Willie, you're such a romantic! If it were up to you we would all wear the guides' clothing, stalk the woods for deer and fish for trout in the stream for our supper. Never mind the caviar and biscuits, the fine French wine, the cigars! Who needs them when we have all of this to please us!" Ella let out a laugh. William frowned at her.

"Have your fun now, but listen carefully, when we arrive at Osprey Island try to stay quiet. I need to talk to old Murray and see what this business is of his letting Alvah Dunning build a cabin and icehouse. I'm not sure what Alvah is up to, but father has asked me to look into it for cousin Charles. He wants to purchase this island to build his own home and sell off the rest to father. I need your cooperation. For once, pretend you're in North Creek, not a London tea parlor, and act like a simpleton."

"Yes William, anything you say." Ella stifled a laugh, put on her most serious face, and half-bowed to him from her seated position on the end of the boat.

They landed on shore and Murray greeted them with a hearty handshake.

"It is a pleasure to be in the company of another writer," he said to Ella.

"Why yes, I am writing a book of poetry and a book on Dante," she replied, delighted that someone was interested enough to comment on her passion.

"Well, I write adventures myself," Murray said.

"Like Tom Sawyer?"

"No, more like do it yourself adventures. I'm trying to get people to understand and appreciate the allure of this place. 'The wilderness provides the perfect relaxation which all jaded minds require'," he said, quoting from his book.

"So I understand," Ella said.

William brought the conversation back to business. "I see there are some new cabins on the property since we last came out to visit Henry."

"Alvah has taken up residence, and I allowed him to build a small cabin and icehouse for his guiding business. You know how popular he is with the Bostonians and New Yorkers," Murray said. "Besides, I'm not planning on staying here. I'll be moving on to other locations, seeking out other places to visit in these woods. Osprey Island was always a way-stop for me. Alvah can have it to himself."

Ella left the men to discuss business and wandered around to see what else was on the island. She walked along the shore, picking up pieces of shale and skimming them over the surface of the water as Ike had showed her. The island was deserted. Although she liked the peace, she decided living on an island would be taking solitude too far.

She came upon a canoe, half in the water, half on shore. It was a beautiful craft, covered by some type of gray bark. She wondered how it would float in the water. Unable to resist the impulse, she pushed it offshore and got in, getting her petticoats and sheepskin boots soaked while doing so.

"I should have changed into my walking clothes after those bloody photographs!" And then she was free-floating in the water. She lay down on the bottom of the boat and gazed up at the pillows in the sky. Cocooned from the wind, she felt the sun warming her face and body.

Time was suspended; she couldn't hear a thing except the soft lapping of waves against the side of the craft. Ella searched for a word to describe the moment "Lethean," she said. Pleased with the sound, she repeated it, "Like the River Lethe in Hades, one drink from it and you are completely oblivious of your past troubles," she said to the air. Nothing answered back, until:

"What in tar-nation are you doing in my canoe!"

Startled, Ella bolted upright wondering where she was. Last thing she recalled was daydreaming in a small boat. Scanning the horizon she realized she had fallen asleep and was now in the middle of the lake. How did that happen so quickly and who was this strange man with the beard and sharp eyes, yelling at her from his boat alongside her?

"I am so sorry, sir! I am not sure how I ended up out here," she stammered.

"Well get the hell out of it!" the man yelled.

She hastily grabbed hold of the oar to row back to shore, looking around to see which way she needed to row.

"Here, you idjit woman. I'll row you back to shore, you doing it will take twice as long as it should." He tied a rope to the end of the canoe and towed her back.

Both Murray and William were standing on shore looking concerned.

"What the devil do you think you're doing, Ella?" William was beside himself.

"I am so sorry, William." She turned to the strange looking gangly man that had rescued her. "Thank you for your help."

"That's alright I guess." The strange man calmed down. "I can't fault a person for wanting to look up at the sky, even if it's in my canoe, an even if it's a woman."

Ella immediately liked him. She put her hand out to greet his. "My name is Ella Durant."

"Yes, well, I'd say pleased to meet you, Miss Doo'rant, but I'm not much with likin' people less they's paying me to like 'em. My name is Alvah Dunning. People call me Snake Eyes, named by the Injuns round here and it stuck."

Ella noticed his beady eyes and could see why he got the name. He had rather peculiar, sharp features. On his hip hung a long hunting knife and a rifle was strapped on his back.

"Ella, Alvah here is a legend. Our friends from New York would pay a month's mortgage for the chance to be guided through the woods by this man," William said, hoping the flattery would ease Alvah's temper.

"Well, then," Murray said, "it looks like the get-away canoe and damsel in distress have been rescued, and no one was hurt by it."

"Yeah," Alvah said, turning his back to the group, he spat on the ground, and walked away.

William refused to talk to Ella the whole row back to Pine Knot. Worse, when they arrived Dr. Durant, who had not given her permission to go along with William, was pacing back and forth on the beachfront, seething.

"Your mother has been looking for you," he said, glaring down at her as he helped her out of the boat. Ella stole looks back at William as she walked toward her cabin. He was conferring with their father on the shore, pointing in the direction of Osprey Island. After what seemed like too long, he looked up briefly, and waved to her. Ella smiled, and with a spring in her step, headed toward her cabin. She knew William couldn't stay mad at her.

The next afternoon, Francis Stott and his wife Elizabeth came by in a boat rowed by a guide. After polite greetings all around, the two families retreated to the shade of the dining cabin for tea.

"How goes the hunting, Francis?" Dr. Durant asked.

"Well for the past few days I've been out fishing mostly, planning on taking a chance with Alvah, scouting out deer tomorrow," Stott said.

The name Alvah raised all heads in the Durant family.

"How is the building going?"

"Bluff Point's perfect for us."

"Where's Bluff Point?" Ella asked.

"Right around the bend from here on the lake dear," Elizabeth Stott said. "I know Jennie and the boys will be delighted to have a summer vacation home. It will be a relief from having to stay in these small cabins the guides built."

"Yes, it's about time Bennett followed through with his plans for a hotel on this lake, we sorely need more options for the visitors, especially for the ladies," Dr. Durant said.

Hannah turned to Elizabeth Stott. "I'm afraid we have been without any newspapers to keep in touch with the world. What news do you have from New York?"

"Oh, have you heard that five of Commodore Vanderbilt's offspring are suing for a larger share of the inheritance?" Elizabeth gasped as she placed her teacup back on its saucer.

"Oh dear!" Hannah said.

"Whatever for? The Commodore has made his wishes known. He wrote the will before he died," Dr. Durant said.

"He left the bulk of his estate, ninety million mind you, to one son, William, and then the rest he doled out in various amounts to his children and grandchildren," Elizabeth said. Flushed and excited from all the attention this gossip was creating for her, she paused to re-pin her hat in place as it had tilted off-kilter.

"Appears unfair to me," Ella said.

"Balderdash," Dr. Durant said. "I say it is all a farce. The man created a fortune with his own cunning. He can choose who is best fit to inherit it. That youngest son of his, Cornelius is it? Is an imbecile if you ask me. Borrowing money from wealthy friends using the Vanderbilt name as collateral when he had no intention of ever paying it back. He doesn't deserve the inheritance."

"The worst of it is that his children are dragging their father's character through the mud in their deliberations. They've found themselves some high priced lawyers who have hired some equally high priced doctors who are going to testify that the Commodore was unfit and insane at the time he drafted his will," Francis Stott said.

"I suppose the children believe that by denigrating his character they will earn sympathy from the judge?" Hannah said.

"That is not the all of it!" exclaimed Elizabeth. "They are claiming he was arrogant, over-bearing, and selfish."

"So what else is new? Again I say, it is not the weak of heart that amass fortunes in today's world." Dr. Durant directed his steely eyes first at Hannah and then William.

"You may be right, Thomas. But I don't agree with how he set up his will. He must have known that giving the bulk of his estate to one son would cause problems. The rest of it — ten million — may seem like a lot of money to us, but the Vanderbilt children are acting like scullery dogs fighting over scraps of food. It is shameful. And it is all being made public thanks to the *New York Times*," Francis Stott said.

"Maybe he would have been better off leaving this world without a will," Ella said.

All eyes turned on Ella.

"Don't be daft, Ella," William scoffed. "You don't leave this world with a hundred million dollar estate and no will."

"Think about it though. If he left no will, the children would contest it anyway. But they would be dragging each other's names through the mud to gain a judge's approval, and not their father's," Ella said.

They were all silenced by this. Hannah eyed her husband over her teacup, waiting for his response. He stayed silent. So did William.

"Now there is a clever idea indeed," Elizabeth said.

Dr. Durant had had enough of the conversation. He rose to tell the guides to get the boats ready.

"The weather is perfect right now for a row, no wind," he said.

Ella and Hannah went back to the cabin to change into walking skirts. Hannah picked up one of the small umbrellas she had brought to protect against the sun.

"You might think about using one as well. Your skin is too dark already," she said to Ella.

"I have a hat on, that should suffice. Besides, I can't help it if I have Papa's skin color," Ella retorted. Hannah shoved an umbrella into her hand.

The guides loaded the packs of food and drink into the boats and the party took off. Ella tried to get into the boat with William but Dr. Durant reprimanded her.

"William is with me. Go with your mother," he said.

Ella wasn't sure but she thought she heard Charlie Bennett snicker.

"I want to hear all about your book of poetry when we picnic on Golden Beach," Elizabeth Stott said as she climbed into the boat with as much delicacy as her layered petticoats allowed.

They rowed to South Bay and landed at a place the natives called Golden Beach. The party put down blankets in the lean-to on shore. William and Ella walked the beach while the adults rested.

"I don't understand it all. Why is father taking us on a tour around the lake as if he is prospecting for gold?" Ella picked up a small stone, threw it into the lake and watched it plink into the water.

"Not gold, land. Just take a look around," William said. "Except for a few hundred acres he already owns here, the land around Raquette is all owned by the state. And if it isn't owned by the state, then the state doesn't know who owns it because people like Charlie Bennett and Alvah Dunning build these cabins and lean-tos in the woods and set up camp. It's squatters rights."

"Hah, that would never happen in England," Ella snorted.

"We're not in England anymore, Ella," William said.

"Yes, I know that all *too* well," she said.

"Here it's the wild frontier, each man to his own. I have yet to see a game warden."

"How exactly do people around here make a living? This land isn't arable, and being a guide could hardly keep a family fed," Ella said.

"Logging, guiding, trapping," William said.

"William, Ella, come sit with us and have some lemonade," Mrs. Stott called to them. They ended their conversation and walked back to the lean-to.

Ella was allowed to ride in the boat with William on the way back. While admiring the cedar-lined lakeshore, she saw a small cabin set back in the woods on a knoll made of logs cloaked in bark, nestled between the trees.

She pointed it out to William. "Who lives there?"

"That was one of Bennett's cabins," William said. "Father just acquired it from him."

"It was a land-swap," Bennett shouted from the stern.

As they rowed past, Ella saw Louise emerge from the front door, sweeping dirt out and down the wooden steps. She wore a white blouse and a long slim skirt that silhouetted her small figure. Louise looked up when she heard their voices echo over the water. Her eyes locked on William's.

By late August the chilly air descended on the cabins at nightfall, which came earlier and earlier each evening. It was time to leave Camp Pine Knot. Ella regretted having to return to her dreary life in North Creek. At Pine Knot she spent time writing because her mother didn't insist she dress for afternoon tea. And instead of the incessant chatter of her mother and Margaret, she could listen to the waves lapping along the shore. Not as majestic as the sea in England, but still soothing.

But the cabin she and her mother shared was only insulated

with sphagnum moss, and there was no fireplace, which made their departure inevitable.

While Dr. and Mrs. Durant instructed the guides and servants where to put their luggage, Ella searched for William. He hadn't shown up with his packs. When he did arrive to say good-bye, he wasn't dressed for travel nor did he have any luggage.

"Aren't you coming?" Ella said.

William shook his head. "I'm staying behind through the fall. I want to be here when the leaves are all off the trees and continue with construction. I'm meeting with some local carpenters and masons. I told the Stotts I'd advise them on their building plans, and this is the best time of year to get a lay of the land on Bluff Point."

Ella frowned. William had taken on the look of a native. He wore a felt cap with the front brim curled up at his forehead, wool knickers and tall hiking boots made of stiff-looking leather. His shirt was identical to Ike's and the other guides — a long sleeved brown flannel. Not exactly the attire he was used to wearing. She wondered what had happened to his silk hat, frock coat and vest, his trousers, linen shirt with a collar and ascot.

"Don't worry, the guides and servants are staying behind as well. Besides," he whispered conspiratorially in her ear, "I can be free of him for awhile, there's no telegraph here." William nodded in their father's direction.

"But what about your job with the Railroad and apartment in New York City?" Ella said.

"Father wants Pine Knot developed enough that he can entertain his business associates by next summer. Potential investors, you know."

"But then where shall I stay if you're not in New York City?"

"Stay with Uncle Charles and cousin Estelle, or what about your friend Fran Murphy? Just make sure, whatever you do, you have an escort of whom father approves."

"Hah, Papa would never approve if I showed up at the Opera on the arm of Poultney Bigelow! I still cannot figure out why he detests the man."

"It's not him, Ella, it's his father John. John Bigelow has been writing some scathing reviews in the *New York Evening Post* about the Erie Canal 'Ring', a group of contractors he claims are skimming off money from the state for maintenance contracts on the Erie Canal. Many of these men in the so-called 'Ring of Corruption' are father's associates."

"He really knows how to pick his friends doesn't he? Yes, Poultney's told me all about this Erie Canal scandal," Ella said. "But that has nothing to do with Poultney. I'd say Papa's real gripe is that Poultney's an intellectual, not a railroad tycoon."

"Time to go," he said kissing her on the forehead. "I'll see you at Christmas. And then I'll tell you all about the grand plans I have for this place."

Ella wondered about Louise and where she was staying. Before she could ask him, Ike came and took her pack, "We're going now, Miss Doo'Rant." Ella followed the boy to the boat, looking back at William. He was already striding away, down a shoreline trail that led deep into the woods.

CAMP KIRBY
MAY 2010

Avery trekked through the woods, her backpack laden with gear, to the White pine she hoped was a roosting site of the saw-whet owl. If she was right, perhaps a pair were mating in the vicinity of this tree. The small gray, fur-covered pellets she had dissected last evening by the lantern light had the remnants of mice bones. Avery observed the telltale signs that they were saw-whet pellets and not another raptor. There was the presence of only the skull in some pellets, and the bottom half of the body in others. Saw-whets tend to eat the head of their prey first and leave the rest for another meal. And there were also remnants of junco and chickadees, the small birds of prey the saw-whet favored.

At the site, she took out the mist net and bungee cord she needed to set up to capture the little owl. She scanned the forest, trying to identify the best location. Unfortunately the poles had not been packed along with the rest of her supplies, and to set up the nets she would need to use the low hanging branches of some trees she could throw a rope up into and tie the net on. Ahead of her two pines stood ten meters apart between which she could drape the net. Avery decided it was a good spot. She planned to use an audio lure to bring the owl — or owls — in. If they were nesting, the males would be defending their territory.

When she reached the trees she saw that none had low-hanging branches she could throw a rope up to, and they were not great climbing trees either. Her only option was to shinny up them, something she was not looking forward to. What she needed was a ladder.

"Might as well get started," she said out loud.

Working the net and cord over her neck she gripped the tree with her arms extended. She planted her feet on the tree forming a V with her body.

"Here goes nothing."

Inching her feet upward, her hands followed suit.

She smiled. This might work after all.

She did it again, gaining another foot up the tree trunk. After three more shinnies, she lost her footing and fell off the tree, landing hard on her butt. The jolt from the fall rattled up her spine to her brain.

"Damn it!" she shouted, rubbing where it hurt.

"Need a hand?" It was Jake, standing off in the distance.

At first Avery was startled. Then she was angry. "What the hell are you doing sneaking up on me like that? And how long have you been there?" She stood up and swatted the duff off her bottom.

Jake stood there looking guilty. "What are you doing?"

"I just lost my balance and fell," she said, annoyed she had to explain anything to him.

"Yeah, I can see that. Would it help if you had a ladder?" Jake asked.

Avery looked around for Frank.

"What brings you here?" Avery asked.

"Tom asked me to tell you to stop by his office later. He has some news about saw-whet sightings."

Avery's heart skipped a beat with excitement. But she didn't want to let Jake off that easy. "Well, I'd appreciate it if you'd just leave me to my work – alone." Avery was apprehensive about his real motive, as well as angry at his intrusion. This guy had some nerve.

He shrugged. "Suit yourself then. I was going to offer to bring you a ladder, but if you don't want my help, I'll leave you to it." He walked away.

Avery's annoyance was tinged with regret — she could use that ladder.

Not one to give up, her next attempt included using her thighs as well as feet to counteract her arms. She bent her knees and laced her legs one at a time around the trunk of the tree, then grabbed hold and started to shinny up again. This time she had more luck with it. Her thighs were pure muscle from all the fieldwork and compensated for her lack of upper-body strength. When she reached the height she wanted, she wrapped the bungee cord around the tree and hooked both ends into the net's grommet.

"There!" she shouted at the tree.

Now she had to work her way slowly down the trunk to the forest floor. It was going smoothly until after about a third of the way down something caught her eye – a bird flitting by – and she started to slide. Her hands raked against the rough bark as she descended. She tried to slow the fall by gripping the trunk with her thighs. This caused intense pain as the friction made itself felt through the denim of her jeans. She finally hit the ground. "That's it. I'm not climbing up there again."

Back at Camp Kirby, Avery discovered a ladder leaning up against the side of the cabin — waiting to be used, but neither Frank or Jake were around to ask if she could borrow it. She glanced at her watch. It was lunchtime, they had probably taken off for Camp Huntington to eat. She thought of looking for the two men but her hands and legs were throbbing and she needed to attend to them first.

She rinsed her hands at the kitchen sink, gently trying to remove the sticky tree sap. It was painful. Her hands were red and raw, with slivers of wood embedded in her palms. She took a break from the cleansing, grabbed a yogurt from the refrigerator and went out on the porch to collect her thoughts.

I need to go to the nurse's station.

It was still lunch hour. She would wait until one and then hike the mile trail along the shoreline to the campus facility. In the meantime, to quiet her mind, she went inside to fetch Minnie's diary from under her bed.

June 2, 1893

Today my charge arrived in a wooden canoe, paddling it to shore and pulling it up along the bank. He walked up to the cabin with his small case and took off his ragged cap to introduce himself. His name is Nate. He is eleven years of age. It is hard to believe I am just six years his senior! William specifically requested that I tutor him this summer. Last year, I worked with all of the Durant children, but given the circumstances of my blossoming relationship with William, this would not be wise.

Nate is a very dark, serious boy. He is an orphan being brought up by his uncle on Raquette Lake somewhere.

"How'd you do ma'am," he said, "My name is Nate and Mr. Doo'rant asks me to help ya out here in the woods."

"Why good day to you Nate," I replied with a smile. "Yes, I could use some help. I am not much of a pioneer and there are a lot of chores to keep up with around here. I will appreciate your assistance. Let me show you where you will be staying."

And I showed him to the loft and his bedroom. He unpacked the few things he had brought with him, including his rifle, which he set on the front porch. He then proceeded to gather wood from the forest and chop it by the fire pit at the water's edge. I sat on the porch and watched with amazement at how quickly he worked without interruption. Not once did he stop to ask for a glass of water or inquire about anything. When he finished with that project he went to work in the cabin, restocking the wood for the stove, and the wood rack by the hearth, taking account of the supplies, and even putting away my morning dishes.

"Ma'am I plan to head back to the Raquette Lake store to gather more supplies. Would you like me to bring you anything in particular?"

"Did you bring any books with you Nate?"

"Books? No ma'am. But I got a book that I try to read that Mr. Doo'rant gave me once."

"Lovely! Then why don't you bring that book with you on your way back from the store Nate? You do know that Mr. Durant asked me to tutor you this summer?"

"Yea, ma'am, but I wasn't planning on it myself. I've gone to school some and learned to read n' write."

"Well, we will start today, after we have something to eat, so bring the book with you," I told him.

I am especially glad to have someone here at night. There are bears in the woods and I can hear them shuffling around the cabin area, searching for food scraps. William has left strict instructions with me never to leave any food scraps out and around the cabin. When he came to see me last night we burned all our scraps in the open fire. We store all the food in a bear box with a padlock. Now that Nate is here he can take care of these small inconveniences.

It will also be good to have a companion. While I waited for William last evening I sat on the front porch. The insects were ruthless, but I needed to do something with myself besides sit inside waiting anxiously for William to show up. I thought I could hear the laughter coming from one of the hotels in the distance and echoing off the lake. I am afraid of becoming too lonely at this cabin away from everything. I suppose it will be alright. William and I can see each other secretly this way without Janet knowing about our affair.

Minnie

Avery put Minnie's diary back in its hiding place and hiked the mile through the woods to Camp Huntington.

"So you're the lucky one hanging out at Camp Kirby all summer are ya?" The nurse attending to Avery was named Sally. She was a pretty, white haired, elderly woman.

"Yes, I'm conducting research on owl nesting habits and Kirby is a secluded spot to do my work," Avery answered.

"Secluded, I'd say. Make sure you check in with us once in awhile so we know you're still alive ok? Now let me see."

Avery winced as Sally took off the bandages she had so sloppily put on.

"My goodness, what were you doing to cause this?" Sally asked, cleaning the wounds and using a tweezer to extract the small slivers of pine bark from her palm.

"I was trying to stay put in a tree," Avery said.

"Doesn't look like you had much luck." Sally smiled at her. "You know the story behind Camp Kirby don't you?"

Avery averted her eyes, not wanting to reveal how much she really did know by now. "I think I've heard it, yes."

"Well, it's true," Sally locked eyes with her. "Don't let anyone tell you otherwise. I know for a fact it's true."

"You do?" said Avery, curious now. "And how's that?"

"Because Minnie Everette Kirby was my great-grandfather's tutor," Sally said with seriousness. Then she lightened up as she gingerly wrapped clean white gauze around her palms, and firmly, but gently fastened them.

Avery held back the barrage of questions she wanted to ask, mostly because Sally kept on talking without offering a break in the conversation.

"Minnie was the family's governess at one time and then Durant hired her to tutor my great grandfather – Mr. Durant was always looking out for his help. Minnie wasn't his mistress though, contrary to what they think around here. I've heard the stories from my own grandmother. They spent the summer there together, Minnie and my great-grandfather Nate. William would check on them periodically. My great-grandfather was an orphan, he lived with his uncle's family but there were many mouths to feed. At times there was little food. Mr. Durant took care of my family."

"Now, that should do it." Sally finished her handiwork and put the tweezers back in the tray where they came from. "By the way, have you met my son yet?"

"Not sure, I haven't met many people around here," Avery said.

"Well, he does odd jobs for the College but mostly he helps run the family store in town, name's Jake. You'll probably run into him, he's going to be doing some repairs to the loft at Camp Kirby this summer with my brother Frank."

Avery kept quiet. She felt guilty for not sharing Minnie's diary with Sally, but she didn't know where to begin. How does one explain something that should have been made known the minute she found it? What could she say now that Sally had told her all of this: "Oh yes, I think I've heard of Minnie. You're wrong though; William kept her at the cabin. How do I know this? Well actually, I found her diary in the hole of a tree."

Then again, why did she feel so protective of Minnie anyway?

It could wait. No one needs to know yet that I have proof that Minnie really was William West Durant's mistress.

"Thank you Sally, it was nice to meet you," Avery said. "I'd love to hear more about your great-grandfather and Minnie some day, but I better get back to Camp Kirby."

"Oh, dear, I'm full of stories, just stop by anytime, I can fill you in," Sally laughed. "Good-bye now. And good luck finding those owls of yours."

Avery went looking for Tom and found him walking back to his office.

"Hey Avery." He looked down at her hands.

"What happened to you?"

"Oh, it's nothing, just scraped them climbing a tree."

"Really, Avery, don't be doing stupid things out there at Kirby. You know if you need help or equipment or whatever, you can tell me. We're here to help. And I think you should try to check in more often, eat lunch or dinner with us once a day so we know you're ok."

"Well, now that Jake is following my every move out there you don't have to worry," Avery shot back.

Tom's brows flicked up in surprise. "What exactly do you mean by that?"

She immediately regretted the remark, aware of how Tom might interpret it and she didn't want to get Jake in trouble.

"Nothing. Nothing, Tom, forget it, I'm not sure why I said that. Anyway, yes please, I could use a ladder, until my poles for the mist nets arrive. What was it you wanted to tell me?"

Tom seemed relieved to talk about something else. "Well Kim Baker, you remember meeting her? She is the mycologist teaching a course here this summer. She saw that flyer you passed around about saw-whet sightings and says she knows where there might be a nest. Says she and her students found some pellets the other day while hunting for mushrooms."

"Great! Do you have the pellets somewhere?"

He smiled "Follow me."

They walked to his office, following the winding, well-laid out paths. At least ten units were still standing from the Durant time period. They passed the Durant Cottage – the main cabin for William and his wife when it was called Pine Knot. Each building was connected to the other by these pathways, a design to encourage people to leave their rooms in order to socialize as well as engage with the outdoors. If you were a guest at Pine Knot, you never dined in your cabin. The cabins were only for sleeping. If you wanted to eat, you had to leave your sleeping cabin to go to the Dining Hall. And if you wanted to play cards, you went to the Swiss chalet, a housing complex for the Durant guests.

Tom opened the drawer of his desk and pulled out a baggie containing the pellets. Avery held the bag up to the light. The pellets were just the right size for a saw-whet.

"Where did Kim find these?" she asked Tom.

"By the *Barque of the Pine*," he said.

The *Barque of the Pine* was the Durant houseboat. It rested on land now, about a quarter mile from the main buildings of

Huntington.

"I'll talk to Kim when I get the chance and check out the site as soon as possible. Do you know where she is now?" Avery asked.

"She was down at the lakefront about ten minutes ago, her class is heading out in canoes to South Bay."

"I'll stop by tonight for dinner then. Thanks Tom," Avery said and took the bag of pellets with her to head back to Kirby and finish off what she'd started that morning with the mist net.

Frank and Jake weren't at the camp, and the ladder was missing. Instead of waiting for them, she decided to scout out new locations for the presence of saw-whet activity, figuring she could get to the mist net again tomorrow. It was getting warm, she took off her sweatshirt and sprayed Deet all over her exposed arms, to deter the black flies, and hiked into the woods. Within minutes she came upon Frank and Jake. Before she could get out a greeting Frank spoke.

"Left the ladder for you, Avery. Jake said you might need it." Frank lifted his cap as he passed her on the path. Jake didn't say a word, just smiled.

She turned around to face them. "Thanks!" she called out. Frank gave her a backhand wave as they walked away.

NORTH CREEK, NY
DECEMBER 1877

William arrived for Christmas supper but didn't have an opportunity to talk to Ella before they were called to the dining room to eat. He had been staying for the past few weeks at his apartment in New York City after working all autumn at Pine Knot.

The four family members gathered at the table. The first course was a consommé, followed by trout, and then roast duck. They ate in eerie silence, the only sounds coming from the kitchen as the staff prepared and presented each course.

Eventually, Hannah made an attempt at conversation.

"Wonderful sermon at church tonight wasn't it?"

"Yes, Mother, it was, wasn't it? Pastor Brown did a wonderful job raising everyone's spirits for the holiday," Ella said, throwing her a conversational bone. Ella and William stole glances at each other from across the table, both impatient for the dinner to be over so they could talk in private. Dr. Durant, quietly consuming his food, spoke up at the mention of church.

"Yes, speaking of church, William, I have been discussing the idea with Francis Stott of building an Episcopalian chapel on Raquette."

"Good idea, Father. Maybe we should also consider a Catholic chapel for the workmen and their families?"

"If you think it would keep them happy," Dr. Durant said. "I've already selected a site on the lake and have commissioned

Josiah Cady's firm in New York to draw up the plans. Construction on *that* property should start this summer."

His intonation stopped conversation as everyone guessed what was coming next. When Mrs. McFarland brought out the dessert — Dobosh torte — Dr. Durant leaned back in his chair. The time had come to pepper William with questions.

"So tell me, William, how is the progress on the buildings coming along?"

"Very well," William said. "It will take more time but we will have a few dwellings ready for the summer."

"What does that mean exactly? How many cabins are you building? We only need one for the family and guests," Dr. Durant said.

"It means I know exactly what needs to be done. Some buildings, the icehouse for example, are complete and we will start construction on the second floor of the main lodge right after the first thaw."

Ella and Mrs. Durant fiddled with the torte, their appetite suppressed by the palpable tension compressing the air. Mrs. McFarland swept into the room.

"Is there anything else I can get you all on this lovely Christmas evening?" Her perfectly timed entrance briefly squelched the brewing storm.

"No thank you Mrs. McFarland." Dr. Durant waved her away. "You may clear things up and then please enjoy the rest of the evening with your husband."

"Why thank you, Doctor Durant. I think we will."

Mrs. McFarland cleared the dessert plates and came back with a new pot of coffee, which she placed on the table in front of him. "Merry Christmas, all of you."

"Merry Christmas," the Durants replied in unison.

"I don't understand, William," Dr. Durant continued when Mrs. McFarland had left the room. "You've been in the woods for the past three months. You must have something to show me, some bloody drawing of the house we are to live in."

William's expression was a mixture of trepidation and

determination. "I'm not building you a large house or mansion. Pine Knot isn't Newport or the Hamptons. The landscape in the Adirondacks is unique and requires a different approach for the construction of buildings, unless you want to cut all of the trees that make the site so attractive in the first place."

"If you have to cut some trees to make the place habitable, cut some damn trees. It's not as if there aren't more where they came from," Dr. Durant retorted.

Ella studied William. His hands were trembling as he picked up his coffee cup before continuing.

"I am making separate sleeping quarters for you and mother, and a hall for socializing that will also have bedrooms for guests. There will be a few small cottages for Ella and me. I plan to enclose the dining hall in glass."

"Confound it, William!" Dr. Durant shouted, pounding his fist on the table, causing the glasses on the table to shake. "This all sounds grand indeed, but when will it be finished?"

Ella shrank in her seat. Mrs. Durant let out a small cry.

"Pet, it's Christmas, can't this wait?" she beseeched her husband.

"Ella, Hannah, leave us at once," Dr. Durant said, looking stonily at William.

Ella rose from her seat and glared at her father who paid no attention. She put her hand on William's shoulder as she parted.

"Listen to me," Dr. Durant said evenly once the women had departed. "I've seen the bills for the labor. You're spending a fortune on Pine Knot. You don't need to hand pick and carve every tree for heaven's sake. And it would be cheaper to get your lumber delivered from one of the local mills. What we need to focus on is bringing in prospective investors. I have the company attorneys trying to purchase another 20,000 acres from the state in Township 40. If they succeed we will own much of the land around Raquette. This area will be the hub of our transportation system. Once this is done, we can turn our energy to building a steamboat line that will carry people in from Blue Mountain Lake."

"I understand your anxiety, Father. But I assure you—"

"I don't want your assurances. I want a place to bring investors which will showcase all that the Adirondacks has to offer in sport and leisure." Dr. Durant cast a steely glare down the table at his son. "When you go back to Pine Knot in February, keep out of that Lawrence girl's tent and get busy."

William's head shot up to meet his father's gaze.

Dr. Durant smiled grimly. "I'm neither blind nor stupid." He rose from his seat, pulled the hem of his vest down over his trousers, and strode toward the door. He turned before leaving. "If you don't get on with it, you'll find that your credit at the Union Club is delinquent, and the Fifth Avenue Hotel will no longer take your reservation." With that he exited, leaving William sitting alone in the large dining room looking down at his coffee cup.

"She's not in a tent, she's staying in your hunting cabin Father, and it has a front porch now," William said to the empty room.

Dr. Durant knocked gently then entered Hannah's bedchamber. She was sitting at her vanity table brushing out her long brown hair. He came up behind her, put his hands on her shoulders and kissed her lightly on the neck.

"Merry Christmas, Hannah."

She stiffened. "Your affection is ill-timed, Thomas."

He peered at her reflection in the mirror. She slammed her brush down on the vanity and walked away from him to take off her robe.

"My dear, let's not argue tonight," he said.

"A bit late for that isn't it?"

"Don't be sore with me, Hannah, not on Christmas. You know how William annoys me at times. I can't help it if I show my aggravation."

"Haven't I told you time and time again that all the wealth you have accumulated will cease to matter if you don't have your family's love?" Hannah slipped her robe off and climbed into her bed. She arranged the covers over her legs and stared at her husband.

"Let's not discuss this now. You are the one that asked me to send you and the children abroad to be with your family while I built the railroad. You are the one that said you couldn't raise them in the midst of a civil war."

"Yes, and you did everything a good husband would do by providing for us. But your absence was felt severely. And even though William is a disappointment to you, I raised him to be a gentleman."

Dr. Durant sat down on Hannah's fainting couch and sighed.

"A gentleman, I agree. But he idles away his time. Why is it that both our children consider themselves above the positions I intend for them?"

"Don't you dare blame me for that!" Hannah took hold of her long mane and tossed it off her chest.

"I would agree that Ella has never been sensible," she said. "But William is another thing. What good was it to have expensive tutors teaching him German, French and Italian, when you were not around to teach him how to carry out family business in the clubs of New York where people can barely speak proper English?"

Dr. Durant was about to protest but she stopped him before he could say anything. "Besides," she said rearranging the covers so that they came up to her neck, "William is a meticulous planner, you would know that if you had spent more time with us. You should have seen the itinerary he put together for the British Consuls in Egypt for the Fete at Karnak."

"Oh I saw it alright, you forget that I paid for that extravagance. Rockets, fireworks and colored lights. Enough food and beverages to entertain a legion. I still can't figure out how much he paid Sheik Abdallah of Karnak to access the temple."

She stopped fussing with her blankets and aimed her penetrating eyes at his. "I heard it was a brilliant affair. Your son knows how to entertain. His attention to detail is just what you need to accomplish your enterprise in the Adirondacks. You may have no confidence in your son, but I trust him to do what is needed for Pine Knot."

Dr. Durant came up to the bed and sat down next to Hannah. "Let's talk about something else shall we?" He put his hand on her cheek, trying to console her and end the debate.

Hannah removed it and reached to dim the oil lamp next to the bed. "Good night, Thomas."

He stood up. He would never force himself on her. Besides, he knew Hannah well enough to know when she was this cold there was no warming up the bed.

The next evening William and Ella were sitting in the drawing room by the fire. Dinner that evening had been uneventful. Their parents had gone to the neighbors to socialize.

Ella looked at her brother, his legs crossed, staring forlornly into the fire, and waited until he was ready to speak.

"Your muse from Malden-on-the-Hudson gave me this letter." William reached into his coat pocket and retrieved a sealed envelope. He handed it to Ella.

Her heart skipped a beat. She was eager to open it but didn't want to do so in front of William. "When did you see Poultney?"

"Last week, at the Union Club. I had dinner with him and his father John."

"Don't tell father or he'll have a fit! I send correspondence to Poultney but he never replies because he knows his letters are intercepted."

"Well, the Erie Canal Ring scandal has died down. So I went ahead and invited Poultney to visit us this summer at Pine Knot."

Ella's spirits lifted. If William extended the invitation it would be conventional, maybe then her father wouldn't object.

"I told him he had better come on some pretense other than to visit you. I suggested he bring a companion with him as well, and then it would not be so obvious you were the object of his journey. Anna Leonowens has been inquiring about visiting, I suggested he accompany her."

"Anna Leonowens who wrote the *Romance of the Harem*? How do you know her?"

"She's been making the circuit, speaking at various functions in New York City. People say she's a bit sensationalist in her account of her life as governess for the King of Siam. I happen to enjoy her stories of the court life there."

"Thank you, William!" Ella leapt up from her chair and hugged her brother. "I'm so sorry father was cruel to you on Christmas! He's been a tyrant lately. He has forbidden me from visiting my friends in New York City without you to accompany me. I have been stuck here at North Creek since we left Pine Knot in August. I can't begin to tell you how happy this news makes me. I can wait for Poultney as long as I know he is thinking of me as I am thinking of him."

William hugged her back, before moving her to arm's length and studying her face. "One word of caution, Ella. Don't hold your hopes out for Poultney. He has other would-be maidens waiting in the wings for his advances."

Ella didn't ask for details. She wasn't naïve but she also wanted her feelings spared.

When she got back to her room she tore open the envelope and read his letter.

My Dear Ella,
How is my swarthy debutante faring? I am working hard at Yale, trying to concentrate on my studies and looking forward to the holidays. As you know I am also Captain of the crew team and the practices are exhausting. I cannot wait until we can get out on the River Thames. No, not the Thames you are used to dear girl, this one is in Connecticut. We Americans like to copy the British I suppose by naming our rivers after theirs.

You must know by now that William has invited me to escort Mrs. Leonowens to your famous Pine Knot camp this summer. I look forward to our adventures in the Northern Woods. William tells me he has grand plans for the site.

Perhaps you might show off your marksmanship to me? I hear you are quite the shot – or so your brother brags.

I already know you are going to be a famous writer one day. So tell me, what are your other talents? Or maybe it would be wiser not to tell me, as my imagination is running amok!

I have to run, one of my chums is calling me to dinner. Until we meet again!

Yours affectionately,
Poultney Bigelow

New Year's Eve was humming with the arrival of Dr. Durant's brother Charles, his wife Margaret, daughter Estelle and three sons: Charles Jr., Frederick and Howard. The excitement over their arrival, along with neighbors and the family lawyer, John Barbour and his wife, was a welcome change from the pall Dr. Durant had managed to cast over the household since Christmas dinner. The cousins had taken the overnight train from New York City to Saratoga and on to the North Creek station on the railroad built by Dr. Durant. He made sure his personal sleigh was at the station as the roads, covered with snow and ice, were impassable by coach.

The guests stepped into the entranceway, and the servants helped each out of their coats. William and Ella welcomed their guests and led them to the drawing room.

"The train ride was a much needed improvement over the stage I must say," cousin Frederick said as he shook his uncle's hand. "All told it took us close to fifteen hours. I'm sure it has cut the time in half at least."

"That's what I do, Frederick, make life easier for people. Now tell me, how are the plans for the Prospect House on Blue Mountain? Has Edison signed on to build us a dynamo generator for the lighting?" Dr. Durant got right down to business.

William and Ella helped carry the gifts of chocolate, fruit baskets and cakes to the front parlor where the decorated tree was standing. Cousin Charles sought out William.

"William you look splendid, the months away from the city have done wonders."

"Thank you," William said.

"And how is Pine Knot coming along?"

"We'll have accommodations for guests by summer."

"Good to hear it. Tell me, did you see much of Alvah this Fall?"

"He's been busy guiding," William responded. "So, no I haven't seen much of him. He did occasionally stop by the camp to talk with the other guides but he stays clear of me. I don't think he considers me a 'friend'."

"Humph, friend indeed. He'll not negotiate with me about Osprey Island and he'll not give it up. I'm not sure what the devil he wants. He could up and leave and, with the money I'd pay him, build another squatter's camp on any of the land nearby."

"Yes, he'd be in good company wouldn't he?" William said dryly.

"I'm not sure if you've heard yet," Charles Jr. leaned in to talk so that he wouldn't be overheard. "But the Adirondack Company hasn't had much luck with the state over that land purchase in Township 40, that 20,000 acres your father wants around Raquette."

"Where did you hear this?"

Charles Jr. shrugged. "Rumors at the social clubs, that's all. It could be meaningless."

"Charles, Uncle Thomas wants to speak with you," Charles' mother came over to where they were standing.

"Excuse me," he said to William, and strolled over to chat with his uncle.

The New Year's Eve meal consisted of shallot soup, fried perch, filet de bouef, and petit onions in cream sauce. And for the beverage, wine from the Rhine Valley. "Nothing compares to this fine dinner you've served here brother!" Charles Sr. raved. "Mrs. McFarland, you have outdone yourself again!"

After dessert the ladies went to the parlor, and the men retreated to Dr. Durant's private study to smoke cigars and drink the Nordhäuser whiskey he had acquired for the occasion.

The men sat around in their smoking jackets surrounded by the deep aroma of the imported cigars. Dr. Durant asked his brother how his sugar refinery business was doing in the city and then turned to William.

"William, Frederick will be following you to Blue Mountain this February. He has business to attend to at Prospect Point."

William turned his attention to Frederick. "You're serious about building this hotel then?"

"Why yes. And I need to meet with some local lumbermen about setting up a mill. I'll need all of the wood cut locally for the building. This hotel will rival all others, including Paul Smith's on the Lower St. Regis. I plan to build a hotel to accommodate five hundred guests."

"At Blue Mountain?" William said. "Frederick, you do realize it's still a rugged outpost."

"Just the reason to build William," Dr. Durant interrupted. "Your cousin has a vision."

William was not convinced it was the best vision for the area. But he wouldn't intervene in his cousin's plans, not when his father was behind them.

"It's close to midnight, why don't we join the ladies in the parlor?" William suggested.

The men reluctantly replaced their smoking jackets with frock coats and found the women waiting, champagne in hand, to toast the coming New Year.

"William, cousin Estelle has a wonderful idea," Ella said when they entered. "Let's all go tobogganing tomorrow at father's mill!"

"At the mill? Why the mill?" Hannah asked.

"Haven't you noticed? People in town sled at the base of the mountain."

"I'm not sure I like the idea," Dr. Durant said.

"It'll be fine, Father," William assured him. "We have enough toboggans, and we can load them on the sleighs after lunch tomorrow. Some fresh air would do us all good."

"Yes, besides, Thomas, I wouldn't mind racing you," Charles Sr. said.

Dr. Durant laughed. "You were never able to outrun me on a sled when we were boys, what makes you think anything has changed?" It brightened everyone's mood to see him enjoy talking about something other than his grand schemes. They raised their champagne flutes and toasted in the new year.

The sky was bright when the Durant families rode in the sleigh to the edge of town where the mill was located. They passed small buildings, shanties put up by the mill workers and prospectors working at the garnet mines.

Dr. Durant pointed to a sign, Barton Mines as they passed it. "They plan to mine the garnet and crush it for making sandpaper and other abrasives."

"Who owns it?" Charles was curious.

"A man from Philadelphia. Haven't met him yet."

The brothers admired the growing town, and the opportunities it afforded entrepreneurial-minded men like themselves. Besides the shanties and small houses that were springing up everywhere, there was a bank, a hotel, and Episcopal, Baptist and Catholic churches. North Creek had a ways to go before it was anywhere near the size of some of the smaller cities like Saratoga, and for Ella and Mrs. Durant, it was a far cry from their life in London. Settlement was for the pioneering spirits only. But as a base of operations, it was an ideal location for Dr. Durant to be near his investments in the Adirondacks.

The horses stopped at the mill. It was stationed along North Creek river at the base of Gore Mountain. The location allowed for easy access to the forest and to the waters of the river — the transportation system for the milled logs to float en masse to the Hudson River and then Erie Canal to be dropped off at the hamlets and cities along the way that were eager for the wood.

"You've really developed the mill, Thomas," Charles Sr. said.

Children from the settlements were making the most of the holiday and the snowy hills behind the mill. Large swaths appeared where the loggers had made paths for their horse-drawn sledges to gain access to the forest. The loggers would cut trees and stack the logs on the horse-drawn sledges to be brought down the mountain to the mill. These logger trails provided a perfect runway for the toboggans.

Ella and Estelle were first to reach the summit along the ridge. The view was far-reaching, the air crisply devoid of moisture. North Creek appeared a fraction of its true size from up here. The North Creek river, jammed with ice, had a few logs that had not made it out to the Hudson and were tossing about in the current.

The cousins maneuvered into the toboggan carefully so as not to let it slide out from under them. Ella was in front with Estelle behind, holding on to her waist. They pushed at the snow with their hands and let fly. Once at the bottom, they leaned over to get off the sled before it hit any of the people milling about.

"That was fun, let's do it again!" Estelle said. She was flushed from the cold and excitement.

Her brother Howard grabbed the rope. "My turn with William." And the two men climbed the hill. Their mothers stayed in the sleigh with heavy wool blankets over their laps, watching the action and drinking tea Mrs. McFarland had prepared. Doctor Durant and his brother forgot how daring they had been in their youth and only climbed partway up the hill. Ella and Estelle waited patiently, and as soon as William and Howard landed, wrested the toboggan away to ascend the hill once more.

When they got to the top they saw a group of boys off to the side, away from the rest of the crowd and heading in a different direction with their toboggans. Ella was curious.

"Let's see where those boys are off to." She didn't wait for

Estelle to respond, took hold of the rope and dragged the sled along to follow the trail of the ragamuffins.

They were walking along the ridge of the mountain and it made Estelle nervous to be following them.

"Maybe we should head back? Our brothers will be looking for us at the bottom and wondering where the devil we went."

Ella ignored her pleas and kept trudging through the deep snow. Although the boys were making a path, it was not as worn down as the sledding hill. Wherever they were going was not often trodden. This intrigued Ella. Estelle however was miserable. She wore the wrong footwear for the deep snow. With each step the snow came over the tops of her boots and slid down her stockinged feet where it landed on the ball of her foot and melted, creating a cold, wet clammy feeling which grew worse with each step.

"Ella, please stop, I'm barely keeping up in this snow!" Estelle pleaded with her cousin. This was not the first time Ella had gotten her into mischief. Estelle recalled one of their rare visits to the States while living abroad, when her Aunt Hannah, Miss Molineaux, Ella and William had stayed in New York City. Their families went for a picnic in Central Park. Dr. Durant of course was absent — out west working on completion of the transcontinental railroad.

Ella talked Estelle into taking off her shoes and stockings and wading into a pond to capture the swans. It seemed like a good idea at the time. Their parents were not paying any attention to them, and the boys were off flying kites. But the fun came to a screeching halt when Miss Molineaux discovered where they were and shouted at them to get out of the pond, causing such a ruckus that her parents and Aunt Hannah came running over to see what was going on.

Estelle had been severely punished when she got home. Her father had taken the strap to her. Ella, as she recalled, was barely reprimanded. Aunt Hannah chastised her and wouldn't allow her to attend the theater that evening. Now here she was following her miscreant cousin one more time, if only to save Ella from herself.

"Shush, Estelle," Ella turned to her. "I want to see where these boys are going. You can turn back if you like."

Estelle knew it was no use trying to persuade Ella to change her mind but she was not about to leave her tracking down unfamiliar pubescent boys alone. The lads stopped suddenly and were pointing into the woods down the hill.

"What are you all up to?" Ella said as they came upon them.

The boys were startled that they had been followed.

"We're going sledding, is all," a round-faced, ruddy-cheeked one said.

Ella looked at where they were heading with their sleds. It was a small path in the woods, very steep and very narrow — at most six feet wide. It was a deer path, worn away by cloven feet, the undergrowth eaten so there were no saplings growing along the run. The trail, however, was lined with very old, very big trees.

"Why on earth would you want to sled down that path?" Estelle said.

"Why not?" a tall boy answered for the rest.

"We call it suicide hill," another said.

"Yes no wonder," Estelle smirked. "You're not going down that hill boys, that would be crazy."

"We've done it before, haven't we fellas?" the tall one remarked. They all nodded in agreement.

"It's a ritual, every time we come we go down at least once."

"Let's try it, Estelle!" Ella was entranced.

"You aren't serious? You're not going down that hill! Just look at it! There are trees all around, one slip up and you would head right into one of them."

"Nah, it's not like that. You go pretty fast and as long as you stay steady you make it ok to the bottom. We've never had a problem, have we boys?" the ruddy complexioned one was convinced.

Estelle was not. "Ella, let's get out of here. If these boys want to commit suicide let them." She tugged at her cousin's arm.

"No," Ella said.

"Yes!" Estelle answered, and she snatched the rope of the toboggan from Ella and started to walk away. "Are you coming or not?" She turned around to make sure Ella would follow.

Ella looked at her, then down the hill, and then at the boys.

"Can I use your sled?" she asked the tall one.

He handed her his rope.

"Ella, no!" Estelle shouted.

It was too late. Ella took hold of the rope, climbed onboard the toboggan and pushed herself off before she lost her nerve.

It only took a second before her stomach lurched to her throat. Her peripheral vision was a blur of brown trees whizzing by, as if they were moving, not her. Her muscles were taut, if she dared move she knew she would head right into one of them. It was terrifying and exhilarating at the same time. She heard someone yelling in the distance, moved her head to see who it was, and then everything went black.

CAMP KIRBY
MAY 2010

Avery spent the afternoon waiting by the mist net. She planted herself a few meters away at the base of a large maple and played the lure recording of a male call every twenty minutes, hoping it would cause the nesting male to make himself known while trying to protect his territory. Leaning against the trunk of the old maple and looking into its canopy above she could both see and hear the wind rustling the branches of the not-quite-yet-leafed-out tree. It was still spring in the North Woods. The cold nights kept the buds from blooming too early.

Avery soaked in the sun shining down through the canopy, warming everything in its wake as she waited. The mosquito netting over her head helped to keep the black flies at bay, but it was annoying to look through. She took it off. It was better to have a clear view of the beautiful day. The forest wildflowers were in bloom, eager to take advantage of the fleeting opportunity to photosynthesize before the maple leaves shaded the forest floor. All around her were trillium, Jack-in-the-Pulpit and her favorite, bloodroot — a plant that got its namesake from the reddish sap in its root used as a dye by Native Americans. This glorious flowering showcase, she knew from her years of tramping through the North Woods as a girl, was a short-lived scene.

Her reverie was broken by the sound of a male saw-whet responding to the lure. Its 'toot, toot, toot' wasn't hard to recognize. Avery took out her binoculars to search for the small owl in the trees but spotted nothing. After a couple of hours of waiting she took the mist net down. At least now she knew there was a male in the vicinity, which meant there was probably a nest and he would be busy scouting for food for the chicks tonight. She carried the ladder back to Kirby and searched for Jake and Frank to thank them, but they had gone.

Avery set off through the woods to Huntington for dinner.

Kim Baker found her in the dining hall. "There you are!"

Avery sat with Kim and her students for dinner. Their stories and laughter made Avery feel ten years younger. She was enjoying it so much she decided to come back more often. Being alone at Kirby was great, but the company lightened her spirits.

After dinner, the crowds of students left the dining hall to meet up at Metcalf house for a roaring fire, games, and cards, while the few that had KP duty remained behind to clean. Avery and Kim headed over to where the Durant family houseboat — the *Barque of the Pine* — rested on land, where Kim had found the saw-whet pellets.

"He seems to have had an affinity for the chalet style," Kim remarked as they walked by Metcalf Hall. They stopped for a moment to stand and admire the log cabin with decorative motifs, including a large W made out of bent limbs that graced the rails and roof.

Continuing on they passed the private quarters of William and his wife Janet. This cabin was sheathed in bark. It also had an elaborate front porch. Avery remembered seeing a picture of William walking down the front steps in a book about the Great Camps of the Adirondacks that sat on a coffee table at her grandfather's camp. It was a photo taken in 1889 by Ray Stoddard who worked for the Durants on occasion, marketing their Adirondack properties. "I know he used all local material, not just because it was cheaper and more accessible. I think William West Durant believed what he was building should stand the test of time, and he chose the wood for that purpose. I read that he'd spend days in the forest looking for just the right tree to cut. The college is lucky none of this has burnt to the ground," she said.

"How'd he prevent the wood from rotting in this climate?" Kim asked.

"He used a special formula of beeswax that protected the wood from the elements."

"It obviously worked," Kim said.

"It sure did," Avery said, looking around at the numerous cabins and construction still standing after a century of wind, rain, snow and sleet. Mammoth trees that had been standing when William was building, stood as sentinels to the passing time.

They passed the trapper's log cabin; a solid looking affair with a low angled roof and front porch that was not as decorative as the others but just as rustic looking.

"I wonder who lived there?" Avery said aloud.

They arrived at the *Barque* as dusk was about to fall and went into the houseboat to explore briefly.

Like the other buildings on the grounds, the houseboat was enveloped in cedar bark. The interior had pine paneling. There were two small bedrooms, a small kitchen and two baths. It reminded Avery of a child's playhouse.

"Who used this?" Kim asked.

"Well," Avery said, "the story goes that William would launch the *Barque* with his wife Janet in it out into the middle of the lake while he biked over to Camp Kirby to have a rendezvous with his mistress Minnie."

"Is there any evidence he had a mistress?"

"Just some rumors as far as I know," Avery said absently.

"I'd need more than anecdotal proof myself," Kim said as they left the beached vessel to look for more signs of the saw-whet before it got too dark.

After a short search they found a pine with a small hole about ten feet off the ground. Avery pulled out her binoculars and sure enough there was a female saw-whet, quietly sitting on her brood. Giving the binoculars to Kim, she pointed at the tree. Kim suppressed a squeal of delight.

"This is much more exciting than combing the ground for

mushrooms," she said.

Avery used her flashlight to walk back to Camp Kirby. She was thrilled by the discovery of a nesting saw-whet. It meant another chance to capture a male. It was late when she arrived back at Kirby. She boiled water for tea, turned on the propane lantern in her room and settled down to read more of Minnie's diary.

June 3, 1893

Nate came back from the store with butter, bread, potatoes, and onion. He plans to fish later this morning for our supper. William left word with Nate that he would join us this evening. I cannot wait to see him!

Nate is a better reader than he let on. His aunt has taught him well. Yesterday afternoon we spent time reading the book William gave him: Murray's "Adventures in the Wilderness". I must say I have never read it myself so it is very interesting to read the book that made the Adirondacks so popular. Here is an excerpt:

"Not until you reach the Raquette do you get a glimpse of a wilderness that rivals Switzerland."

I thought that odd at first when I read it; who would compare this outpost of a region, so harsh and bare in the winter, to the beauty of Switzerland? I wonder if that is why William brought a Swiss music box to show me? He told me he uses it as a model for some of his buildings. William seems obsessed with his building plans. Lately, he talks more about that than our future together.

Minnie

June 4, 1893

Last evening was magical! Nate made William and me a wonderful supper of lake trout fried in butter with onions and potatoes. Nate's father, I learned, was once a lumberman. When I asked what happened to him Nate said, "He was swallowed up by the woods." I could not help but laugh, until I saw how he looked on at me so earnestly. I said, "Nate, the woods don't swallow people up."

"Yes ma'am, they can, and they did. They done swallowed up my Pa," he said with such seriousness for a boy. I don't dare ask what happened to his poor mother. I asked William last night and he was rather vague about it, said that Nate's father 'ran off'. Poor Nate. It does seem though that he has plenty of men folk that are like fathers to him. He tells me that his Uncle Ike teaches him the arts of trapping, hunting and angling.

William told me more about his plans for Uncas. He spent last fall surveying the land around Mohegan Lake so he could start construction this Summer.

Nate had gone into the cabin by then, and we were sitting idly by a fire he made for us by the lakefront. I felt all warm inside sitting next to him. He is so fair, tall and handsome. And he is so kind to me and Nate. I felt the urge to kiss him, but before I could turn my lips toward his he abruptly stood up and told me he must get back to Pine Knot before Janet wondered where he was. He lies and tells them he is checking on the progress of the renovations of this small hunting cabin. He told me Janet is very tied up with the children and spends her nights sleeping on the Barque of the Pine, to get away from the biting insects. He told me that if she is not on the Barque, then he is. The two of them hardly speak. I do not think they share a bed anymore.

Minnie

The next morning Avery woke up to the yodel of the common

loons echoing across the lake. She made coffee in the percolator and sat on the front porch to take in the view and inhale the aroma of balsam and cedar. The loons wailed again. She pointed the binoculars in the direction of the sound and squinted into the lens, looking for the beady red eyes, the ring of white around the neck, and speckled white-on-black plumage. She landed on them: two birds bobbing around at the shore in front of the dock. Mates.

The lake looked tempting, and she knew the water in the solar shower would not be warm yet. She retrieved her towel, left it on the beach and walked toward to the water's edge. She waded in until the water reached her calves. It was freezing cold, at most fifty degrees Fahrenheit. It would not warm up until July. She went in further. The cold sent shivers up her legs and into her chest. It reminded her of when she was a little girl at her grandfather's cabin on Schroon Lake and she and her brother would dare each other to be the first one in for the season. A few steps further and the water was at her waist. She just needed to do a quick dive and it would be over.

"Hey, what the hell are you doing?"

Avery was shocked, not only from the cold. It was Jake, as startled by her nakedness as she was by his presence. Her surprise turned to anger. She quickly ran out of the water and grabbed the towel, wrapped it around herself and started for the cabin.

"Hey, Avery, really, what're ya doing?" Jake asked her as she fumed past him on the shore.

She turned to look at him. My, he had dark eyes. His good looks however did not compensate for his intrusive behavior. *What the hell was he doing here this early in the morning?*

"I was about to go for a quick swim, obviously," she said.

"Well, I'm sorry I scared you but that's crazy," he said. "I was in a wetsuit yesterday helping a neighbor put his dock in and I can tell you even with a wetsuit I was numb from the cold. You shouldn't be taking chances like that out here with no one around to watch you."

She raised her brows. "Why worry when you have that covered?" She stormed off toward the cabin, stopped for a moment and turned. "Just what *are* you doing here this early?"

Jake glanced around for an answer, setting his eyes on a tall pine hoping it would provide one. "I, I thought I'd come and maybe share a cup of coffee on your porch before I start work?"

Avery softened a bit. He seemed so — sincere.

"Coffee's in the kitchen. I'm going to shower." She left him standing there.

He can figure out whether or not I want to share a cup, she said to herself as she went to the back of the cabin to use the shower stall. When she was done she snuck into the front parlor to look out the window. Jake hadn't left. He was sitting on the porch, coffee mug in hand. She felt a small jolt of excitement.

Returning to her room, she quickly dressed in her field clothes: jeans and sweatshirt. She put her wet hair in a braid and grabbed a mug of coffee for herself. With the stealth of an owl, Avery stepped out onto the front porch and sat down next to him to enjoy the view of the rising sun.

"Nice of you to dress up for me. Although what you had on before wasn't all that bad," Jake smiled as he took a sip of coffee.

"Watch it buster," Avery said, looking out at the lake smiling.

"I tell ya what, I'll make it up to you. Let me split some of that wood over there." He nodded his head in the direction of the large woodpile that Avery had not gotten to since last time he saw her working on it.

"Deal," she said.

"Ok, I'll get to it after we are done working for the day."

"And maybe if you're nice, I'll make you dinner," Avery said. And this time she smiled directly at him.

Avery found Tom helping students get into the canoes at the beachfront.

"Mail arrived this morning for you," he informed her.

She followed Tom to his office and retrieved the package her advisor, Dr. Martin, sent. Inside were the poles and a letter.

Dear Avery:

I hope all is going well with your research. Sorry you left these poles behind; I hope it has not delayed your research. I must admit you have set yourself up for quite the challenge. Eighty percent of the time only females are caught in these nets. Hopefully your work will shed some light as to why.

Best of luck, and please keep me apprised of your progress.

Dr. Martin

Avery looked at her watch. Nine am. It was still early enough to trap some owls. Poles in hand, she went out to set up her mist net and audio lure by the *Barque of the Pine*. Instead of admiring her surroundings while waiting to capture the owl, she sat under a Balsam fir and took Minnie's diary out of her pack.

June 10, 1893

I haven't been able to write for a few days, as I have been very busy with Nate. And when I am not with Nate, I am with William. Lately he has been coming by more often. Now instead of visiting with me only in the early evening, he has been stopping by in the middle of the day. He just sits with me on the porch and stews in his thoughts while Nate goes out in his small canoe to catch fish. He tries not to be cross with me, but he doesn't like it if I ask him too many questions about our future, or his life with Janet.

If he does talk, it is about Camp Uncas. It sounds like it is really coming along. He told me he had a road built so his men could get into the interior where the camp sits on Mohegan Lake. He said it is not accessible by boat. But the six-mile road is so narrow and treacherous it is hard to bring material in and out with a horse or mule. So he had a few of his men use the yokes from the boats and put them on their shoulders with slings to carry in the sawed spruce timber he had chosen for the window frames. He said that his two best men carried three logs apiece this way. I dared not ask why the wood near Uncas was not good enough to use. As it is he has his men setting up blacksmith shops on site so that they can make all of the hardware for the door handles and knobs. William, I've come to understand, is a perfectionist.

Minnie

June 15, 1893

Tonight Nate and I did something that would make William very angry with us if he found out. Nate took me hunting by jacklight. We were reading about it in "Adventures in the Wilderness". It all sounded very exciting to me so I asked Nate whether he had ever done it before.

"Yes ma'am."

"Well is it like the book says?" I asked him.

"Yes, ma'am, but harder sometimes."

It was after supper and I knew William was not to come this evening, so I begged Nate to show me how it is done. He was not happy about doing it though. He kept glancing at the path leading to Pine Knot, worried he would see William come walking through the woods. I told him, "Don't worry Nate, he is not coming tonight, and if he did and does not see us I will tell him we went for a short canoe ride to get away from the mosquitoes."

And so we set off on our little adventure. Nate had a jacklight all rigged on his little boat. It is an odd thing, just like the book describes it: a piece of wood carved in a crescent moon shape with a birch bark wrapped around it and a hole dug in the bottom for a light to rest in. Nate had a small oil lantern in his. He strung it on the end of a pole that was nailed into the bow of the boat, but he did not light it yet.

We paddled over to Golden Beach and found a small inlet to the lake we could barely make out in the dusk. A few deer were eating the water lilies at the edge of the shore. We were so quiet in our canoe they did not hear us. Then, as it got darker, I lit the small lantern. We waited in the boat, just sat there quietly, letting the boat float in the water. It was so calm. And then it happened, a deer on the water's edge gazed up and saw the light and was mesmerized by it. It was a buck. He couldn't take his eyes off the light. Nate paddled closer to him. We were about twenty feet away and he still was not spooked. I raised the rifle Ike had loaded for me so we would be ready for this moment. And then I fired. It had been so long since I had shot a deer, but all of my training as a girl came back to me. Nate was so excited! He couldn't believe my marksmanship. Ike scrambled out and we managed to lift the deer into the boat. We hurried back to camp where Ike put it in the padlocked icehouse for protection against the bears and wolves. There will be venison for dinner tomorrow — not that I need to worry about being fed here. I told Nate to take some of the meat to his family after he butchers it.

Nate made me promise I would lie and tell William that he shot the deer during the day if asked. He said that Mr. Durant would be very upset if he knew we were out jacklighting.

Minnie

Avery closed the small diary when she heard some noise at the net. Inspecting it she found a bird, but it wasn't a saw-whet. She checked her watch, it was too late to net any more and she needed to figure out what she was making for dinner.

NORTH CREEK, NY
JANUARY 1878

Ella woke up to find William sitting next to her bed reading. Everything was hazy and her head hurt. She tried to lift herself up and winced in pain at the effort.

"Can't ever sit still can you, Ella?" William said. He was smiling with relief.

"Good lord my head hurts. What happened?" Ella said, placing a hand over her eyes to ward off the sun shining through the windows. "Close the shutters, *please.*"

William got up and shut the light out. He came back and took her hand in his own. "You scared us all, father especially. I don't think I've ever seen him so distraught. You're lucky he was there. All of his medical training came back to him. He wouldn't allow us to move you until he was sure you hadn't broken your neck. And he immediately acted to make sure you didn't go into shock, taking his heavy coat off and placing it on top of you. He bundled you up and carried you to the sleigh. He wouldn't let anyone else touch you. Mother of course was hysterical, I think she believed you would die. Now I know where your propensity for drama comes from."

Ella smiled.

"The good news is you're not going to die."

"Thank you for informing me of the obvious," Ella said sarcastically.

"You do however have a concussion."

"But what happened? Last I remember I was flying down a hill and my stomach was lurching from the excitement of it all."

"What happened? We were all waiting at the bottom of the hill for you and Estelle to show, wondering where the devil you were, when suddenly you came flying out of a patch of woods like a horse let loose from a barn fire. Your toboggan must have hit a patch of ice and you swerved one way and it went another. You went tumbling down the hill, and the toboggan came crashing down after you, hitting you on the head when you finally landed — face first in the snow. It was quite comical really. Until we all realized you weren't moving."

"How long have I been in bed? And where's Estelle?" She lifted herself up slightly onto her elbows and then collapsed back on her pillow.

"You've been asleep since the accident yesterday. And Estelle left this morning with the rest of them. Uncle Charles was snarling at her, telling her she should have known better than to follow you around, and to grow up or something like that," William laughed.

Ella started to laugh as well, but stopped as it hurt too much. "Oh poor Estelle. She will never learn will she?"

"No, and neither will you my dear. Now you have really done it. I was planning on bringing you with me when I head back to New York City. I had father talked into it as well until this incident."

Ella tried to sit up again but couldn't. "Please William," she pleaded from her bed, "don't leave me here! Wait until I'm better."

"Can't. I have to get back on railroad business, wining and dining some politicians at the club."

"But I'm sure by tomorrow I'll be up and around."

William kissed her lightly on her forehead. "It wouldn't matter. Father's furious with you. You're not going anywhere until he brings you up to Pine Knot this summer."

"But where will you be for the next few months? Are you staying in New York?"

"No. I plan to leave New York City by mid-February. I'm traveling with cousin Frederick to Blue Mountain and then on to the lake to start construction on the main house at Pine Knot." He glanced at the door in a conspiratorial manner, "Don't say anything to father but it will be modeled after a Swiss cottage."

"Really, our own playhouse? Like the one at Osborne for the Queen's children? How charming," Ella said wanly. She rubbed her temples, it didn't help the pain.

"Not exactly, but modeled after it, yes. Good–bye then." He got up to leave.

"Good-bye," Ella said, and closed her eyes. Even in the dark of the room keeping her eyes open was too much to bear. She was quieted by the thought of her father tending to her. She wished she'd been conscious enough to experience what that was like.

PINE KNOT
SPRING 1878

William and Frederick took off at dawn with Dr. Durant's large sleigh on a cold morning.

"As the days grow longer the storms grow stronger," Frederick quoted. Two powerful horses were dragging them north to Blue Mountain in a galling wind and snowstorm. They were bundled in wool coats and had a blanket thrown over their legs. William wore the fur vest, hats and mittens that Louise had made him. Jem Stone, who was given the task of driving, knew enough now to cover himself head to toe as well. It was hard to see for more than a few yards ahead; the going was slow. It had been a blustery winter and spring was slow to arrive. The region was experiencing more snow than it had for as long as the locals could recall. It made hunting for deer and turkey difficult, as they were deep in the woods and tracking was arduous.

Many were worried the deer would suffer terribly, the fawns would die from lack of fat reserves and the does would be lost to starvation. The harvest would be slim come summer. William made sure his caretakers at Pine Knot were supplying the deer in and around Long Point with some feed stored in the icehouse for just this reason, a trick he had learned in Europe. This act of humanity was reserved for the wealthy however, as others just tried to cope with the vegetables they had stored in their cellars last fall. Meat was not the only scarcity. Usually men could chop a hole in the ice and gain access to the fish. But the constant snowstorms were making it difficult, on top of which the ice on the lakes and streams in the Northern Woods was over three feet thick in parts.

The men didn't talk much as they made their way to Blue Mountain. When they finally arrived at Holland House the owners welcomed them with warm milk and tea.

"Good lord that was a miserable trip," William lamented as he shook the snow and icicles off of his long coat.

They took a seat by the fire and drank their tea.

"Isn't that Verplanck Colvin with Alvah Dunning?" Frederick stared at two snow-covered men entering the dining room. He waved down the barmaid.

"Madam, is that the famous surveyor Verplanck Colvin?"

"Yes sir, he's a regular here. He and Alvah just come back from a trip up Mount Seward."

William was in awe. Who in their right minds would be out surveying the elevation of mountains in the Northern Woods in the middle of snowstorms?

"Can I get you gentleman anything else?"

"Yes, do you have something a bit stronger than milk and tea? Cognac perhaps?" William waited for a reply but the woman was visibly puzzled by his request. "You do have cognac here don't you?"

"Cognac sir? I'm not sure," she said. "Let me ask the owner." She hurried off.

"Should we ask the gentlemen to join us?" William said.

"I will," Frederick replied. He got up and walked over to the two men standing by the fire, shook their hands and asked them to join William and Stone at their table.

While they made acquaintances the owner came over. "I hear you men would like brandy?"

"That would be wonderful. What do you have?" William asked.

"Nothing the likes of what you might be used to sir, but it works well for taking the chill off," he said, putting down five glasses and a bottle of clear liquid.

"Stilled this myself," he boasted.

The men gulped it down. The liquid tore at their throats and tasted lightly of apples. It did the trick though; William felt it warming his stomach lining with its tingly sensation. The owner was right, it wasn't what he was used to, but he didn't care at that point.

The caretaker's wife served them venison stewed with potatoes and onions. It was a meal fit for kings when you've spent the past day in the wind and cold.

"So tell me Verplanck, how long have you been at this surveying?" William asked once he was finished eating and sipping on a glass of below-par sherry.

Verplanck, still eating, wiped his mouth. The man was a voracious eater.

"I've been surveying these mountains for six years now."

"Six years? Why does it take that long to figure out the height of a mountain?"

Verplanck laughed ruefully. "Because I'm using my own money, when I have any. The state has barely paid my wage these past few years. The unappreciative idiots in Albany have no idea what I'm contributing in terms of knowledge of the vast resources this region has to offer."

"I would think the men in Albany are all too aware of what the region has to offer," William remarked.

"Oh, yes, they see the lumber and iron ore deposits. That's not what I'm talking about. These forest streams feed the St. Lawrence and Hudson rivers. The snows that blanket the mountains will avalanche without the trees to hold the soil in place. Come spring thaw everything will come barreling down the hills taking the sides of the mountain with it, clogging up the waterways and polluting the streams. One only has to look at what has happened in the primeval forests of Europe to realize the catastrophe that awaits us. Especially if people like your father, who own most of the acreage around here, have their way."

This apocalyptic forecast took William aback. He hadn't considered his father a destroyer of the earth. But then, even after three years in America, William still felt he had only a cursory knowledge of his father's business dealings.

He kept so much from him, giving orders of who to dine with and when, telling him when he needed to travel from New York City to Saratoga to transfer documents from one company lawyer to the next. His talk of a steamboat line over Christmas was the latest announcement.

What William did know was that the Adirondack Railroad Co. land holdings were his father's pride and joy. He wanted nothing more than to open this vast wilderness up so that people could enjoy it.

"Truly you jest," William said in defense of his father.

"Take a look around. You're heading to Raquette Lake tomorrow? You'll see that the Marion has been dammed for navigation. And the loggers are denuding the forests around Eagle and Utowana Lakes. Township 40 is the central hub for transporting logs either north to the St. Lawrence or south to the Hudson. There's a reason your father seeks the 20,000 acres the state doesn't want to give up."

"Industry is what makes this country strong," William retorted.

Verplanck shook his head sadly. "I've seen the views from the highest peaks here and would disagree with you," he said.

Frederick changed the subject abruptly. "Alvah, tell us what you're doing here with Verplanck?"

Alvah lifted his head up from his glass. "I've been keeping Colvin here from dying in the cold and gettin' himself killed by a catamount."

"A mountain lion!" William's eyes lit up. "Tell us man! Did you encounter one recently? I've yet to see one of these great cats."

"That's because they're mostly gone from here. The bounty on their heads is worth more than a wolf," Verplanck said.

"We came upon one a couple of days ago near the summit of Seward," Alvah said. "He was eating the carcass of a deer."

"Had to shoot him unfortunately," Verplanck said.

"Were you able to bring him down? Do you have his coat?"

William asked.

Alvah shook his head slowly. "Too far up the mountain, we could never carry him off. And we had no time to skin it in the storms that were coming down on us, not when we still had work to do. Pity, could've gotten close to forty for him."

The morning air was icy cold, the sky a brilliant blue as William and Stone loaded the sleigh. Each inhale formed ice in their nostrils, each exhale gave off steam.

"I'll have Stone come back for you in a day or two Frederick," William said. "In the meantime, good luck with your negotiations."

"Thank you, William. And I hope once I have the title to the land for Prospect House you'll lend a hand on the design and construction," Frederick said, lifting one of William's bags into the sled.

"I'll see you in the spring, if it ever decides to come," William said.

"I don't know, today is starting to feel a bit like it, even with the cold air," Frederick said, looking into the sky.

"We need to get going if we want to make Pine Knot before sunset," Stone said.

"Yes, let's head out," William said and climbed into the sleigh.

Although the wind usually did a good job of sweeping the snow from the lakes, the recent storm left a white carpet on top of the ice.

They passed a number of lumbermen on horse-drawn sledges loaded with logs heading east toward the rivers that flowed into the Hudson. Once the loggers reached their destination, they would bank the logs along the riverside until the spring thaw when they would herd the harvest downstream to the nearest mill.

William saw Verplanck was right, the dam at the mouth of the

Marion was almost complete. He knew it was his father's doing, presumably part of the steamboat business. He made a mental note to find out more when he next went to visit the family lawyer John Barbour in Saratoga.

The sun was beaming down by the time they were traveling on the Marion River. The air started to warm up considerably, a typical February day in the North Woods. They reached Raquette as the sun was setting behind the mountains — casting long, dark shadows on the lake. The snow, which had been melting under the glare of the sun all day, froze, forming a thin crust on top which made it hard for the horses to trudge through. The sleigh slogged along, crushing the snow with a sound like thousands of eggshells breaking in its wake.

William put his head up to catch the last rays of sun before it disappeared behind the range. He was anticipating the welcoming reception from Louise. He had told her and Wood he would be back by mid-February and that they should plan for his arrival.

"Sir," Stone woke William from his daydreaming. "Look, up ahead."

Two dots in the snow were chasing a deer. They were making their way easily on snowshoes on the lake. The deer however, was slowed down by the hardening snow. Each step was followed by a crash through the crust and an attempt to breach the deep snow; a drain on its energy reserves. It was hardly able to keep ahead of the two boys.

It was Ike, and an urchin of a boy that must have been his younger brother. Stone halted the sleigh and William shouted to them to stop. The boys gawked at William. Red-faced and panting, they were surprised by the large sleigh, and annoyed that they were being hailed to stop.

"What the devil are you two boys doing out here tracking that deer like a pack of staghounds?" William demanded.

"We's crustin' deer, Mr. Doo'rant," Ike answered. His younger brother shook his head in agreement and watched in despair as the deer started heading for the woods.

William glared down at the boys and then at the deer. "What

kind of sport is this? That deer has no chance in this snow."

Ike shook his head. "We ain't doing it for sport sir. We're doing it to feed our family."

"Yes sir, Mr. Doo'rant, sir. We haven't had meat in a month. It's been too much snow and stormin' for us to find any game," the younger brother said.

"And our mother's been sick," Ike added solemnly.

"Get in," William said. The boys untied the straps to their snowshoes and got in the sleigh. They were gaunt.

"We'll catch up with it," William directed Stone to follow the hapless animal.

Within minutes the sleigh was upon the deer. William gave Ike the go ahead to shoot the pitiable creature. At that point it was the most humane thing to do. A wolf would have made a quick meal out of it once it reached the woods and collapsed from exhaustion.

"I'll take you back home tomorrow morning," William said. It was getting too late to travel, and he needed to unload his gear at Pine Knot. "Do your parents know where you are?"

The boys shook their heads no. "They aren't worried though. Pa won't leave the house with my Mama being sick and all. He told us to go out and find some meat cause he can't trap or hunt. He knows we won't come home 'til we found some," Ike said.

William frowned. He wondered what Louise was doing then, if she would be able to meet him at Pine Knot as planned.

Jerome Wood greeted them when they arrived at Pine Knot. He and the boys helped unload the supplies: ice saws, picks and tongs to harvest and carry out chunks of ice from the lake before it melted — all to be stored in the icehouse on a bed of sawdust William had laid out last fall. They had dragged along a small sledge for the ice-cutting job and Stone was leaving behind a horse.

They also unloaded nails, carpentry tools, large saws for taking down trees, measuring tools, and food: deviled ham, cheeses, boiled quail eggs, smoked meat, fowl, wine and whiskey.

They took the deer to the icehouse and locked it until the morning when it could be butchered. Wood opened one of the cabins and lit a fire in the stove. The smoke trailed out of a crude pipe that went through a small hole in the ceiling. William decided one of the first things he would start on would be the frame for the fireplace. It would be the center of attention in the guesthouse, the chalet. He had one of his craftsmen — a Finn he met last fall — collecting granite, and it was to be delivered by horse and sled before the ice gave out on the lakes.

The spruce and cedar logs he had selected personally while walking the woods around Long Point had been cut and stacked along the shoreline, bark intact, waiting for the thaw.

The two industrious brothers had gutted, skinned, and carved up the deer before the other men had risen. Stone and William took the boys back to their home, relying on their navigational skills to lead the sleigh to their dwelling in the woods.

They headed south from Raquette until they reached Eighth Lake where the Lawrence family had a home in a small clearing in the woods.

"Thank you Mr. Doo'rant. My Pa will be much obliged to ya," Ike said as he climbed out of the sleigh.

"Wait Ike, I know your father needs you to hunt and trap for him while your mother is sick," William stopped Ike from scurrying off. "I'd like to talk to him about the use of your services as well. For payment I can bring your family food supplies every week with the sled."

Ike knew this was a good offer. He and his family would be fed, and he would be able to carry game back in a sleigh instead of dragging it through the snow and chancing an encounter with a wolf or worse, a bear coming out of hibernation, starving. "Come on in sir."

William dismounted from the sleigh, took a crate of items out of the back, and walked up to the structure where the Lawrence family lived. It was strange. A wooden shack attached to a domed building, sided with bark. Stone gave him a questioning look. "Wait here, and don't question me. I know what I'm doing,"

William said to him and then followed the boys to the entrance.

William ducked his head at the doorway as he followed Ike into his abode. The roof of the entrance was flat, and the sides were made of logs. There were shelves along the walls that held trapping gear. But once they stepped out of it they entered the domed structure, twenty feet long, with four poles along the ceiling spanning the width of the room used as supports for the cascading walls, each pole tied with strips of bark to the vertical posts coming out of the ground in the center of the house. Some type of pliable wood created the domed roofline above.

The interior space was symmetrical: the width of the interior was equal to the height and length. Each side of the domed longhouse was identical: beds on each side elevated on log platforms lined the walls and above the beds, shelves that stored the family belongings, including clothes, snowshoes and furs. In the center was a hearth with a small black pot hanging over the fire and other cooking implements. There was a canoe made out of bark hanging from the rafters.

A flap of bark over the smoke hole in the ceiling kept the snow out. The smoke from the fire pit had accumulated over the course of the winter and left a haze. The air smelled slightly acrid.

Intermingled with body odor was the tangy-crisp smell of balsam, a few boughs of it hung from the rafter beams and were burning in the fire to ward off the stink that lingered in the air. Louise's grandmother was on the ground by Ike's mother's bed, holding a cup to her mouth and trying to get her to drink from it. She was singing a light melody he had heard Louise sing before, a Mohawk song. Nailed on the wall above her bed was a crucifix. The crude plank floor was covered in deer and bear skin. The bed coverings were furs from bear, wolves and other woodland mammals. Mink perhaps? Or that strange weasel they called a marten? William recognized beaver pelts — a legacy from ancestors, since beavers were extinct in the region.

From the depths of the long building William made out small dark heads, the children's hollow-looking eyes casting scared stares his way, wondering who this strange, tall man was.

122

"I don't mean to intrude," William said.

Isaac's dark eyes were full of sorrow. William felt a stab of sympathy for the man and his plight. He was responsible for feeding five children yet couldn't bear to leave the side of the woman he loved, who, from what William could tell, was clearly dying. She was pale and delirious, her face had patches of red. It was probably an infection of some sort. William had seen the symptoms of septic shock before. It was always fatal.

"I'd like to help," William told Isaac. He handed him the crate. It was filled with eggs, butter, sugar, flour and pork salt. William knew the family could use the staples. The venison wasn't enough.

Isaac shook his head no.

"You don't understand, I'd like to bring Ike and Louise back to my camp to work for me over the next few months. I'll pay by making sure you're stocked with food for the children. I'll deliver the food with Louise and Ike every week." William hadn't even thought to ask whether Louise would want this arrangement, leaving her mother on her deathbed. He assumed she would rather be with him, an assumption confirmed when he met her eyes.

Isaac considered the offer. There was Sarah, Louise's younger sister by three years, all of fourteen, to help around the cabin, and Emaline, although she was a mere ten. Louise was his rock though. But it would also mean two less mouths to feed, and from what he knew of William he was an honest man, and Louise loved him.

"Sit down, let's eat and drink together. Jake — go tell the driver to come in," Isaac placed his hands on the floor, a request for William to sit next to him.

William and Stone were given warm moccasins and asked to remove their boots. Louise took boiling water from the pit and poured it over bright red Staghorn sumac berries to steep for a tea. Her grandmother called out instructions while she was preparing the tea. William recognized a mixture of French and their native Mohawk language.

"Yes Mémé," Louise said. She took a small tin from one of the shelves and scooped a teaspoon of maple sugar into each mug. The children licked their lips. They had been treated to the sugar sparingly since their mother took ill. Any leftover supplies from last spring were used to flavor the bitter tinctures their grandmother made for her.

William felt uncomfortable taking advantage of the family's hospitality. He looked at Stone, a signal it was time to leave. But just as they were about to get up, Isaac sat down on the floor by the fire pit, lit a pipe of tobacco and began telling his family's story. They had no choice but stay, thinking it would be rude to leave in the middle of his tale.

"The Mohawks are one of the Six Nations of the Iroquois, we call ourselves the Haudenosaunee – the people of the Longhouse." He waved his arms toward the ceiling to indicate this was still the case. "I was raised in Kahnawake near Montreal. My parents had four children. I was the only son. Louise's mother, Clara, is French. My family adopted her when she was twelve, abandoned by her father who was a widowed trapper. I married her three years later."

"My father taught me how to trap and hunt. But then the Canadian government told him he couldn't anymore. They drew a line around our village." Isaac used the end of his pipe to draw a circle in the fur. "They told my father he had to stay in the line and farm with my mother and sisters." He stabbed the center of the makeshift circle.

"He died a heartbroken man. My sisters and their husbands left to go west where there was more game. My mother remembered coming to the Adirondacks every summer to see her New York relatives. She told me to bring her back here. She said there would be plenty of game. After traveling many days we found a clearing in the woods. The lumbermen had been here. This is a perfect place for deer as they like to eat the young saplings that sprout up when the sun can reach the forest floor."

"It was a good place to build the longhouse. The wood," Isaac gestured toward the ceiling and the curved, young ash and spruce branches that held the roof in place, "is best when it's young and pliable."

He built his longhouse and took up trapping. When that was not enough, he worked as a guide. Clara kept the house, tended the garden and taught her children how to read and write in English, while their Mémé taught the Lawrence children the Mohawk language and traditions.

When Isaac was done telling his story, Louise and Ike wasted no time gathering their belongings, guns and traps, and the few items of clothing they had to bring. They took off for Pine Knot with William and Stone.

"I need you to relay this to my father." William handed Stone a card the next day. "It clearly states my intentions so don't worry about being reprimanded. I'll need you to bring back the smaller sleigh. My father has several at the mill in North Creek. Pick one that suits the terrain here, a cutter should work well. We'll need it for several reasons that I hadn't foreseen. My letter explains it all. And tell him our meat supplies are low. I have left him with a list of food items we will need until the thaw. And I want them delivered as soon as possible. Come back with the cutter, I'll meet you at Holland House in a week."

Stone wondered how the devil he was going to explain these arrangements. He just hoped Dr. Durant would be preoccupied with his own business dealings and not ask too many questions.

Clara Lawrence didn't survive the month of February. William drove Ike and Louise home one day to find that Isaac had already buried her. He felt helpless standing in the longhouse when Sarah told Louise and she wailed in her sister's arms. Ike was in shock. He left to find his mother's grave and didn't come back.

Finally, William, realizing how out of place he was amongst the mourners, left to scope out a few small lakes he had seen on his travels. He made a camp in the woods with a tent and waited until morning to retrieve Louise and Ike and head back to Pine Knot.

When the spring melt did come weeks later, the workmen followed because William sent word out that he would offer twice the pay they would get driving logs downstream. These lumbermen, William came to understand, were like many he encountered in the United States: first or second-generation immigrants from Ireland, Germany, Scandinavia and Italy, a jumble of cultures. It was not uncommon to meet a man with a surname unrelated to the origin of his Christian one. When he was introduced to Patrick DeLuca, William had trouble discerning which country the man regarded as his homeland. Pierre Smith could be French Canadian or just another bloke from Vermont fleeing a string of bad crops to seek his fortune with his axe in the woods. And they brought other tools of their trade: axes, spuds, hand saws, adzes and lathes. Besides felling a tree they knew how to join and finish logs, carve wood and stretch bark. They made their sleeping arrangements in makeshift lean-tos and shanties and worked hard every day alongside William, helping to shape his vision of Pine Knot.

After the death of her mother, Louise instinctively assumed the role of matriarch at Pine Knot. Her quiet directions were always obeyed. She knew what the men needed, what they wanted from her. And her maternal skills were well received. She healed their wounds using the herbs her grandmother gave her, made meals out of wild game and fish, mended their shoes and clothes.

Louise was also William's companion. They stayed in the hunting cabin as they had done together the previous autumn. Growing up in a longhouse didn't allow for privacy and Louise was well versed in the desires of man and wife. It was natural for her to spend nights in the bed of the man she loved, who took care of her and her family. The only time she would not sleep with William was right before and while bleeding. Then, she slept by herself in the other room as her grandmother had instructed her.

Every night after the food had been put away and the men had settled into their routines by the campfire, William, Louise and Ike would walk the mile path along the shore to the hunting cabin.

When they got to the cabin in the evening, Louise would sing Ike to sleep and afterwards enter the bedroom she shared with William where he would wait for her, listening in a chair to her soft lilting voice, barely able to stay awake himself after a long day of building, constructing and commanding his workmen.

Sometimes she would give him a tonic made of the macerated inner bark of the mountain ash, mixed with water, whiskey and sugar. It was a favorite of all the men at the camp. He never asked, she always knew when he needed it. The strong drink surged through his veins and roused his senses. When she was ready for bed she would lift the lid of the Swiss music box and undress in front of William to the tinkling sound. Louise was not hindered by useless garments. She wore a long skirt with deer hide breeches underneath it — there was no need for a bustle, there was no one to show it off to in the woods — a chemise and blouse. When it was very cold she wore a tunic over her blouse made of deerskin or fur. And she always had on a small wooden charm of a turtle. Sarah had made it for her. It was a symbol of their clan.

After she undressed she would help William take off his clothes: shoes, trousers, shirt, and then lead him to their bed. She would massage his shoulders, his back, his head. They would lie down together, their warm bodies creating enough heat to keep the cold night at bay. Sometimes they would make love, other times they were too tired. It didn't matter to Louise, she had everything she needed from him. His complete devotion to her and her family. He would never let them starve.

The Finn came by skis to Pine Knot one bright morning in March. By this time the laborers were making headway on the chalet. The fireplace was framed and waiting for the granite stone Johannes Koskinen had promised William would be ready by Spring.

Johannes reached for William's hand in greeting. William took it but was slightly disappointed by the fact that he came without a horse and sled filled with the rock he needed for the chimney and hearth.

"Where's the granite you promised, Koskinen?" William asked.

"Follow me," Johannes said. William strapped on snowshoes and followed him into the woods. They passed a stand of sugar maples in a swampy area near the camp. Louise and Ike had slashed trees with their axe, and nailed buckets made of birch bark underneath to collect the dripping sap. In the evenings they came out to collect the buckets of sap and boil it down to make sugar.

"Where there's spruce there's granite," Johannes said in his broken English. Unsure what he was talking about, William just nodded in agreement and kept walking.

Finally they came upon an area on Long Point where the bedrock was visible. It was swampy, and there were stands of larch and Black spruce trees. The Finn motioned to William to follow him to a clearing where an outcrop of granite stood. There he showed William what he had done. Before the last frost he used an auger to drill small holes in the granite. He filled the holes with water and plugged them with hemp. When the water froze it expanded, putting pressure along the seam of the rock. Johannes lifted his sledgehammer in the air above the granite and split it in pieces.

It took more hammering to get enough rock for the fireplace but by the end of the week Johannes, using a horse and sled, brought enough back to Pine Knot for the men to finish the fireplace and chimney.

Now it was time to start on his parents' and Ella's cabin. William was making good progress. But he had only enough men and time to complete these three buildings and close the dining area with windows. The glass would be arriving from Saratoga by rail to North Creek and a stage was bringing it to Blue Mountain. He had workmen frame the windows with limbs he had found while scouring the forests. Where possible he made the frames decorative, and continued the designs on the rails of the porches. He liked the idea of designing with the forest's supplies. It allowed him to explore and not have to rely on the mills too much for the finished wood products. Indeed, in some cases he left the bark intact which provided the primitive feel to the cabins William desired.

Pine Knot was coming along, but it still wasn't done to his satisfaction. He wanted to install benches, gazebos, and window boxes, all reminiscent of the English gardens of his youth. That would have to wait. He needed to make good progress or his father would abandon him as the builder and hire it out to someone else.

Every day William learned something new about the local environment that he incorporated into his plans. One morning he found Louise and Ike by the shoreline pounding away at strips of ash wood they had soaked in the lake for two days. Louise was pounding a strip with a hammer and then handing it over to Ike who used an adz to smooth it out.

"My father uses the adz on the bark of his longhouse so that it repels the rain," Louise told him.

William liked the way the tool shaped the wood. "This would work well on our siding," he said.

The mix of cultures at Pine Knot meant that collectively people knew the elixirs the forest provided and taught each other. While Ike and Louise collected the sweet sap of the maples, the Scandinavians tapped the birch and added it to their drinks. Bark, William came to find out, had many uses besides siding. The lumbermen chewed on the sweet birch bark to cleanse their palate and that of slippery elm to quench thirst.

Johannes showed William how to collect the white chalky substance from the outer bark of the paper birch, betulin, he called it. "It makes a good preservative when mixed with pine pitch and beeswax," he said. William immediately sent word to his father to have beeswax delivered and had the men mix up great batches of the substance. They applied the concoction on the exterior of the logs of the buildings.

He was enjoying himself so much amongst these people who made their livelihoods from the woods that he almost forgot he was a Durant. He slipped into the role of husband to Louise and commander to the woodsmen that were building Pine Knot. Reality struck when a letter came from his father with instructions for him to build a small boat.

"It is only April yet your mother has already started complaining of the insects that she envisions in her head will be swarming Pine Knot when she arrives three months hence," he wrote William. "Make me a floating house that I can launch out on the water, away from the biting insects — with your mother and her companion Margaret on it."

Where his father got the idea for a floating house William had no idea but it was an unwanted distraction. He didn't want to waste the good wood he had handpicked for construction. His reserves were starting to dwindle. It was then William recalled that one day while walking in the woods he had come upon an area that was victim to a forest fire. The pioneering birch grew well in the open canopy and he used the bark for the ceilings of the chalet. The charred remnants of the White pine trees could be recycled for the boat. He called the floating house barge the *Barque of the Pine*.

Part Three

CAMP HUNTINGTON
MAY 2010

He was trapped, and docile. It took Avery a moment to realize she had one, a saw-whet tangled quietly in the mist nest waiting for its fate. Owls' specialized feathers allow them to fly without sound so she would never have known if she hadn't been checking the net every half hour.

She put on gloves and disengaged the bird gently from the net, put him in a small sack and brought him into the *Barque of the Pine* where she had set up her equipment. The *Barque* was a perfect lab. It sat shaded by tall pines and the low, overhanging roof and small windows kept the inside dark.

She pulled out an ultraviolet light to estimate the bird's age. The pigment of new saw-whet feathers fluoresces a pink glow in the light and fades with age. This one's feathers were luminescing a pink glow under the black light. She recorded the age as one year old, a juvenile.

It was definitely a male, as he weighed in on the scale at less than seventy-five grams; a female would be closer to one hundred. Avery blew on his downy chest feathers to look for the telltale yellow of a fat deposit, indicating that prey is plentiful. He was a plump one all right; the field mice were abundant around the *Barque*. When she was done recording, she put a small aluminum alloy band around his tiny leg with a serial number for tracking. If he ever did leave his territory in the North Woods to migrate south, maybe a bird-bander in Pennsylvania would capture him one day and they could share stories.

"All done little guy," she said. Lifting him in the air at the door of the *Barque* she was both sad and exhilarated that she finally had a live bird banded. The creature, which had shown no emotion during the whole ordeal, bit her wrist before he flew off.

It was a productive morning. By 11 am she had captured and banded four more owls: three males and one female. Satisfied and hungry, she decided to call it a day. Since luck was on her side, maybe this evening she would give it another try at the site near Camp Kirby. She returned to Huntington to eat lunch with the co-eds before heading back to her small cabin in the woods. After lunch she took a break on the porch of her cabin and stole a few minutes to read more of the diary.

June 16, 1893

I woke up to the lonely wail of the loons. They frighten me sometimes, the loons, they call to each other every morning as if they are lost. And it reminds me of William. Sometimes he appears lost.

For instance, last night he came to see me very late. Nate had long since gone to bed. William tapped lightly on the door leading to my room.

I was startled by his tapping, it took me a moment to realize someone was outside my room on the porch. I put on my robe and went to him. He was as wet as a mop and smelled like cigar smoke and campfire.

He was exhausted. I know that he and Janet have been doing a lot of entertaining this summer. President Harrison has stayed at Pine Knot more than once while on a hunting expedition. And numerous friends and family from New York City are planning to visit when the black flies have gone. Or so William has informed me. He does not want so much company, he told me, while he is working on finishing Camp Uncas, but he has to entertain to keep these people interested in investing in his land holdings. I really don't understand it all.

"Oh Minnie," he said and hugged me, causing me to get drenched as well. He went to the chair in the corner and took off his shoes before sitting back in the chair to look at me standing in the middle of the room. I was still so shocked to see him here at this time of night.

After what seemed like a long time of me standing there in the middle of the room, shivering, waiting for him to say something, he took my hand and led me to my bed and tucked me in and sat down on the bed next to me. We listened to the soft patter of the rain on the roof and looked out the window at the drizzle. I had my arms over his chest.

"I will stay with you until you fall asleep," he said.

When I woke up this morning he was gone. And that is when I heard the loons calling.

Minnie

June 20, 1893

Nate has been my constant companion while I pine away here waiting for my next visit from William. Tonight we sat on the porch after supper. We read about the guides of the Adirondacks that Nate is so proud of. This funny little book, Murray's Adventures, was written over twenty years ago, yet Nate reads it like it's his talisman. He was especially proud of Murray's description of the independent guide, as it reminds him of his Uncle.

"...a more honest, cheerful and patient class of men cannot be found the world over. Born and bred as many of them were in this wilderness, skilled in ....woodcraft, ...handy with the rod,...superb at the paddle. Bronzed and hardy, fearless of danger...uncontaminated with the vicious habits of civilized life..."

I would hate to be the one to tell poor Nate that they are a dying breed as the hotels hire them as servants to the masses that arrive each summer, no longer just the men on an outing: the women and children are in tow as well. And the tourists spend their time not in a boat or portaging from one lake to the next but sitting on the verandas of places like Under the Hemlocks or Paul Smith's Hotel, waiting for tea and the next social event of the day where they can put on their finest clothes and act like they are back home. I know all of this because I heard the guides complaining about it while I was a governess for William's children.

But all of this turmoil is hard to explain to an eleven year old orphan boy who wants to believe his father was swallowed up by the woods and who doesn't even know how his mother died.

I held him close to me as we watched the sunset.

Minnie

"Hmmm," Avery hummed to herself, intrigued by the way this affair was shaping into something. She yawned, then put the small diary back in her pack and went into the cabin to take a short nap before going out again to scout for more owls.

CAMP PINE KNOT
SUMMER 1878

William greeted the guests and his sister Ella at the dock at Pine Knot. He was thinner, glowing, and more muscular, the happiest Ella had seen him since their early days in England. "Welcome!" he said as he raised his arms in the air to embrace her.

"Oh, William, you look marvelous, I missed you so much!" She hugged her brother, took his hands in hers and feeling how coarse they were, held the palms of his hands up. "Look at this, your hands are so rough and calloused. What have you been doing all spring?"

"This place is beautiful," Anna Leonowens said, looking around.

"Yes, let me show you to the guest house," William said. He walked the group to guest quarters with Louise trailing close behind.

"It's right out of the Alps!" Poultney exclaimed with wonder at the building William was transforming from a one to two-story chalet.

"Yes," William said with pride, "my workmen have indispensible knowledge of the lumber here, what works best, where and how to join the logs together. I've shown them a small model of a chalet, explained my vision, and they go right to work on it." He led the guests to their cabins.

"When does father plan to arrive?" William asked Ella later while they sat on the front porch of the new cottage he had built for her.

"He said he would be here by June," she said. "He was a bit vague about his arrangements."

"Father, vague? What a surprise!"

"Hello there! So this is where you're hiding." It was Poultney. Not one to rest, he'd gone looking for Ella and William as soon as he was done unpacking his things. William gave them a tour, showing them all the buildings, except the cabin in the woods he shared with Louise, who had long since gone to the kitchen to make supper for the guests. Loud voices, hammers, and saws were the background music; the place was alive with construction. There'd been numerous improvements. Even Papa should be satisfied, Ella thought. The glass windows were in place on the dining hall, a couple of new outhouses were being built and placed in the woods behind the cabins, and the guest quarters were brilliantly done, neither too polished, nor too rustic.

"What's this?" Ella asked when they reached the shore where the men were building a small cabin on top of massive logs lashed together with hemp.

"This, dear girl, is mother's escape from the insects while she stays at Pine Knot," William told Ella. "It's a houseboat, as requested by our father." The three snickered as they envisioned Mrs. Durant with Margaret out on the lake.

"Well, I think we should be the first to christen it," Poultney said.

"Yes, it'd be a good idea, make sure it floats and all that. When the water warms up a little more we can launch it and idle out on the lake for a day," William said.

They headed to the dining hall for a supper of fish and venison and the good wine Ella had brought from North Creek.

"What do you think?" Ella was sitting with Poultney on the front porch of the chalet waiting to hear his critique of her latest poem: *Moon and Sea*.

"Lugubrious," Poultney said, languidly handing her journal

back.

"How so?" Ella said.

"It just is."

"No it's not, not all of it anyway."

"Yes, it is. Let's see, 'We sat together watching the glorious scene; And if each longed to reach the other's hand 'twas only known to the moon and sobbing sea'. Now if that isn't mournful I don't know what is," he said.

"You never have anything nice to say about my writing. Did you notice that? You look for faults."

"That's not true. I just don't extol you and you don't like it."

"That's not the point! And you have no sense of good writing when you see it, Poultney," she said.

"Really Ella, you asked what I thought of your poem. I told you and you can't take it. Do you want my opinion or not?"

She crossed her arms over her chest, brooding. Poultney looked through the canopy of trees at the white trilliums sprinkled like powdered sugar on the forest floor.

He paused and glanced sideways at her before continuing. "Ella, every poem you've sent me to read lately has been a little self-indulgent. You need to get out of North Creek more often."

"You know as well as I do I'd love that, but father won't allow me to go anywhere without a chaperone, and William's been busy." She gestured to indicate Pine Knot as the reason she was a prisoner in North Creek.

Poultney shook his head and threw his arms wide. "Look around you. There's plenty here to draw on for your poetry if you need inspiration. Much better I'd think than pining over that lad of yours from Scotland or wherever. 'Come maiden, weep with me for love is slain' and all that." Poultney mock-slashed his throat with his pointer finger and grimaced.

Ella was not amused. "I've written poems about this place. I started on a piece called Raquette," she said defensively.

"Well why don't you let me read that then instead of your unrequited love poems."

"I might, if I felt you wouldn't make fun of it." Ella picked up

138

her journal and descended the porch steps in a huff. Poultney sighed. She'd be back, eventually.

William came up just as she was leaving.

"What happened?" he asked Poultney.

Poultney shrugged.

"You upset her again?" William said.

"It doesn't take much," Poultney replied.

"Perhaps, but try not to antagonize her too much, old chap. It's never fun when Ella's in a snit."

"Humph," Poultney agreed.

They stared out at the lake.

"Where is Louise from?" Anna asked William as they sat in the living room of the chalet, close to the roaring flames in the fireplace with a decanter of sherry at hand ready to be poured. Poultney and Ella came in from a short walk around the camp.

"She's part Mohawk," William said. As if on cue, Louise entered. She sat down in a chair in the corner, picked up some mending and started to stitch.

"Louise dear, come here will you please?" Anna said.

Louise was not at all surprised by the request. Something about Anna made her think they might share something in common. Ella sat down while Poultney poured them all some sherry before taking a seat himself.

"None for Louise?" Anna asked William.

"I don't drink alcohol," Louise answered.

"Well, my dear, you hardly know what you're missing. So tell us your story. How did you end up here at Pine Knot?"

Louise proceeded to tell them how she and Ike met William through Charlie Bennett and then became his servants. She left out that she shared William's bed. Only Ike knew that William followed her into the woods to the small hunting cabin. He had instructed Louise to keep their relationship hidden. He said it was for her own protection. "These people, my family and our friends, they will not understand."

This baffled Louise. She didn't know the customs of marriage that William's culture supported. What she knew from her time in the Northern Woods was what she saw. Men and women lived as one because they wanted to be together, to have a family, to stay alive. You grew in love because you had to with your mate. There were not many choices. Official documents, ceremonies, these were all foreign to her. Her mother never talked about it, her grandmother only told her about the feasts they had in the longhouse to celebrate the unions of her aunts to her uncles. She did not witness any of these occasions. What she had with William was in step with what people did in the Adirondacks: they landed somewhere, settled, and made a home and family. The conventions that existed in the Adirondack woods were tenacity and common sense. If you didn't have these, you didn't survive.

The tranquil days were over as soon as Dr. Durant arrived. Although gracious to his guests, he harangued William with questions about the progress of the buildings from the minute he landed on the dock at Pine Knot. The foursome found refuge on the *Barque*. They packed up their things, brought Louise and Ike along for the ride and told the Doctor it would be best if he stayed behind to watch over the workmen. It took five men to push the massive floating log hut off the beach and into the water with the party on it. They waved and lingered on shore to watch as Ike used the long pole to push the boat out to the open waters.

"I wonder if those oars we made will be enough to row them to shore," one of them remarked. Then they lumbered back to work with regret that they couldn't be Ike, for although William drove them hard, he shared in the burden. The ferocious-looking Dr. Durant just sat in his chair barking orders.

That evening as the group sat around the fire laughing about their day, Louise prepared the special tonic she made out of the bark of Mountain ash.

"This is delicious," Dr. Durant said, lifting his glass in the air.

"What's in this concoction?"

"It's made with the bark of the Mountain ash," William said.

"You've got me drinking bark?" He spat some out of his mouth and it dribbled onto his beard. He wiped it off his chin with a handkerchief. "My God, William, you've been in the woods too long, you're becoming one of the natives. Louise — get me a straight whiskey, now!"

Louise, who had resumed her role as servant, was sitting in the corner mending. She looked up, startled by the order and Dr. Durant's intonation. So was William. For the past few months he realized, no one had ordered Louise to do anything. She did what she needed to do when it needed to be done. If she didn't do something it was because the deed was uncalled for.

William knew it was a bad idea for Louise to serve his father anything more. He'd clearly had too much wine at dinner. "It's not as if you're chewing on bark, it's macerated after all." He got up and made his father another drink, watering it down.

"What the devil does that mean? I'm no cook."

Anna saved the day. "Louise, this drink is lovely. And so are you." She turned to Dr. Durant, "It means, Thomas, that she soaked the bark in sugar water before adding it to your rye."

"Humph." He didn't agree but he was in too good a mood to argue. Something about the air in the Adirondacks settled him. The French wine helped too. He finished the tonic in two gulps and asked for another one. "Here's to slaying the coeruleus!" He raised his second glass to the special tonic.

"What on earth is that?" Anna asked.

"The part of the brain that causes stress and panic. I have to admit that this tonic, along with the mountain air and the clear lake water, seems to address those ills quite well."

They all toasted their agreement.

A week went by and then it was time for Anna to leave. Poultney was escorting her home to New York City.

"I'll be back in August," he promised Ella.

"August is too long."

"While I'm gone you can think of me and write. Just try to be a bit more upbeat will you? As far as I can tell there is nothing unrequited about our love." He smiled at her.

Ella smiled.

"I left an Ode to the Adirondacks in your guest book. It's for William," Anna said as she joined Ella and Poultney on the docks with one of her bags. Ike followed with the rest of her luggage. Louise, who had been a faithful companion ever since Anna asked her story, was there as well.

"I wrote it in Sanskrit. It's vaguely reminiscent of the story of King Nala," Anna said. "I saw the play in India and I will never forget the beautiful girl who played the princess Damayanti. Louise reminds me of her." She turned to Louise who blushed at being the center of attention.

Ella wondered why she would write her Ode in Sanskrit. No one would be able to translate it. In the Hindu story, Ella recalled from reading a translation, King Nala must leave the princess in the forest to protect her from his own misfortune.

William came to say good-bye. "I'm sorry my father isn't here to say good-bye. He's still in his cabin, I'm afraid he's not feeling well."

"Yes, wine and rye will do that to you," Ella said.

William opened his mouth to chastise his sister, but changed his mind and refrained.

"I know it may be a long while before you have a guest here that can read Sanskrit," Anna said, "but I'll tell you how it ends. 'Like a wife, the forest is the best medicine for a man that is afflicted. For the forest heals all, 'tis the truth I speak'." She turned to William and Ella. "Thank you for hosting me, and please thank your father as well." With that, she got into the small steamboat with Poultney. Ella waved good bye to Poultney as she watched them row away. William and Louise took a walk in the woods.

"It's time we head back to North Creek and the city," Dr. Durant said to Ella and William over dinner one evening.

William feigned indifference. "Yes, I know what you mean," he answered. "I'm getting a bit antsy up here with no other companions but the workmen. But do you think it wise to leave them here alone? We have numerous supplies that could easily be purloined." William knew and trusted his men, as he had weeded out those he didn't, but he needed his father to doubt so that it would be his idea, not William's, to stay.

"Hmm, you may have a point. It's not like I can leave Stone behind. I need him to drive the carriage back. Where are Wood and Bennett?"

"Charlie Bennett is busy building his hotel. And Wood must be guiding. I haven't seen or heard from him all Spring. And that's another thing to consider. The buildings are not all furnished. I was planning on meeting with one of the Stott's craftsman. I hear he makes quality furnishings. We'll save ourselves a lot of money if we can at least have some of the furniture made locally."

"Well, then. When did you plan to do all of this? Maybe I can wait another week." The idea of staying another week pleased Dr. Durant.

But not William. He wanted him gone. "Sadly, it will take longer than that. I'm not sure when the Stotts arrive. And Frederick asked me to check in with him on his plans for the Prospect House on Blue Mountain."

"Oh yes, I forgot about that. I saw Frederick on the way in and he mentioned you were coming to offer guidance. You should see what he has already developed."

William could just imagine from all of the grand plans he had heard the guides talking about; it sounded like one of the hotels on Fifth Avenue, but in Blue Mountain.

"I'd like to stay behind as well," Ella piped in.

Oh God, William thought, she's going to ruin it. I had it all planned to ask father if she could stay and now he'll say no automatically.

"No." Dr. Durant didn't even bother to look at her.

"But Papa! What am I supposed to do back at North Creek? I'll be so bored!"

"Ella, leave us. Now!" he ordered.

Ella opened her mouth to speak but stopped her verbal tirade when she saw the look William gave her. It said: *Shut up. I'll handle this.* And so she did. She got up as daintily as her fury would allow and left the table.

"You know," William said once she was safely out of earshot, "as much as I would hate to be distracted by Ella, you may be doing mother and yourself a favor leaving her behind with me at Pine Knot as well."

"How so?" The doctor put a forkful of venison in his mouth.

"I know she pesters mother about how bored she is at home."

William knew that Ella would get his mother into a frenzy about how miserable life was in North Creek, enough so that his father would eventually relent to their requests to visit New York City. But these excursions, sporadic as they were, cost him a fortune. The women always seemed to need, and purchase, the latest fashions in the windows of the many shops that lined 5th Avenue. William knew his father would be glad not to have to listen to their banter about these trips at the dinner table. Besides, it would save him the angst of paying the bills.

"Maybe that's not such a bad idea after all. You stay here, with your sister. I am warning you though, I expect to see some progress when I come back in August. You must have this place in shape by then. Don't let Ella distract you from your work."

William sighed and accepted his father's decision with good grace. "Of course, Father. I understand," William said. "And as if there wasn't enough to do already, Ella informed me that Howard and Estelle may visit and Poultney plans to come back and bring a schoolmate from Yale."

"Good. The more the merrier. As our guests spread the news with their friends how wonderful the experience is, we'll win more investors in our properties."

"We will indeed," William smiled inwardly.

144

Ella and William gazed out at the horizon from the boat, lost in their own thoughts as the rising sun cast a mirrored reflection of trees on the water. They were on their way to see cousin Frederick. Ike left them off at the mouth of the Marion river. From there they had a short walk over the rapids to meet the new steamboat, part of the Durant transportation system, waiting to take them to Blue Mountain Lake and Frederick's Prospect House Hotel.

"What is all of this steam business costing?" Ella turned her attention away from the horizon to William.

William shrugged. "The company lawyers, Sutphen and Barbour deal in numbers. I just assist in the logistics. I'm adding another steamboat to our line to carry passengers onto Raquette Lake. No more guideboats."

"And what will we gain from it?"

"We shall see more people coming to the area and investing in our land once we make it easier for them to travel. Now that father has lost his chance at the 20,000 acres around here, our last hope may be this steamboat line and the land holdings we can sell."

"I wonder if we'll ever see England again," Ella sighed, "or are we destined to remain in this wild place?" She reached for a maple leaf hanging from a branch above her on the path.

"I used to wonder that as well," William said.

"Jack and Bill Napier would like the hunting here though, wouldn't they?" she said. "Do you think my lady friends would enjoy these views?"

William stopped her. "You do realize that even if you ever do make it back to England, our friends, your friends, will be married off and settled into their affairs. The days of masked balls and dances are behind us."

Ella smacked the leaf playfully across his face. "My goodness, you sound like an old man. You're only twenty-eight. Most men your age are only starting to think about marriage."

William scuffed a twig with his foot and contemplated what Ella said, then reached down to pick it up.

"Not true. Jack and Bill Napier were married this year after all. It is about time for me as well I think."

"You can't be serious! Who would you marry?" Ella was incredulous, as far as she knew William was not courting anyone in New York, so who then was he talking about? Could it be Louise? She shook off the notion knowing what William already did —their parents would never allow it.

"I used to think about returning to England all the time," he said, continuing to walk while twirling the twig between his thumb and pointer finger. "But I've come to realize that our life in America is all that we have to look forward to now." He tossed the twig in the air ahead of them. "Maybe though it was all meant to be this way," William looked around him. "Although it's not the Isle of Wight, these woods aren't such a bad place to spend idle time."

"Dear brother, *you* may enjoy being a gadabout in the woods, but *I* do not. Which reminds me, when will you go back to living in New York City so I can stay with you?"

"So you can rendezvous with Poultney?"

"Poultney has other affairs I'm sure. Besides, he told me he plans to attend law school at Columbia once he finishes at Yale. He'll be too preoccupied to spend time with me."

It was William's turn to laugh. "He'll find the time I am sure."

When they arrived at Prospect House Frederick was consulting with one of his workmen on the massive front porch.

"Three hundred rooms — an electric light and running water in each!" He walked his cousins through the hotel, once in awhile pointing out something to William and asking him what he thought. It stood six stories tall, and there were two levels of decks overlooking the water. William gaped at the enormity of the structure. The ceilings in the ballroom reminded him of those they'd seen in the aristocratic households of Europe.

"We will hold grand dances, it will be *The Place to Be* in the summer."

William was quiet on the way back. Besides the tour of the hotel, he couldn't help but notice the new mill Frederick had erected on site and the forests around the hotel were being cut to provide the wood for construction. The roads were deeply rutted from the supplies being carried in by horse and wagon. And all of the people working on-site turned the area into a minor city: tents and shanties, men drinking, smoking, and cursing. He'd never seen anything like it before —except once — when they went to visit their father while he was building the transcontinental line out west.

"Why does he have to make it so big?" Ella was reading his thoughts.

"I don't know. Durant trait I suppose. I'm sure father is goading him along. I know he was the one that asked Thomas Edison to build the steam generator that will provide the electricity. And that alone will take enormous amounts of wood to run."

"Did you miss your Muse from Malden-on-the-Hudson?" Poultney whispered in Ella's ear as he climbed out of the boat onto the shore of Pine Knot weeks later.

"No. If anything, not communicating with you has done wonders for my writing. Less irritation to deal with. I've never liked pests," Ella teased.

"Sir? Do you know where you and your friend are staying?" Ike inquired of Poultney, glancing at his friend from Yale. It was going to be a busy couple of weeks. Besides Poultney and his friend Steven, other guests were already here: cousins Howard and Estelle, and Ella's friend Fran Murphy, Hannah Durant and Margaret, and Reverend Dix was arriving any day with his wife Emily.

William had done his best to finish the construction and furnish the chalet and a cabin specifically for the men to go for after dinner smoking and playing cards. There were private cabins as well: one for Ella and one for his parents. He knew his father would be pleased.

Poultney shrugged at Ike and glanced at Ella, looking for a clue to where he and Steven were staying. William provided the answer as he came up to the group, sunburned and wearing his workman's attire.

"The men are all staying in the chalet, it's not quite complete but should do – Ella and the other young ladies are in a cabin down the pathway." He motioned toward the path and shook the men's hands all around.

"William." Poultney took his hand. "You look years younger. And where is your silk top hat you are never without in the clubs?"

"No need for that here," William said.

"Promise me you'll take us on an overnight trip. We brought tents," Poultney said.

"Of course we will, and more," William assured them all. "We may even provide some swimming lessons on the *Barque*. Now you must all be hungry for some supper. Louise has been busy cooking."

"So tell me, Poultney, what've you been doing without me these past several weeks? It must be pure torture not receiving my poems so you can tear them apart," Ella teased as they went for a walk in the woods later that day.

"Actually, I read 'Raquette'. You did a brilliant job describing the place. 'Here in the depths, Oh Lethean Lake! We drop our griefs, our vain regret! As from an evil dream we wake, tasting health's sweetness, learning at last life's completeness.'" Poultney swooned.

"My, my, you've memorized my work. And you're complimenting it! How unusual for you."

"Not really, my dear. If I spent too much time praising you, you'd never like me. You're all about the challenge. Besides, the poem shows you're finally getting over your lost love in England, or Scotland, or wherever he was from. That makes me happy."

"Don't be too happy just yet, Poultney." Ella smiled. "I may be over him, but I'm not head over heels for you. You play cat and mouse with me too much for my liking. I don't want to be batted around like a plaything for your amusement," Ella said with a slight smile.

Poultney threw his head back and let out a hearty guffaw. "Ella," he said, "you are more than a mouse to my cat-like cravings."

They walked the shoreline path that led away from Pine Knot and before too long found themselves in front of the hunting cabin.

Ella had not seen it since the summer before when she was on the boat with William. It was much improved. There was a porch and glass windows that faced the lake. They went inside. Two rooms split the front of the cabin; one was a small bedroom with two cots, the other a parlor. Behind the small bedroom was a kitchen and behind the parlor was a master bedroom. The two could not squelch their curiosity — they went to the master bedroom. And there it was: a bed the likes of which neither had ever seen before. Similar furniture was scattered throughout Pine Knot but this bed was a piece of art. It was sculpted out of wood with ornate geometric patterns of inlaid woods decking the headboard.

"My God, it's a marriage bed!" Poultney said.

Ella saw William's Swiss chalet music box, the one he had intended to give to Florence, on the dresser and felt the need to get out of there. Ella was embarrassed for William and their intrusion on what must be his private lair.

Poultney turned to her, his eyes full of desire. Ella caught her breath.

"Should we try it out?" he asked.

"Poultney," Ella was flustered by his proposal, "don't jest with me."

He put his arms around her waist and kissed her passionately. Then he reached for her bodice. "You're not wearing a corset are you?" He breathed on her neck.

She blushed, aroused, and scared to death of his presence. She kissed him back. "No, I never do," she whispered. "Not here anyway."

He started to untie her bodice so he could see what was underneath her blouse. As surprised as she was, Ella didn't stop him.

Just then they heard voices in the woods. It was William and Louise, walking toward to the cabin to rest for a short while before the afternoon's events. If they went through the front they would be found out. This was one situation that Ella would not be able to talk her way out of.

Ella and Poultney looked for an escape and saw the door leading out of the master bedroom. An easy exit, how had they missed it before? They stifled their laughter until they were a safe distance from the cabin and then exhaled in the woods.

Ella finally composed herself so she could put her bodice back in place. She was shocked at how quickly and easily she had responded to his desire. Still giggling, they took each other's hand and walked back to Pine Knot.

Louise and William's group of friends waited patiently onshore next to the beached canoes while William and Ella discussed logistics with their parents. They had loaded up all the gear they would need for an overnight camping trip to a place William had discovered, a small lake not too far from Pine Knot. They had all gotten up early in anticipation of taking off at dawn and were about to get into the canoes and take off when the Durants showed up and called Ella and William aside. And it didn't look like the negotiations were going all that well.

"It's just like him to try to put a stop to our fun," Fran Murphy said.

"If you ask my opinion, I would guess Ella never told Aunt Hannah the ladies were part of this expedition," Estelle said to her brother Howard.

Steven let off a low whistle and Poultney started to pace about anxiously. Ike batted at a fly that was hovering over him while he sat in a canoe.

"You never told us you planned to bring the ladies on this jaunt of yours," Hannah said to William.

Ella opened her mouth to speak but William took hold of her forearm and squeezed it lightly.

"Mother, I'm not sure what all the fuss is about. The young ladies are quite safe. As you can see, I have my rifle strapped to my back, so does Ike and so does Poultney. And Ike knows these waterways better than any guide around here. We are not going that far."

"It's not their safety I'm worried about son, it's their reputations," Hannah said.

"Pffft," Ella said. William squeezed her arm harder, this time digging his fingers into her skin. She let out a small squeal.

"Your mother is right," Dr. Durant said. "Tell the ladies to get their things, including Louise. You cannot take them with you into the woods."

"Father, be reasonable. Look at us." William waved at their group of friends waiting on the shore. "We've been planning this since they arrived last week. Estelle especially has been looking forward to it."

"Well who will cook for our guests if you take Louise?" Dr. Durant said.

"I've arranged for a cook from Antlers to come and help out while Louise is away."

"Humph, maybe we'll finally get somebody that knows how to cook a béarnaise sauce," Hannah said.

"And Fran Murphy told me she wanted to scout out land to talk her father into buying from us," William said, ignoring his mother's insult of Louise's cooking. "You know how enthralled she is with Pine Knot."

Dr. Durant's face brightened as he contemplated the prospect. "Oh alright then."

Hannah let out an unhappy sigh.

Just then Poultney came bounding up to them, all ruddy cheeked and tousled hair. "Is there any trouble?"

"Nothing that concerns you," Hannah said.

"Well looks like we are all ready to go then!" Poultney said.

"Curb your enthusiasm young man," Dr. Durant said.

Blushing, Poultney looked from Ella to William for support and finding none said, "Ok, I will get back to the canoes and wait for you both."

"The nerve of that boy!" Hannah said when he left.

"William, I am counting on you to chaperone these ladies and make sure they are safely in their tents by a decent hour," Dr. Durant said.

"Of course, Papa, what else—" Ella started, but didn't finish her sentence because William gripped her arm tightly and started to lead her away.

"We will see you tomorrow evening!" he called back to his parents as he pulled Ella along with him.

"You'd think by now Ella you would have learned to keep your mouth shut when I am negotiating with father," he said.

Ella wrenched her arm away from his and stormed away.

"*Tout va bien maintenant?*" Poultney asked her as she headed toward one of the canoes.

"*Ouais. Ça va.*" She waved her hand in the air as she climbed into the bow of one of them.

Poultney was about to jump into the stern behind her when William stopped him. "As Ella said, everything is fine. We are taking off now. Ike, you ride with Ella," he said.

Poultney got into the stern of the canoe with Fran and pushed off.

They canoed through one of the inlets and stopped when the stream became narrow and ended at a waterfall. There they got out to portage in the woods a short distance before getting back into the canoes on the other side.

After a few more portages they reached the lake.

The clear lake sat like a bowl in a basin of green forest.

"What an enchanting place!" Estelle said.

After they had set up their tents the ladies went in search of wood while the men tried their luck with their fishing rods.

That evening Louise fried perch and trout over the fire. Afterwards, Ike took the left over food supplies and packed them in a sack he had brought especially for the occasion. It was tied with a long rope that he could use to hoist it into a tree. They watched in awe as he shinnied like a monkey up a White pine and swung the rope over a thin branch about ten feet off the ground. The rope dropped to the forest floor where Louise picked it up and tied it to a nearby sapling, anchoring the sack over the limb in midair.

"What are they doing?" Fran asked William.

"They are securing our food from bears and raccoons by leaving it hanging on the tree limb," he said.

That evening they sat, leaning against some large logs that the men had dragged over by the campfire and listened to Steven play folk tunes on his banjo.

He strummed a tune that Estelle recognized. She crooned along with him:

We're tenting tonight on the old camp ground,
Give us a song to cheer
Our weary hearts, a song of home
And friends we love so dear
Many are the hearts that are weary tonight,
Wishing for the war to cease;
Many are the hearts looking for the right,
To see the dawn of peace.
Dying tonight, dying tonight,
Dying on the old camp ground

The last line hung over them as the hushed group waited for the sound of the humming strings to vanish in the air.

"That was lovely, Estelle. Where did you learn it?" Ella asked.

"Oh that is an old civil war ditty they taught us in school,"

Estelle said. "You missed those years, Ella."

The only sound then was the cicadas and crickets buzzing in time with the flicker of the fireflies.

"Well," Steve slapped the palm of his hands on his lap, "I'm off to bed."

The others followed his lead and one by one said good night until only William, Ella and Poultney remained around the fire.

William waited for them to go to their respective tents, knowing that Louise was waiting for him in his. He watched as Ella inched closer to Poultney.

"I think it's time we called it quits as well don't you agree?" he said to them.

"Don't wait up for us, William, we are going to enjoy the fire a little longer," she said.

William simmered in his seat. He didn't want to cause a scene but he did not trust these two. In the meantime, Louise was waiting for him, having agreed to sneak into his tent once it was dark enough so that nobody would see her.

He gave up. "Ok." He got up to leave and stopped by the bucket of water. "Poultney, old chap, would you mind dousing the fire before you retire for the night?"

"Of course. And I will be sure to escort Ella back to her tent."

"That's what I'm afraid of, old boy," William said.

"William, really," Ella said.

"Good night you two, don't stay up too late." William left them.

As soon as he was out of sight Ella moved next to Poultney. "I'm shivering," she said facing the glowing fire.

"Dear me, we can't have that," Poultney said, putting his arms around her.

They looked up at the stars. "Did you know Emerson wrote a poem called Adirondacs about a trip just like this one."

"Hmmm, yes I've read it," Ella said as she reached her hand up to Poultney's face and caressed his cheek with the back of her hand.

"Of course you had, I should have known," Poultney said. "I

fancy myself a writer as well."

"You do?"

"Yes even though my father would like me to pursue law. I'd much rather spend my time writing. Like you." He looked down at her.

"Like me indeed," she said, smiling.

"Tell me why are you so fascinated with Dante? Is it because he is a poet as well?" he asked.

"Well that yes, and the fact that we share a name. His real name was Durante you know."

"No I didn't know that," Poultney said.

He leaned down to kiss her.

Ella responded by reaching until their lips locked and they kissed, deeply.

"Oh my," Ella said when she stopped to breath. "I think this is what my father was worried would happen."

Poultney smiled and put his hands on her hips to turn her slightly so she was in front of him. He ran his hands up and down her slender waist and she moaned softly.

"Ahem." William appeared out of the inky blackness, holding the bucket of water above the fire. "Do I use this to douse the fire or you, Poultney?" he said.

"No need, William, I've got a handle on it." Poultney gently pushed Ella away from him.

"Yes, that's precisely what I'm worried about," William said.

Poultney scrambled to his feet and took the bucket from William. He poured the water over the fire and they listened as the coals hissed and then went dark.

"Ella, I'll escort you to your tent now." William walked over to Ella, took her arm, lifted her off the ground and led her to her tent, holding her steady so she wouldn't trip along the way, leaving Poultney standing by the dead coals.

A few weeks later, when it was time to leave, Poultney pulled Ella aside.

"Here, I want you to see my work of art," he said. "It's for your guestbook."

He showed her the sketches he had done of their adventures that summer. There was a picture of the canoe they had taken out at sunset. That was a beautiful evening, Ella remembered. Poultney had rigged a pole with a sail so they could catch the last restless breeze of the evening. In the sketch he wrote the word 'Kismet' on the sail.

There was a sketch of their friends swimming off the deck of the *Barque* and a picture of the men tramping through the woods with the canoes hoisted on their shoulders during their camping trip.

Ella loved the drawing. "I'll put this in our guestbook. What's this saying written in the banner above it all?"

"It's Latin: We slay the evil coeruleus," Poultney said. He glanced around before stealing a kiss from her when he knew nobody was looking.

CAMP KIRBY
JUNE 2010

They were sitting at the White pine waiting for the saw-whet to appear.

"He sounds like the alarm on a truck when it's backing up," Jake said.

Every time she played the audio lure the owl responded. Once or twice she spotted him flitting about in the trees, but never into her net.

"This doesn't make any sense," Avery scowled. It was becoming a contest: her against this elusive saw-whet. All the others were willing to be captured, tagged and let go, why not this little bugger?

"Maybe he wasn't meant to be captured," Jake said, looking up into the trees when he heard the owl call. "If I were you I wouldn't lose too much sleep over it." He looked at her slyly.

Avery laughed back.

The two had consummated their relationship weeks before. One Saturday night he showed up on her porch with a bottle of wine, a basket of local cheeses and warm bread from the bakery.

"A peace offering, and thank you for the great dinner the other night," he said, raising the basket in the air so she could see it from behind the screen door to the cabin.

"Thanks," she said, opening the door. "You didn't need to do that though, after all you split the rest of the wood for me."

"I didn't mind that," Jake said as he entered the cabin.

Avery didn't mind it either. He had split all the wood for her, sweating so much that he had to take his shirt off, revealing his lean torso. Avery couldn't help herself; she stood on the front porch, staring at his back muscles while he lifted the maul up and down over the pieces of wood, until she finally tore herself away to make dinner. And when they sat down to eat afterward, he acted like he had never eaten so well before, praising her cooking the whole time. He was pleasant company. They talked all evening and then he took her out on his boat so they could gaze up at the stars.

"I was just about to shower. Would you like to open the wine for us? The wine glasses are on the top right shelf in the kitchen. I'll be back in a minute." She went to the outside solar shower to rinse off the day's fieldwork, tingling inside that he had surprised her with another visit.

She peeled off her clothes and stepped into the small shower stall. Normally she would take a swim but there had been a storm earlier in the day that had stirred up all the sediment, turning the lake an ugly dark brown.

After washing and brushing her hair she searched for something to wear that wasn't a sweatshirt or jeans. The first thing she spotted after putting on her underwear was her robe.

"Why not?" she murmured to herself.

She walked out on the porch where Jake was waiting patiently for her, stood in front of him, and reached for a glass of wine. He handed it to her and gulped. The thin, black cotton robe clung to her body. It had several small buttons that started between her cleavage and ended right above her thighs. He saw a glimpse of her black lace bra as she leaned over to take the glass and a flash of thigh where the robe parted as she sat down. She took hold of the hem and wrapped it around her as she propped her legs up in a cross-legged position on the wicker settee across from him.

"Mmmmm, this is good," she said raising her glass, "what is it?"

"It's a rosé, French."

"I like it! Where'd you find this?"

"Old Forge. We do have wine in the Adirondacks you know."

"I know," Avery, said, "you forget I grew up coming here in the summers. I told you that at dinner, remember? My grandfather had a place on Schroon Lake."

Jake had to think back a minute. What he remembered about that dinner was watching her cook and thinking about how she had looked naked.

"I have to confess I'm not much of a wine drinker so I asked my cousin. She drinks a lot of wine."

"Thoughtful." Avery smiled over the rim of her glass.

He noticed when she got up from the settee her wet hair curled above her shoulders. "Would you like me to take this inside and cut up the bread?" Another flash of thigh as she approached him.

Jake took a sip of wine before answering. "If you like."

She went inside the cabin to cut the bread. He could hear her opening and shutting drawers and cupboards in the kitchen. He turned his attention to the lake hoping the still waters would calm his nerves. Earlier that day the waves were tumultuous. Kind of how he felt right now. *What was she doing to him?*

He heard the *WW Durant* tour boat honk its horn as it passed the cabin and he waved at the tourists standing on the deck.

"Here you go." Avery came out onto the porch and leaned over him again. *Damn.*

Suddenly Avery stood up and locked eyes with his. The carnal energy was apparent. "It was awfully hot and muggy before that storm today wasn't it?"

"Yeah, steamy," Jake replied.

"What do you think of my robe?"

Jake cleared his throat, "Umm, it's very, hot."

"Yes," Avery said as she stood in front of him and unbuttoned the top button. The light cotton clung to the curvature of her breasts.

Jake gulped the rest of his wine. "That's making me even warmer."

Avery unbuttoned the bottom button, a flash of thigh and black lace. And then the next one, continuing until only the last button remained undone. He could see it straining to pop out of its enclosure. Jake stood up, undid it, and wrapped his arms inside the robe around her waist until they reached the small of her back. The only thing between his hands and her was the black lace. He brushed off the robe and it slid to the floor. He lifted her off her feet and carried her into the bedroom. She opened the door with her free hand on the way in.

That was two weeks ago, and they had been together almost every night since.

They picked themselves up from the forest floor, swished the dirt off their backsides, and headed back to Camp Kirby.

"Hey take a look at this," he beamed. "A great hiding place for a raccoon." Jake had found the cavernous hole in the pine where Minnie's diary was hidden for more than a hundred years.

Avery gave off an awkward laugh. "Oh, yeah, I've seen this before. As a matter of fact I found —"

"Hey look at this!" Jake pulled a shelf fungus off the pine.

"The backs of these make a great artist's palette." He was a child holding on to a special find from the forest.

She had seen these at Camp Huntington; the students collected the white half-moon fungus that extruded from dead trees and sketched drawings on the back for display in the cabins.

"It's beautiful." Avery hesitated, undecided. Should she tell him now? She decided it could wait. She didn't have to tell him where she found it. When the time was right she would know.

June 30, 1893

Nate found an owl's nest. He came running to the cabin this morning from the woods to tell me. He was out setting traps and thought he heard the sound of a saw-whet. After exploring, he found a nest with the mother sitting quietly on her brood. He pulled me from my reading to show me. The nest was a short walk in the woods behind the cabin in a

*White pine. The mother owl was just sitting there with her eyes closed,
so still.*

*"They play dead," Nate said. We watched in wonder for awhile to see if
she would flinch. When she didn't I told Nate we should leave her alone.*

*The guests are arriving tonight at Pine Knot and William has informed
me that he will not be able to see me for a few days. Between construction
at Uncas and the company he keeps he has hardly found time for me
lately. I know I must be patient until the time comes when he will
divorce Janet and take me to live with him at Uncas. But when will it be?*

Minnie

"Oh good lord!" Avery said. Poor Minnie was starting to sound
like a dimwit.

She checked her watch. Jake would be returning shortly. After
sitting with her under the pine looking for the saw-whet he'd run
out to the store for some supplies and Avery took the opportunity
to read a bit more.

Some of the things she read about Minnie and William were
starting to disturb her. From what she knew about William's life
after selling Pine Knot, it didn't bode well for Minnie. Her diary
was a soap opera Avery couldn't get enough of.

July 4, 1893

*There is much merriment at Pine Knot. I imagine I hear the tinkling of
glass and laughter, but I cannot partake of any of it. William and Janet
are entertaining friends from New York City: the Huntingtons and the
Forbes. William said this whole affair was costing him a fortune and he
would rather be with me or at least working on Uncas. He said he had to
order two cases of fine French wine, not to mention cigars, caviar and
whiskey.*

And Janet has not been much of a help lately. She is having what her Doctor has diagnosed as 'hysterical fits.' I guess it is an ailment of high society types because I do not recall my mother ever having those. Dr. Pratt has been attending to her for the past few months and William is furious with her for not being the hostess he feels she should be under the circumstances.

Ella is causing him many troubles as well. William doesn't talk much about it but I do remember last summer after he came back to Pine Knot from his yacht excursion he was summoned by a lawyer to appear in court regarding her demands for money from their father's estate. He lamented to me that she has been 'acting up lately' and she is back from England 'harassing' him to no end.

I wish we could just escape to Uncas and leave Pine Knot behind. I know William doesn't like to live the lavish lifestyle that his position demands. He would rather be with me alone in the woods. Just the two of us. As each day passes I feel more lonely and desperate for our life together to begin.

Minnie

"Why are you so tired tonight?" It was a few nights after their visit to the tree and Avery was lying on her side next to Jake in the bed, sweeping circles on his bare chest with her fingertips. She could feel his heart beating rapidly.

"Long day, I guess," Jake said. "Bit worn out after that." He smiled.

Avery turned over on her back and examined the ceiling. She felt glorious. In the meantime though, her work was piling up. Capturing and banding the owls was only part of it. She needed to get over to Camp Huntington for a day and catch up on her research, her emails, and her database. There was no Internet connection at Camp Kirby, no reality really. Time was suspended here. She and Jake were living in a fantasy world that would end in September. Avery shivered and pulled up the covers. *Not going to think about it.*

When she could hear his soft snoring, she snuck out of bed, threw on yoga pants and t-shirt and went into the parlor to read more of Minnie's diary. There were few opportunities now that Jake stayed with her almost every night, unless she took it with her in the field, but that was not always wise either. She never knew when a college student searching the grounds for a mushroom or fern would come upon her, wonder what she was up to and notice the diary.

It had happened once already. One of Kim's students found her sitting under a tree in the South Bay reading the diary, oblivious to anything. An owl could have been flapping helplessly in the mist net and she wouldn't have known, that's how engrossed she was. It was almost unhealthy. And the secrecy was only compounded by the fact that she knew she should show this to Sally, or Jake, or somebody at Camp Huntington. The legend of Minnie would finally be uncovered. But she wasn't ready, yet.

July 10, 1893

Tonight I complained to William that I was unhappy here just whiling away my time with Nate. We have already finished reading Murray's book. I think I was especially melancholy when I read one of the last stories about a spontaneous dance that he and his fellow travelers had one evening at their hotel. All the merriment and cheer he described, he and his fellow companions whooping and hollerin' it up with the ladies who were also staying at the hotel, and after a day of hunting in the woods – it all sounded like such fun. It reminded me of the dances at the Grange Hall in Potsdam. We had the best fiddler around, and all the young people knew how to square dance. How I miss my family!

"A dance is what you want, then a dance you shall have!" William said to cheer me up.

He opened up the music box, took hold of my waist and waltzed me around the room as it played Brahms. Nate came in and started to laugh at us.

"Young man, do you even know how to dance?" William asked him.

Nate shook his head no.

"Then let me show you." And he swung me around and counted in time, 1,2,3; 1,2,3. We danced around the room. I was delirious with happiness. Then William gave me over to Nate. He was awfully shy and awkward about it, but after a bit of instruction and encouragement on my part he found his footing with me.

It was a romantic evening. Afterwards Nate made us a fire by the water and we sat and watched the moon rise in the sky.

Minnie

"What're you doing?" Jake was suddenly standing in the doorway to the parlor. "Are you alright, Avery?"

"Yes, you startled me that's all." Avery shifted in her seat to cover Minnie's diary that she quickly stashed under her bottom.

"What were you reading?" He came over to her. She shifted again to make sure he couldn't see it.

"Nothing important, just some journal about the saw-whet owl." She hoped her voice did not betray her deceit.

Jake gave her an I-don't-quite-get-you look.

"I forgot to tell you. Must've been because I was too preoccupied." Jake smiled and went into the bedroom to retrieve a book.

"I found this today in the loft, hidden in the wall. It was covered up when they last renovated." He handed Avery an old book: *Adventures in the Wilderness* by W.H. Murray.

Avery turned it over in her hand. This was Nate's book!

"Look, Jake, it's inscribed."

There inside the front cover was William West Durant's handwriting. It said: "To Nate, I hope you enjoy these stories as much as I did when I read them." It was signed William Durant.

"You can show it to your mother. Proof that your great-great grandfather Nate really did live here in Camp Kirby at one time."

CAMP PINE KNOT
AUGUST 1881

The trees were dying. It was the first thing Ella noticed on her return trip to Pine Knot. She, Poultney and Martha Parker, her friend from New York City, were heading to her family camp via the Durant steamboat line. This was a clandestine affair. Her father had closed the camp for most of the summer, leaving a skeleton crew to look after the grounds and had forbidden her from visiting until he and Mrs. Durant were back from a trip to New York City. But he refused to take Ella along with them and this was her way of getting back at the old despot. *Who cared if she spent a couple of weeks up here with her friends anyway?* It wasn't as if anyone was using it. William was away on business in Saratoga and told her he didn't have time to accompany her anywhere for the next month until he tied up some 'loose ends' for father. The house at North Creek was desolate. She was doing everyone a favor, really, checking in on the place, making sure Jerome Wood was overseeing things properly and no vagrants were taking over their food supplies.

"What's wrong with those trees?" Poultney said.

"I'm not sure." Ella sadly cast her eyes about looking for the stately specimens of Red maples, larch, and beech she remembered from her last trip to Pine Knot. But the trees lining the river were devoid of leaves and unidentifiable.

"It's the dam and the dredging," a strange man said to the group. He was a guide. Probably heading to one of the camps or hotels on Raquette to work.

"The dam?" Poultney asked.

"The Durants put in a dam and dredged the Marion to make it navigable. Otherwise I'd be carrying my boat most of the way instead of dragging it behind this steamer." The man motioned with his head to the back of the steamboat where his boat was being dragged by a long rope.

"So the dams have raised the water levels and drowned the trees," Poultney observed.

A harbinger for what was ahead? Ella hoped not. She had thought this trip would rekindle what she and Poultney first started the last time they came to Pine Knot. It was, quite frankly, the last chance for the two of them. He was in his final year at Columbia law school and then he planned to head off to London as a correspondent for *Harper's Magazine*. If only he would ask for her hand in marriage she could go with him, and return to the life she once knew.

He was an enigma to her really. Why he wouldn't confess he was in love with her was beyond her comprehension. All of the signs were there. But she had to admit their similarities also made them bad bedfellows. She was strong willed and independent and as much as he pretended to find that endearing she knew deep down he'd rather marry a soft-spoken society girl he could boss around. And that was not her, never was. They fought all the time because of it. It was almost as if they thrived on the challenge of teasing each other endlessly. She did love him, dearly. If only he would see that and accept her for who she was.

"It's wonderful to be back here!" Poultney exclaimed to the startled staff when they arrived by steamboat on the docks of Pine Knot. Louise was there.

"I thought you said the camp was closed for the season. Does Louise live here now?" Poultney whispered in Ella's ear.

"How am I supposed to know? I hardly see William anymore. He's either in Saratoga or New York conducting business for the railroad company. I haven't had a chance to talk to him in months."

"Well I'd say there is another reason you haven't seen too much of William lately," Poultney sniggered.

"That's not funny, Poultney. If father found out Louise was living at Pine Knot he would be livid," Ella fumed. But that was not the worst of it, she knew. He would send Louise back to Eighth Lake and disown William if he wasn't more careful about whom he chose to bed. If that happened she would have no one to rely on any more.

Jerome Wood was reluctant to open up the camp for Ella and her friends, knowing it wasn't what Dr. Durant wanted. Only Louise seemed serene about the arrangement. She made sure Ella and her friends had what they needed and instructed the work crew to stop construction so they could open up the cabins and collect wood to be put at the hearth. She sent Ike to Bennett's new hotel called Under the Hemlocks for the provisions they needed for the guests, as supplies were low and told him to track down their sister Emaline so she could help out as well.

Ella always marveled at how everyone listened to Louise without question. She had some kind of mystical power over the place. Even her father would bite his tongue around Louise. The only one that seemed to scare the girl off was her mother. Hannah had threatened more than once to replace Louise, complaining to Dr. Durant that her cooking was too native.

For the next few days the group spent idle time enjoying the peace of Pine Knot. They swam, went fishing and canoed. One late afternoon, while Ella was resting in a hammock slung between two trees on shore, a boat pulled up with two of Poultney's friends: Steven and Harry. Harry's sister Frances was also on the boat. Ella was startled to see them. *Who told them we were here?*

"Allo there!" Harry stood up in his boat and almost tipped it over. The guide rowing the boat gestured for him to settle down. Fran held up a bottle.

"We've brought you some libations!"

"Well then, welcome ashore!" Poultney called to the group, eyeing their arrival from his reading spot on the porch of the chalet.

Ella put her hand over her eyes to see the group through the glare of the sun. Steven was also holding some bottles in his hand.

"We've brought some Clicquot!" He held one up.

The guide expertly landed the party onshore and went to find Ike. Poultney, Martha and Ella walked up to greet the crew.

"What are you all doing on Raquette?" Ella asked.

"We're staying at Antlers Hotel and heard a rumor that you were at Pine Knot." Steven winked at Poultney, kissed Ella on each cheek, and followed up with the same greeting on Martha. Ella stole a glance at Poultney. He shrugged as if to say, how would I know they'd show up?

"So we hired a guide to bring us here," Fran finished for Steven.

"*Veuve*, hmmmm, it'll do," Poultney said, taking one of the bottles out of Fran's hands and holding it up for inspection.

Ella took the other bottle from Fran and helped her out of the beached boat.

"Let's gather at the chalet. I'll have Ike make us a fire as the air is getting chilly," Ella said and led the group off the beach. She left them at the chalet and went to the kitchen to find Louise leaning over a bread board kneading dough. Louise smiled as Ella entered.

"Louise," Ella said and started looking through the cabinets. "I thought I overheard my brother say he ordered champagne flutes, do you know where they are?"

Louise was puzzled. "Flutes?" She kept her hands in the dough.

Ella opened a cabinet door and saw only claret glasses. "Glasses, Louise, for drinking." Ella started to throw open every cabinet door. It was bad enough to have friends arrive unannounced, another not to have the right supplies to entertain. She was sure William had ordered champagne flutes.

After tackling all of the upper cabinet doors and leaving those wide open, Ella started in on the bottom, becoming more and more agitated at her own lack of preparation for this trip with her friends. It was not working out as she had planned. Poultney was barely paying any attention to her. He was too preoccupied flirting with *Martha*. She was beginning to think coming to Pine Knot was a disastrous idea.

Louise put a flour-dusted hand on her shoulder. "Here," she held up the small narrow-shaped stemware. "It was in a box delivered last month from New York City. I hadn't unpacked it yet. I was waiting for William to tell me what they were for."

Ella noticed the box on the floor by the back door to the kitchen. There was a case of glasses, waiting to be used. She sighed with relief and went over to quickly unpack and rinse them for her company. She hadn't expected this trek to the woods to be so much work.

"Louise, stop what you're doing and prepare whatever food there is to accompany afternoon refreshments." Ella gathered as many glasses as she could in two hands, brought them to the sink and cast her eyes around the kitchen. "Where is Emaline?"

"She had to go back to the hotel to work," Louise said. "I could only have her here for a few days."

"Well that's understandable, she doesn't work for us. But is there any other help here besides you and Ike and the workmen?"

"No Miss Ella. We weren't expecting company," Louise said, brushing her hands on the apron. She went over to help Ella who was standing, furiously rinsing the glasses under the water pump. The two women worked side by side.

"Louise," Ella ventured, "does William come to visit you here often?"

"Oh yes," Louise beamed. "He comes at least twice a month."

"So you are living here now?"

"I've been here through all the seasons." Louise looked at Ella quizzically, not comprehending why she was asking these questions.

So that is why William was never available when Ella asked to come visit him in New York City. He wasn't there as often as he claimed. He was here. With Louise.

"Where the devil are you Ella?" It was Poultney. He came

bounding into the kitchen. Ella was annoyed by his interruption. He was the one that had invited the guests unbeknownst to her. It was his fault they were unprepared.

"You go now. I'll prepare some food and bring it when you're ready," Louise said as she dried her hands.

"Thank you, Louise." Ella put seven glasses on a tray and handed it over to Poultney. "Take this to our friends. I have to find Ike to set up the dining room, as Emaline is no longer here and as you can see," she added with irritation, "we are short-staffed and over booked." She walked out the door to find Ike.

Steven had found the violin that was stashed away in the corner and started playing a soft melody.

"There's my girl!" Steven said when Ella arrived back from giving Ike instructions. The friends were all gathered around the fire.

"She's mine right now." Poultney took the opportunity to lighten Ella's mood, taking her into his arms and sweeping her around the room. "Play us a waltz Steven!" he shouted. Ella blushed and pushed Poultney away.

"Not 'til someone gets me a glass and we have a toast," Steven said, putting the violin down.

Harry opened a bottle and Fran poured the champagne into the glasses.

"Here's to the Adirondacks," Steven raised his glass along with the others, "and the great company it lures into its deep forested interior."

"Here, here," Harry said.

"*Prost!*" Poultney said putting the glass to his lips and downing it in two swigs. "Now back to the music!"

Steven gulped his champagne and picked up the violin to play a waltz.

Poultney grabbed Ella as she was about to take another sip of her champagne. She set it down quickly to avoid spilling it, and was gathered up by Poultney. Harry grabbed Fran and the foursome danced while Martha pouted in her seat.

"My turn," Martha said.

"Let me have at it," Harry took the violin from Steven and started in on a tune.

Poultney let go of Ella and took Martha's hand. "My dear lady." He bowed in a mock gesture of deference.

Steven saw the look of disappointment on Ella's face and went to her. "Will you do me the honor then?"

The dancing went on with intervals of drinking until Louise came in to tell them there was trout for supper and it was ready to be served in the dining cabin. The fish had been freshly caught by Ike and was accompanied by fresh baked bread and butter. By then they had finished off four bottles of champagne and were famished.

The merriment stopped briefly as they all sat down to eat. Ella sat next to Martha and across from Poultney so she could monitor their flirtations.

"I overheard some people talking at the hotel. They were saying that the Adirondack air brings a cure for consumption," Harry said between mouthfuls of food. "Something about the smell of balsam."

"They got that from Marc Cook's article in *Harper's* didn't they?" Poultney asked.

"Yes, that's it," Steven said. "That article has sparked an interest in people coming up here to find a cure for the disease."

Martha turned to Steven who was sitting on the other side of her. "I read the article as well. He stayed at Paul Smith's hotel and claimed he was cured by the pure mountain air. It's causing quite a stir. People are madly rushing to Saranac Lake as a result."

"Humph, I would expect *Harper's* to have more important prose to fill their pages than some rubbish about a miracle cure," Poultney said.

"Some of my own friends have been taken ill with this terrible disease. I showed the article to them and they told me they might visit. Why, I would rush here too if I thought it would cure me," Fran said.

172

"Dear girl," Poultney addressed Fran, "only months ago the Czar was assassinated by anarchists and weeks ago President Garfield was shot by a lunatic, and yet people can justify the use of their time reading this drivel?"

A hush fell over the group. Ella, who was feeling a bit hazy from the champagne, thought she saw Martha kick Poultney in the shin under the table.

Ella broke the uncomfortable silence. "Hah," she said. "This Marc Cook, has he been here when it rains non-stop for days? Hardly a place for someone having a coughing fit I would say."

"Yes, it does sound like an odd remedy doesn't it?" Martha said. Everyone quickly murmured their agreement.

Oblivious to the undercurrents, Poultney turned to one of his favorite subjects, his life abroad while his father served as Minister to France.

"I recall the time Prince Wilhelm and I were young lads playing cowboys and Indians in the Bavarian forests," he said a little too loudly.

"Dear God, someone stop him before it's too late!" Ella heard Steven lean over and whisper to Martha. "He's going to wax lyrical about his primary school antics with German royalty again."

"Yes, whenever he's drunk he gets like this, trying to make his youth sound more appealing than ours had ever been," Martha whispered back drolly. They started to giggle.

"When are you heading back to the hotel?" Ella interrupted Poultney.

Harry and Fran perked up. It was getting dark outside.

"I guess we better find our guide," Harry said.

"Nonsense," Ella slurred. "Not until after we have had a campfire. Your guide will know the way back in the dark. These men know the waters like no other, they go hunting at night."

"That would be swell but I'm afraid we are all out of champagne," Steven said. They all cast their eyes about the table at the empty flutes and bottles.

"I brought a few bottles of claret. I can't see any reason not to open them." Poultney said.

"Haven't you had enough, Poultney?" Martha said.

"Nonsense! I'll go fetch Ike to make us a campfire outside," Poultney fired back.

The friends gathered blankets from the beds in the chalet while Poultney went to find Ike and Ella went to the kitchen for claret glasses.

The next morning Ella was sitting in a wicker chair on the lawn beside Poultney and Martha massaging her temples. She had woken up to the torturous sound of the workmen constructing a new roof. Each blow of the hammer to nail pierced her eardrums, sending jolts of pain to her throbbing head.

Suddenly, Alvah Dunning came from out of nowhere and was standing in front of her. Ella looked up and squinted at him.

"Miss Ella," Alvah said, ignoring Poultney and Martha. "Is your brother here?"

"Why Alvah! How nice to see you again," she said.

Ella wondered what he was up to, he didn't usually bother with her brother and he rarely came to Pine Knot unless he was picking up guests for a day of hunting or fishing. But since the day they had met she knew how to charm old Snake Eyes.

"How are you doing? Well, I hope?" she said, giving him the best smile she could muster.

"I'd be better if your cousin wasn't always pestering me about my land there on Osprey. Where's William? I want to chew his ear."

"Yes, I hear Charles has been a bit of a nuisance. My dear cousin, like all Durants, doesn't understand the word no," Ella said.

"Well he'll quickly understan' the end of the barrel of my gun."

"Humph." Poultney intervened in the conversation. "Has it really come to that?"

"Next time he steps on my property? Yeah," he said.

"And tell me, Alvah, what is he asking for exactly?" Poultney said.

"He wants me to vacate so he can build a house. Why he's already started constructin' somethin'. He wants me to give him the land. The land was mine when no one else wanted it. Murray took off and left it all to me." Alvah cocked his head and spit on the ground after making his last point.

"That sounds like squatter's rights to me," Poultney said.

"Excuse my ignorance," Martha chimed in. "I am not sure how it is that anyone can claim a piece of land without a deed, although anything seems possible up here. But if that is the case, why not tell Charles to find another piece of land and use his squatters right as well?"

"Too late for that," Alvah said. "State owns it all 'round here now." He swept his arms in a gesture to encompass the 20,000 plus acres the State had refused to sell to Dr. Durant.

"I say, stick to your guns, Alvah," Poultney said. "Just try not to use one on Ella's cousin."

Martha laughed. Ella refrained. She knew that was the wrong thing to say to Alvah, as it would only encourage his gumption. Poultney needed to shut up or Ella was going to be in trouble with William. Indeed, this whole trip was not what she had expected. Her charms on Poultney were waning. She couldn't seduce him as she once had, without trying. He was falling out of love with her. She knew it instinctively and she wanted to go home.

"Alvah, I'll tell William you came by to see him," Ella said to get him to leave, at once. "It was so nice to see you again."

"Yeah, maybe," Alvah said and walked away.

Alvah rowed back to Osprey pondering over what Ella's friends said. It was true. This was his place. He had obtained it fair and square from Murray. He was the only one on the island until the Durants showed up on Raquette a few years back. Now they wanted it all.

Alvah dragged his spruce bark canoe on shore. It was leaking. They didn't make them like this anymore. He had traded some venison and bear meat for this one from Ike's father. Very few men knew how to make a canoe out of bark anymore, but Isaac Lawrence had skill. Now they had all kinds of fancy boats being built out of Long Lake, and the guides were abandoning these old crafts. He understood why though. They had their usefulness as lightweight crafts to drag over carries, and they could glide over stones and rocks in the tightest of spots without wearing down. But they needed a lot of maintenance. The ends were tied up with the roots of the spruce tree and the seams were held together with the gum. The gunwales were made of narrow pieces of cedar.

Alvah did what he needed to find the holes in the canoe as Isaac showed him years ago. He placed his mouth over the area he thought was leaking and sucked in, detecting air. He found a few holes and marked them with small sticks. He went to his cabin and got out a wad of spruce gum, put it in his mouth and softened it with his chewing. Then he took an old rag, a hot poker from the fireplace and went back to the canoe. Carefully he placed a piece of the rag into the hole, took the soft gum out of his mouth and inserted a wad of it into the rag. He used the hot poker to melt it into place, continuing the procedure until the holes were all filled with the gummy substance.

Hungry, he went back to his cabin to cook bacon and beans. He had traded with Bennett for the pork, given him a few deer mounts for his hotel walls. It amazed Alvah that the city folks liked the look of these heads on the walls as if it was the trophy of the kill rather than the meat that mattered. He was taking the first bite of his bacon and bean sandwich when he heard some men coming on shore. He grabbed his gun and headed for the beach.

"Get off my island," Alvah said as he pointed the barrel of his gun in the direction of the men that were getting out of their boats loaded to the brim with milled wood. Charles had brought a contingent — some locals that were looking for work. Alvah recognized a few of them. They were men just like him, knew these woods like the backs of their hands, been guiding city folk most of their adult lives, but the business was slowing down now that the hotels had arrived. The city folk didn't need these men when they could just plunk a rod into the lake from the end of a dock. Why bother with a canoe and carry? Charles Durant embodied everything that was ruinin' this place for Alvah. He needed to be taught a lesson.

"I said move it!" he added with emphasis when he saw that the men were standing still, looking at Charles for direction on what to do next. None of them were quite sure if Alvah's bad temper would get the best of him, and if what local legend said about him was true: he had a cruel streak. They didn't put it past him to take a shot and they all knew his aim was legendary.

"Alvah, be reasonable," Charles approached him. "I was planning to build a dock right here that we can both use. And think of the possibilities if I do, steamboats can pull up and drop off supplies for both of us when we need them."

"That and tourists. Get off my property."

"Well, you see Alvah," Charles scoffed, "that's where you're wrong. This island belongs to no one right now. Murray never had a deed. Just ask the State Commissioners."

Alvah lifted his gun in the air, aimed it at the boat filled with wood and shot a hole in the gunwale. Splinters of wood went flying in the air. The men were shocked. Alvah meant business.

"The next one will be aimed at a head," Alvah said.

The men wasted no time getting back in their boats and rowing away from Osprey Island.

"You shouldn't have said that to Alvah." Ella was furious with Poultney. They were walking after supper into the woods, purposely avoiding the hunting cabin.

"I'm not sure why you're so upset, it's not as if he's going to kill your cousin. And you have to agree that he has a point. If he doesn't want to sell he doesn't want to sell."

"You have no idea how long my brother has been trying to get Alvah to see Charles' side and give up his land," Ella said.

"Ella." He took hold of her arm to prevent her from walking further. "What's really bothering you?"

"I, I, I don't know," Ella confessed. "It's just that you're almost done with law school and then you're leaving and I won't see you again for a long time. And I think—" She stopped herself before confessing anything further.

"You think what?" Poultney said.

"Oh, nothing," Ella said. She felt dejected. He knew what she wanted to say. He was trying to drive it out of her before he would admit it himself.

"Ella, I have so many responsibilities to deal with. I can't be tied down right now. As much as I would like to be with you, you'll have to be patient and accept us as friends. For now anyway." He kept walking and when he noticed she wasn't following, he looked behind and saw her standing in place.

"Friends?" Ella said. "Why what else would we be then?"

He walked back to her side and took her in his arms. "You know as well as I do. We both want each other." He kissed her and she couldn't help but respond. It wasn't long before they were lying on the carpet of pine needles, passion taking over any sense of propriety. Their clothes were half off when Jerome Wood found them. He had come to tell Ella that William had arrived and was enraged that Pine Knot was open to visitors.

CAMP KIRBY
JULY 2010

When Avery woke up Jake wasn't in bed. That was unusual, it was Saturday. During the week Jake would get up early and meet Frank at Camp Huntington for breakfast, grab tools from the back of his truck that he kept parked in the lot there, and walk back to Camp Kirby to work on the loft. Although Frank, and everybody else for that matter, knew that the two were an item, Jake liked to keep up appearances. He didn't want to be seen coming out of the cabin in the morning when Frank arrived to work. Avery admired him for that. But weekends were different. There was no need to show propriety on a Saturday; no one was around but the two of them. She got out of bed, went to start the coffee perking, and making the most of the unexpected privacy, extracted Minnie's diary from her pack.

July 11, 1893

Nate was not in the cabin when I woke this morning and at first I was alarmed. He is usually up before me, starting the morning fire in the kitchen stove. I shouldn't have been too worried though, because as usual, he was ahead of me. He had started the fire and must have taken off to see if the saw-whet owl was out in the tree, either that or he went early morning fishing. I freshened up, put coffee on and then waited on the porch for him to show up.

It has been very humid lately, storms arrive by the late afternoon. But the mornings are the best time to sit outside and take in the fresh air. Just as I was about to get up to see if the coffee was done perking I saw Nate walking down the path toward Pine Knot with a woman. It took me a few glances to perceive that it was my own cousin, Cornelia! She must have been visiting Janet. How did she know I was here?

We sat and had coffee together and she told me many things that surprised me.

First she told me that Janet has known all along that I am staying here at the hunting cabin. She told Cornelia that William had finally admitted it when a neighbor from Golden Beach asked over tea one day who I was. They must have noticed me and Nate down at the beach. William told Janet that I was staying at the cabin to tutor Nate. Janet knows William is fond of him. I assumed it is because he is an orphan but Cornelia told me that Nate's uncle and aunt were once servants for the Durants and William used to provide for their family when they were destitute.

While I went to get us more coffee Cornelia must have found my diary. I had placed it in the parlor earlier in the day and forgotten about it. From what I could tell she had read my first entry only. I snatched it from her hands.

She was shocked and had such a strange look in her eyes when she flew up from her chair and grabbed a hold of my arms, digging her finger nails into my skin so that it hurt. I must have squealed because she quickly let go and then scolded me for lying to my mother and father.

But I assured her I was telling the truth. I was asked by William to tutor for the summer and this is what I was doing.

Then she said, "You foolish girl! You really believe William will leave Janet for you? He has to keep up appearances! He would never leave his wife for a young governess turned mistress!"

Cornelia made me promise that I would forget about any "silly fantasies and go home at once."

I had to think quick. I didn't want Cornelia to ruin everything so I said, "Of course my diaries are just made up stories. I write down whimsical thoughts when they come to my head, being out here all alone has made me half crazy."

I begged her not to tell my father as long as I promised to return to school because I don't want him to worry about me.

Minnie

July 12, 1893

Last night I was very agitated. William has not come by since Cornelia came to visit. I wonder if he is purposely staying away so that Cornelia does not suspect anything.

Once I knew that Nate was asleep I opened the lid to the Swiss chalet music box and undressed. I put on my nightgown and for a moment stood in front of the mirror to admire my reflection. That's when I felt a cold chill run through me, as if a ghost had come floating into the room to watch me watch myself. And then a screech owl let out a shrieking trill outside my window. It was a desolate sound and it scared me! I jumped into bed under the covers and had a fitful night of sleep.

Minnie

Avery heard Jake's small boat puttering up to the dock. She put Minnie's diary in her pack and walked out to the porch. Maybe he'd gone fishing and was coming back with breakfast.

"Allo there!" She waved from the porch as he tied his boat to the dock.

Jake climbed up the beachfront with a small brown bag in his hand. As he came closer Avery could see it was stained with grease.

"Fish?" she asked him as he approached her on the porch steps.

"No. Better than that," he grinned. "Doughnuts."

"Doughnuts? Where'd you find those? The cook at Huntington made some?"

Jake laughed. "No these are world-famous doughnuts. Only one place around here has them, the General Store in Raquette. People line up every weekend morning to get some of these. I got up early to get some." He approached her on the porch and held up the greasy brown bag to her face. Avery could smell the baked goods inside.

"Mmmmm," she said breathing in the aroma. "That smells delicious. Let me have one." She reached for the bag.

"Not yet." He swiped it away. "They taste best with coffee."

"I can't wait." Avery grabbed the bag from his hands and sat down in one of the Adirondack chairs to open it before he could protest again.

He shrugged and sat down next to her. "Your loss then."

"Oh my God!" Her eyes opened wide as she chewed on the first bite of doughnut. "What is this? It's heaven."

"That's the maple glazed. I told you they were good."

Avery started in on the rest of her doughnut.

"I thought I had gotten to the store early enough to beat the crowds so I couldn't believe it when I arrived and there was already someone ahead of me in line waiting for the baker to arrive with the trays," Jake said.

"Huh," Avery took another bite. "I can see why."

"Anyway, this guy that was ahead of me? He was obnoxious. He practically cleared out one of the trays of doughnuts. I could hear people behind me grumbling as he kept ordering more and more. By the time it was my turn at the counter I grabbed the last two maple glazed."

"That was sinful," Avery said licking her fingers.

"I know, what a jerk," Jake said.

"No, I mean the doughnut," Avery said. "Do you have another one for me?" She rooted around in the bag.

"Did you hear anything I just said?"

"Yes, you got the last two maple doughnuts because some jerk almost started a riot at the General Store."

"I'm not going to give you the last doughnut when I got up early and waited in line for it."

"I'm going to get some coffee." Avery jumped out of her seat.

"Great, can you get me some too?"

"Not unless you share that last doughnut with me," Avery said as the screen door slammed behind her on the way into the cabin.

"Are you kidding me?" Jake turned in his chair and yelled after her. "No way." He looked back at the water smiling.

"Ahhh, this is soooo good." Avery came back a few moments later and was standing at the screen door with her cup of coffee.

Jake got up from his chair. "Give me that," he said.

"No."

He opened the screen door. Avery yelped and ran for the bedroom, dropping her coffee cup on the way. She was halfway into the parlor when he grabbed her, picked her up, carried her into the bedroom and flung her on the bed. He climbed on top of her and kissed her. She tasted faintly like coffee and maple syrup.

"So how do you think Minnie ended up as the Durant's governess?" Avery handed Jake a cup of coffee she had re-heated after their lovemaking and nap. It was two hours old. She placed her cup on the side table next to the bed as she climbed in next to him. Jake sat up, took the coffee out of Avery's hand and took a big sip before answering.

"Her cousin Cornelia was good friends with Janet Durant. She appears in the guest book from 1893."

"Where was Minnie from?"

"She grew up in Potsdam, her father was a minister there."

"What makes everybody think she was Durant's mistress then?"

"They found a candy dish in Camp Kirby with a calling card that said *With best love and wishes for a Merry Christmas' it was signed Minnie Everette Kirby.*"

"How do you know all of this?"

"My mother, and some of the alumni of the college. There are a group of sorority ladies that started a file on Minnie. Every year they seem to dig up something new. That signed book I found in the loft has thrown them all into a tizzy."

"Who told them about the book?"

"I did." Jake gulped down the rest of his coffee and placed the cup on the side table next to him. "I gave it to Tom. It belongs to the college."

Avery didn't mention the diary. Instead she asked, "What ever happened to Minnie?"

"She got her teaching degree from the State University at Potsdam and married a man named Tappan. I guess she was a real socialite."

"Hah!" Avery said, thinking of the small college town on the Canadian border, "I would hardly consider Potsdam a hotbed of social activity."

"Maybe for her time it was," Jake mused. "Why are we talking about Minnie? You always seem to want to talk about her."

"Oh I don't know," Avery squirmed. "I guess you finding that book in the loft has got my imagination going."

"Well, I almost wish I hadn't. My mother won't shut up about it. She wants Frank and me to take the floors up in the loft now and that wasn't part of our construction plan. She thinks there might be more evidence stored under the floorboards."

"Well, that would prolong the job a bit wouldn't it?"

"Yes, it would. You'd like that wouldn't you?" he said reaching to take her into his arms.

"You know—" Avery was about to broach the subject of the diary with him, but then was interrupted.

"Hello, Avery? Are you there?"

Avery and Jake jumped.

"Oh my God it's your mother!" Avery jumped out of bed.

"What's she doing here?" Jake climbed out of bed to put his pants on.

"I don't know, did you tell her you were here?" Avery worked her way into her jeans and bra.

"Of course not! She doesn't know I sleep here. Why would I tell her something like that?"

"Why wouldn't you?"

"Hello! Avery, are you in?" Sally was banging on the front door to the cabin and calling through the screen.

Avery tipped-toed into the parlor to look out the window onto the front porch and returned. "Shit, Jake, she's brought some ladies with her." She wrestled her t-shirt over her head as Jake threw the covers over the bed in an attempt to make it look like they had not been in it. Avery thought it absurd but refrained from saying anything.

"Just go let them in and I'll sneak out the back door," Jake said. They both looked at the door in the bedroom that led to the forest behind the cabin and then at each other. Avery started to giggle.

"Now is not the time!"

"You have to admit it is kind of funny," Avery smirked.

"Thank you for letting us in." Sally looked relieved when Avery finally came to the screen door. "We don't mean to intrude on your work but these ladies are from the Theta Phi sorority and they helped raise the money for the renovations to the loft. I was wondering if I could show them the work going on up there?"

"Of course." Avery opened the screen door and let Sally and the three sorority sisters into the cabin. "Let me show you the way." She led them through the kitchen, glancing out the kitchen window in time to see Jake sneaking through the woods as the ladies ascended the loft stairs ahead of her.

CAMP PINE KNOT
AUGUST 1881

"The problem with your family is they're assuming you should maintain the same standards of conduct as you did in England," Martha said. The two women were in Ella's cabin. Martha was assisting Ella into a corset and dress for her appearance before William.

Ella enjoyed Martha's company, but this trip was proving to be a nightmare, and Martha's inspirational banter wasn't making her feel any better.

"I have no idea what you mean. And right now, I'm in no mood to decipher. Believe me though, my father is thoroughly *American*," Ella said standing with her back toward Martha so she could tie the stays of her corset.

"You spit out American as if it leaves a bad taste in your mouth." Martha pulled the last stay of the corset so tight Ella gasped. "Your family doesn't realize we live in a different world than the one you came from." She finished off the ties and grabbed Ella's dress off the bed. "You have lived here for over five years now. America is not England. Enjoying yourself with friends around campfires unaccompanied by your brother or another male family member doesn't make you a social outcast." She held the dress out for Ella to put on. "And besides, you're hardly a maiden anymore, my word! You're almost thirty. You should be allowed to come and go as you please. Your brother and father's disapproval of you coming to New York City unaccompanied is rather odd."

"They just don't like it when they don't know my whereabouts. Father especially wants to control who I socialize with as friends," Ella said as she put one leg and then another into her gown. She lifted the straps over her shoulders and put her back toward Martha again to button up. She glanced at Martha's reflection in the mirror and held her tongue. She dared not offend her friend by telling her that Papa also disapproved of her friendship with a divorcee. Ella had met Martha at a writers seminar for women organized by Anna Leonowens in New York City. Ella had been thrilled to be part of it even if she did feel like an amateur amongst the other writers. The women that attended the seminar were mostly single: spinsters, widowed, or divorced, like Martha. Dr. Durant didn't approve of Ella attending, calling the event 'frivolous and a waste of money.'

"Didn't you tell William you were coming here?"

"No. He had no idea. I didn't think he would be here. I thought he was in Saratoga on railroad business. It's just like him to show up unexpectedly." Ella thought of Louise and the cabin in the woods. *Wait until her father found out that William was harboring Louise there for his pleasure, year-round.*

"I can't imagine why William would be so upset with you for enjoying the camp. From what I hear, the man spends countless hours at the clubs in New York bragging about this place. Why shouldn't you get to enjoy it as much as he obviously does?"

"My father instructed that the camp stay closed this summer while the workers carried out construction work." She wasn't sure why, but Ella felt it necessary to defend William.

"Well then Ella, you *are* in trouble. Good luck."

Ella knew there was more to grovel about than why she defied her father by coming to Pine Knot. She was nervous when Louise came to tell her William was in his cabin waiting to see her. What had Jerome Wood told him?

"William is going to throw a fit I know it," Ella lamented to Louise as they walked to his cabin.

Louise linked her arm with Ella's and patted her hand. "You

must tell William you love Poultney. He will understand. William has told me many times how much he loves me."

Ella was concerned by her enthusiasm. As smart as she was, Louise was so naïve about the world the Durants inhabited. *Was William leading this poor girl on?* He had to know their parents would never allow him to marry an Indian girl from the Northern Woods.

They stopped in front of William's cabin just as dusk placed its veil over the forest.

Poultney was standing at the rear of the room when they entered; Ella could barely make him out in the gloaming.

"Sit down, Ella." William was also standing.

Ella looked around. William's cabin was better furnished than any other. He had shelves built into the walls and above each door where he kept his many books on architecture, foreign lands, and hunting. Red curtains framed the windows, bear rugs cloaked the floor and hunting trophies of deer head were mounted on the walls. His desk was sided with inlaid twigs and the front was decorated with a large sheath of white birch with his initials WD carved into it. Her eye was automatically drawn to the commanding fireplace, surrounded by stone and a huge mantel made of some piece of wood from the forest. Considering he was supposed to be working in New York City and Saratoga mostly, William was keeping busy at Pine Knot. Ella sat down in one of the rocking chairs.

William wasted no time getting to the point. "Wood has told me everything. In light of these events, and your inability to follow father's orders, I have no choice but to tell him that you were here with your friends."

"Is that all?" Ella said. Why was Poultney just sitting there lurking in the corner? Was he not prepared to defend her honor?

William cleared his throat. "Your relationship with Poultney is over."

"What?" Ella stood up quickly.

"I told you what. You and Poultney are over. He will not be welcome here again and you'll not see him in New York. You either listen to me on this or I tell father everything."

"Tell him what exactly, William? That I'm in love?"

"Really Will," Poultney came out of the shadows, "Ella and I are," he stopped, searching for the right word, "friends."

For a brief moment Ella felt as if her heart stopped pumping the blood in her veins. Then, in one swift rush it all went to her head, carrying everything with it: all the pent up rage she had been feeling since leaving England: Basil Napier's death; being left out of family plans, her life plans in ruins; trapped like an exile in a small, backwoods, nothing town to rot while her parents, friends and brother lived it up in New York City; only to be told by Martha that her upbringing was not adaptable to life in America, and the hypocrisy of William condemning her while having a secret affair with Louise. And now, to top it all, Poultney was denying her. Outrage consumed her.

She lunged at him. In three strides she was close enough to pummel him. Poultney lifted his arms in defense against the barrage of punches she rained down on him.

"Friends, Poultney? 'Just' friends are we? Liar! Liar!" She struck him with all the force she could muster.

It took William a moment to register what was happening, and when he did, he moved between them. He grabbed Ella's arms and pinned them to her waist. "Ella! Get a hold of yourself."

She struggled to break his grip. "No!" she yelled at William.

William was shaken, he knew Ella had a temper but he had never seen her like this before. "Ella, calm down."

He was surprised at the effort it took to prevent her from wrenching out of his grasp. For a moment he thought he might have to slap her when, out of nowhere, Louise intervened. Unbeknownst to all of them, she had been there the whole time. Without a word, she stepped up to William and lifted his hands off Ella. The men stood helpless as Ella collapsed into Louise's embrace. Louise glared at William and led Ella out of the cabin.

"Whew, that woman sure has some temper!" Poultney said.

William stared at the closed door, humbled to the quick by Louise's look of remonstration. He turned around to face Poultney, staring up at him with a smug look on his face. William struck him so hard he went flying across the floor.

After a moment, he walked over to Poultney, took the handkerchief from his pocket and threw it to him. "Here," he said.

Poultney took the linen and wiped the blood from his face and lips.

"Hit by two Durants in one day, that is quite an accomplishment," he quipped. William went to the small rustic table that served as a bar and poured whiskey into a crystal tumbler.

"You want one?" William raised the glass filled with the brown liquid at Poultney.

"Yes." Poultney continued to dab at his mouth as he worked his way into the rocking chair. William brought a tumbler over to Poultney. They raised their glasses in the air in a salute, put the tumblers to their lips and washed the drink down. Poultney winced at the stinging sensation the alcohol left on his cut lip. William retrieved the bottle and pulled up a chair next to Poultney.

"You know I can't marry her," Poultney said.

"I know. But did you have to lead her on, you bloody fool?" William observed his glass was empty and refilled it along with Poultney's.

"It's not that I don't love her." Poultney said as he wiped the blood from his mouth. "It's just that I can't have her. I can't marry a woman that has similar ambitions to mine. We would be competing with each other all of the time, and I would lose." He started to laugh at the irony of his statement, then stopped. It hurt his mouth too much. "Besides, your father would never allow it. I don't have, how should we say, enough capital to bring to the union."

William said nothing. There was nothing to say, Poultney was right.

"What are you going to do about Louise?" Poultney asked.

William's anger flared and he scowled at Poultney but quickly squashed it, realizing Poultney was pointing out the obvious.

"I'm not sure yet," he sighed into his glass. "But if history is any indication, probably what I have always done with the women in my life. Protect them from my father." He and Poultney finished their drink in silence.

Ella and William's relationship remained tepid after Poultney and Martha departed. They rarely spoke, preferring to ignore each other's existence while going about their daily routine. Ella continued her writing while William worked on Pine Knot. There was always something to do. A new wing on a building, repairs to stonework, a change of plans because William didn't approve of a craftsman's work and ordered it to be done over. As time went by William had mostly forgotten about Ella's indiscretion until his cousin Charles came to visit and informed him that Alvah had pulled a gun on him and his workmen.

"I've already put at least $1,000 dollars into it!" He paced the floor of William's cabin in a fit of rage. "How dare he tell me I can't build. Who is the squatter here after all? I have offered him a square deal to move on to another location. His run-down ramshackle house is falling apart as it is. And he has no money to fix it. I say, rebuild somewhere else where no one will notice. He hates Raquette now anyway, always complaining there are too many tourists."

William sat and listened to his cousin's rant. This was not good. His father was on his way to Pine Knot and if he heard what Alvah had done, he'd send the cavalry to boot him off Osprey. It would not go over well with the natives. "Charles, sit down and let's think." He coaxed Charles into a chair.

"What's to think about? Your sister and her friends have riled the man up! He told me as much when he was pointing a gun at my head. Said something like, 'Ella and her New York friends agree I should stand my ground here'."

Christ, William thought, Ella hadn't told him they conversed with Alvah, much less that they excited him into believing he had rights to the island. *How would he explain this to his father?* There was only so much he could do to keep Ella from drowning in her own stupidity.

"Let's keep that to ourselves for now, Charles, while we think this through."

"Think what through? No, I have done enough negotiating with that man. It's time to take action. I can't leave my half-built house and investment without a fight. Who's to say Alvah won't take it over?"

"He wouldn't do any such thing. He may be belligerent, but he is no thief, I assure you, Charles. My men know him well and think highly of him, even if he is anti-social."

Wood appeared at the door and cleared his throat to announce his presence. William wondered how much he had heard of their conversation.

"Dr. Doo'Rant is here and requests to see you, sir."

"Tell him I'll be right there, Wood." William turned to Charles. "Keep your head about this. We'll figure it out."

"What is Ella doing here?" It was the first thing out of his father's mouth upon entering his cabin.

"Hello, Father. Where is mother?"

"She went with Margaret to talk to Ella. Someone has to knock some sense into the girl. I strictly forbade anyone from coming to Pine Knot with friends this summer. The bills we are incurring are outrageous! And what are you doing here as well? Last I heard you were doing business in Saratoga working with Barbour."

William looked away. "I was until I came up here to check on how construction was going on the new kitchen." He stretched the truth slightly. He had been planning to come up this summer, but came sooner than intended when cousin Frederick sent word that Ella had stopped at Prospect House with friends on her way to Pine Knot.

"I tell you we cannot trust that girl. She's too rebellious, has been since the day you all left England. She insists on having her way with everything. Do you know she has been harassing her mother and I to send her back there? As if we can afford the fare and the lifestyle she leads. Personally I think she just wants to chase after that Bigelow character."

William said nothing. He wouldn't betray Ella now. But she owed him for staying silent about her indiscretions. "You can hardly blame her for wanting what she has come to expect. Ella is bored with her life at North Creek, as you and I would be if we had to be there permanently. It's not surprising she goes looking for diversions," he said in her defense.

"Her diversions are damn costly," Dr. Durant grumbled.

"And as for Poultney Bigelow, I think that attraction may have cooled somewhat," William said.

"Well I damn well hope it has. Bigelow is an intellectual. Intellectuals never have money. They just want to marry into it. I'd rather Ella do that." Dr. Durant walked over to a chair and sat down.

"Will, sit down." Dr. Durant motioned to the chair next to him.

William sat.

"I've been thinking. It's time we wrap up the construction projects here at Pine Knot and start developing some of the other land holdings in the Adirondacks. Our lumber and iron ore leases are still providing income but that won't last forever and the State is becoming less generous in its subsidies for new industries."

"Father," William started to protest, knowing where this was leading. "After this summer I'm quite sure there will only be a few more buildings to finish off. You can't expect me to stop what I'm doing here."

"Will, you're not hearing me. I'm not telling you to *stop* construction I'm telling you to *complete* it." He sighed and looked around the cabin. "Where is Louise? I could really use some tea."

"I'll go ask." William slid off his chair and went to the door. He opened it to find Louise standing there with a tray of tea and small sandwiches of smoked salmon. He stepped aside. She moved toward the side table and set the tray down, glanced over at Dr. Durant and nodded; he nodded in return.

"Good day," she said.

"Thank you, Louise," William called to her as she left the cabin.

His father let out a racking cough as William poured their tea.

"That doesn't sound good, have you had the doctor check your lungs lately?" William thought his father looked older than usual, too tired to be leading the masses into the wilderness. What was it that drove the man? Was it his greed or his ambition to conquer any challenge he confronted? Because this venture was turning into too much for him. Was it all for money? He constantly complained about not having enough of it. The challenge? After all he had built a railroad across the United States, what did he need this for?

"You forget I'm a doctor," his father said. "Now back to the subject at hand. I've come to realize I made a mistake in your upbringing."

William handed his father his teacup and sat down.

"I never should have allowed your mother to talk me into sending you to be educated abroad while I was working for the Union Pacific. Chicago schools would have been just as good and you would have learned how to be more shall I say *American*."

William chuckled and his father raised his brows.

"I'm being serious Will. Your mother and her family friends implanted some outrageous idea into your head that you deserve to lead the life of aristocracy. Unlike the gentry you associated with in England, we have to build our empire, we didn't inherit it. This," Dr. Durant gesticulated, "is not your fiefdom."

William frowned. He didn't like where this was going.

"We can't tithe the tenants. Our tenants are trees, and the people that come up here to see them." He paused to take a sip of tea.

"And another thing," he continued, giving William no chance to rebut, "unlike your friends in England we don't get seats in the House of Lords because of our title, we *buy* political influence."

"I get your point, Father. I may not have been educated in America but I know how the government structure works."

"Do you? Tell me, since you came back to the U.S. how many times have you been to Albany to represent our railroad interests?"

William recalled the last time his father instructed him to conduct business with the politicians in Albany. It was his last meeting in Senator Jacobs' office, using the Durant name to persuade the Senator to introduce a bill that would allow cousin Charles to lease Osprey Island from the state, taking any questions of ownership away from Alvah. It was all so undignified. He swore it would be the last time.

"Yes, now you gather my meaning. Will, stop pretending you are some country squire. It's time you took on more responsibility. You need to take over as President of the Adirondack Railroad."

William stood up quickly from his chair. "I'm not sure now is the right time for this."

"Really? Then tell me when is the right time?"

"Well, I don't know." William put his hand to his chin, rubbed it, and started to pace the floor. "There are the remaining cabins to build here—"

"Wood can oversee the rest of the construction project, he has been doing fine without you this summer."

"And then there's the steamboat line at Marion River. We have a contract to build another steamboat specifically for the Raquette and I anticipate a lot of traffic with Bennett's new hotel. And—"

"And our lawyer John Barbour can take care of any of that business from Saratoga," Dr. Durant said. "I've been too lenient with you. Your life is filled with too much leisure. Now is a critical time for us. We have to decide what to do with our land." He rose from his chair and started to pace the floor. His father's movements persuaded William to take a seat.

"We need to consider the best prospects for making money. Sure there are a few wealthy men, friends from the clubs that will want what you have achieved here." He waved his hands in the air. "But the real money is with the middle class."

"Surely you aren't implying we should build a hotel?" William said.

"No, no, not that. The tourists are our future investors Will. We need them to buy our land when the price is right. We need to consider what will attract them to the area to buy land. Most can't afford grand camps like Pine Knot. We need to make plans to subdivide our land holdings while the price of land is still reasonable for the people with less means. Especially before our fellow business partners buy up all the land around here and turn it into private reserves."

William mulled on this. A group of businessmen, friends of his, had recently bought a thousand acres near Pine Knot to turn into a private hunting preserve. Personally, he was in favor of this trend. Who better to steward the land than the people that owned it and had the resources to take care of it? The State Land Commissioners had made a mess of it over the past few decades. The woods were left barren after a cut, fires were now more frequent, and the mining companies raped the land and then abandoned it.

"And the State will take whatever is left." His father was becoming more agitated. "That pesky surveyor Verplanck Colvin and his rabble rousers in Albany are calling for it. Mark, my word Will, if we don't move soon the state will try to take our land from us, and all that I have worked for here will be lost."

"How small do you want the lots?"

Dr. Durant shrugged. "I don't know. One acre, half acre."

"What can we possibly build on a half acre of land that would attract people?"

His father shook his head, exasperated by the questions. "I don't know, that's for you to figure out. But look around you, the guides do it."

"Yes, but they're not our clientele are they?"

"Well maybe they should be!"

He was not making sense, William thought.

Dr. Durant sat down then, tired and gray-faced. "And," he raked his hand through his hair, "I suppose it will come out soon enough." He paused and looked at his son. "The Adirondack Railroad Company is bankrupt. We've spent $6 million building this line and it hasn't turned a profit. Investments have run dry. We won't be bringing the rail to Canada. The tracks we've laid are as far as it will go. A proverbial 'dead end' you might say." He let out a sigh of defeat.

"What do you mean bankrupt?" William asked.

"I mean the till has run dry, William! Why do you think I want you to finish your work here? So you can focus your attention on making money instead of spending it. Which seems to be your favorite pastime."

William gripped the side of his chair. "I've done everything you've asked me to do here, father. Maybe you don't remember but it was you that wanted me to build this compound to attract investors. So what happened?" he said with as much control as possible.

"We've achieved what we needed to get the first leg of the tracks built. But the State has ruined our plans by taking control of the last 20,000 acres. I can't help it if people lose their investment as a result of something over which I have no control."

"What investments? Do you mean the investors in the Adirondack Railroad?"

"Yes, of course. What other Railroad?" Dr. Durant answered. William resented his father's sarcasm.

"We are going to reorganize, William. I'm going to sell you the company, and then we will have title to the land holdings. You need to go to New York City to sign the papers."

William had no idea what his father was scheming. He only knew that once again, it would interfere with his plans. And the last thing he wanted to do in the middle of the summer was visit with William Sutphen, the Adirondack Railroad company lawyer, and sign papers putting him in charge of a failed enterprise. He had better use for his time. Unbeknownst to his father he was planning another project, this one in a very remote area. He was sure it would rival Pine Knot. "But really, I should at least stay through this summer, I—"

"Damn it, you're not listening, it's all planned!" Dr. Durant lurched from his chair with raised fists. He stopped suddenly, stumbled forward, clutched his chest, and started to cough uncontrollably before staggering backwards. His knees buckled and he started to fall. William reacted quickly, reaching his father before he hit the floor and guiding him back to his chair.

"You really need rest. All of this exertion is making you ill," William said as he waited for his father's breathing to ease before letting go of him in the chair.

"I'm not done," Dr. Durant said when his breathing became steady. "You know as well as I do the importance of familial loyalty."

William sat down. *What is he on about now?*

"Believe me I understand that men have particular, how shall I say it — needs. After all, I spent years away from your mother and I always took care of mine."

William could feel the blood rushing to his cheeks. "Father, do we need to discuss this? Especially in your condition."

"But I always came back to her."

"Yes, and her $200,000," William said under his breath. His father was too preoccupied with his own speech to have heard him.

"I would never cause a scandal by staying with a harlot."

"Father, please," William interrupted him before he insulted Louise.

"Figure out what you're going to do about Louise and make your departure plans. Sutphen is expecting you. Now leave." Dr. Durant closed his eyes and held his hands over his chest.

William left his father wheezing in the chair.

"Tea, Hannah? What are you thinking? The man has no manners. What makes you think he would even be comfortable sitting down for tea with you, and how on earth do you propose to convince him to let Charles build?"

"Well, Thomas, the usual Durant method of bullying is not working," Hannah said firmly. "So I'm trying a different approach – tact." She handed Margaret her wrap and settled into a chair facing her husband and William. Dr. Durant never liked it when she called him Thomas, he much preferred Pet. And lately she was more likely to use his given name than this term of endearment.

It was the day after Dr. Durant's coughing fit and William was worried there'd be a repeat, but somehow his mother knew how to handle the man. They were holding a family meeting, minus Ella, to decide what to do about Alvah. The three of them agreed that amends needed to be made but how to go about it was a matter of contention.

"I'm not sure he'll even come, Mother," William said.

"Of course he will, he has a huge crush on Ella," Hannah said.

The men raised their brows at her, considering how preposterous it was, Ella and Alvah together.

"Really, Hannah, using your own daughter to obtain a piece of land. Even I wouldn't stoop that low."

"Oh you wouldn't, wouldn't you?" She shot her husband a challenging look. Surprisingly, his father did not defend himself.

"And what does Ella think about this?" William asked.

"Does it matter what she thinks?" Dr. Durant replied with a dismissive wave of his hand. "I think your mother may be on to something."

CAMP KIRBY
AUGUST 2010

Frank was working a circular saw to cut new floorboards for the loft. The project was almost complete. They had done a good job so far and he was proud of the work. Just as he was about to put another piece of wood to the saw he heard a boat pull up to the dock. He didn't recognize the people in the boat, probably tourists — lost. He shut off the generator as they approached.

"Hello," the man in the boat waved at Frank. "Mind if we come up?"

Frank waved back thinking he hated to be disturbed while working, but they were most likely looking for Golden Beach State Park. Maybe they were visiting friends that were camping there.

A man and woman, both in their fifties Frank guessed, got out of the boat and walked up the path to where he stood.

"We heard this is the cabin where the famous William Durant kept his mistress." The man was too eager. The woman was apprehensive as she smiled at Frank.

"We just thought maybe we would take a look, sorry to disturb you. We didn't think anyone lived here," she said.

"Well." Frank looked around protectively. He didn't want these people to know Avery was staying here by herself even if Jake did spend most nights with her. "I stay here while doing some renovations for the college. This is private property you know."

"Oh yes, we are so sorry to intrude!" The man backtracked.

There was an awkward silence.

"Jim, maybe we should go now." The woman took Jim's arm in hers to lead him away.

"Wait," Frank said. "I don't mean to be rude. How did you find out about this cabin anyway?"

"Well, actually," the man started to chuckle, "I'm an avid fan of great camp architecture. We came up here to tour around the area. We've been staying at Sagamore, and the staff there were talking about Minnie Kirby and William Durant and an old book that was found in the attic just recently confirming the story. So we thought we would take a look."

That concerned Frank. But it was just like his sister Sally to gossip about the book with their nieces who worked at Sagamore. He needed to get over there pronto and tell them to keep their mouths shut. The last thing the College needed, or Avery for that matter, was a bunch of history fanatics tramping around the grounds of Camp Kirby looking for more clues about Minnie. The story was too intriguing, especially to women. He could never figure out why.

"Sorry to disappoint you folks." Frank was not going to feed the frenzy. "But this is private property and we are in the midst of a major construction project. It wouldn't be safe to look around. I think the College opens Camp Huntington up for a tour every summer with the rest of the Great Camps in the area. You may want to check the *Adirondack Almanack* calendar."

"Will do, thanks anyway. Come on Jim." The woman took a firm hold of his arm and started walking toward the boat.

"It used to be the women that took an inordinate interest in Minnie," Frank said under his breath.

"Who was that?" Jake came down from the loft to check on Frank's progress with the wood as the couple was leaving. He wiped his brow with a red bandana he kept in his back pocket.

"Nobody. I think. They were inquiring about Minnie." Frank handed Jake the wood. "I may leave a bit early today and head over to Sagamore to have a talk with your cousins. Seems like your mother has been spreading rumors again."

Jake sighed and took the wood into the cabin and up the stairs.

Avery felt a twinge of guilt for sitting under the old White pine again, waiting for the saw-whet to appear. She was well on her way to developing a thorough database on these owls. Her research so far had netted over 50 owls, the majority males. But this one, he would not be caught. And she didn't have much more time. So she made an attempt at least once a week to lure him in with the hope she would uncover some deep secret he held. Why was he so different from the rest? Where was his mate? She took out the diary while she waited. Maybe that was another reason she came to this spot. In truth, it allowed her time to read Minnie's diary without worrying about stopping to disengage an owl from the net.

July 30, 1893

It is hard to believe it is going to be August in two days! Today Nate and I had our afternoon tea under the White pine. I showed Nate how to prepare tea properly for a picnic. William provided us with portable cake tins so we filled those up with some scones I baked, and jam. He also gave us a small silver teapot with a spirit lamp so we could brew it right in the forest. Nate thought that was so exciting. He said the lamp reminded him of a portable stove his uncle Ike uses when they camp. It was a lovely tea party. He brought the new book William gave him, "The Last of the Mohicans". A love story I believe, I have never read it so I am looking forward to it. William told me he loves that story.

William is arriving any minute now so I must go. Nate is building us a campfire and we are going to feast on trout for dinner. It may be the last time I see William for awhile as he has more guests arriving next week.

Minnie

CAMP PINE KNOT
SUMMER 1881

Alvah glanced around him to make sure no one was watching and picked up the teacup to examine the stamp on the bottom.

"Humph," he grunted. "Wedgwood." He wondered if Wedgwood was in England. Mrs. Durant was from England, he could tell by her accent. He spit out a gob of tobacco juice on the ground next to him; it was probably the last chance he had to do it before the ladies arrived. He never worried about spitting in front of anyone before, but Mrs. Durant might not take kindly to it and she could be caustic. Besides, she had invited him to tea, and although he figured he knew why, he thought it only proper to try to act civil.

Alvah looked around again, squirmed in his chair, and batted away a fly that was hovering over the teacups. His hand clanged into one of the delicate cups and he quickly grabbed it before it fell to the ground and shattered. It was just like the Durants to bring fine china to the woods. Another indication it was time to get out. Things were changing too fast for his liking. Every summer more and more tourists descended on the lake. They arrived by steamboats and stayed at Bennett's new hotels. Antlers and another called Under the Hemlocks. That made Alvah laugh. He knew what it really meant to sleep under a hemlock, with balsam boughs as a bed. Used to be Alvah would guide a few adventuresome souls like ol' Murray who came to the Adirondacks to breathe the fresh mountain air and take in a few deer. Now even Murray was gone; he left Osprey complaining of the same tourists that he had attracted to the area with his damned book!

It was no good anymore. The lakes were clogged with steamboats and guideboats, the rivers were flooded because nobody even knew how to carry anymore, and the women were the worst of all. The wilderness was no place for women and their fine china and tea. *Give me coffee in a tin cup and I'm fine.*

"Alvah, so good of you to join us for afternoon tea."

Alvah was startled out of his musings as Hannah Durant approached the table that had been set out under a maple for the occasion, Ella following close behind. Alvah remembered his manners and stood up as the ladies found their own seats at the table. He took his hat in his hand and held it by the brim.

"Thanks for invitin' me Mrs. Doo'Rant, Miss Ella." He looked in Ella's direction, blushed and sat down across from her. He put his hat on one knee and the linen napkin from the table on the other.

"Of course, we haven't been around much this summer and I wanted to catch up with you. You always know what is what around the Raquette," Mrs. Durant said.

Ella was not her usual animated self Alvah thought as he cleared his throat. He was not much for small talk and he knew why they had invited him for tea, so he told Mrs. Durant what was on his mind.

"Well I've been off guiding some gentlemen from New Yerk City these past few weeks. But when I got back to Osprey there was your nephew and workcrew buildin' a cabin. Seemed as though he was takin' advantage of me in my absence."

He glanced up at Miss Molineaux as she came and put a tray of small yellow cakes and a jar of honey in front of him along with a teapot, sugar bowl and creamer.

"No biscuits or sandwiches Margaret?" Hannah looked down at Louise's cakes unsure of what they were.

"No." Margaret glared at Ella, "The provisions are low due to all the company that's been here recently. There is no flour left.

Louise made cornbread instead."

"Johnnycakes! Louise makes the best." Alvah said.

"Yes, of course she does." Hannah tried to mask her displeasure. She had no idea what Louise had concocted but she did not like the sound of it — at all. However, if it made Alvah happy, all the better.

"Louise's cornbread is famous with the crew here," Ella offered as she poured tea for Alvah and then her mother before pouring a cup for herself. Hannah shot Ella a look that said, why do you even know this?

Ella refrained from offering the hovering Margaret any tea, or a seat. She waited to see if her mother would and hoped she wouldn't. Margaret took the hint and left the party.

"Well, Alvah, I'm so glad then that we could offer you cornbread instead of our usual pastries. This isn't exactly Ranelagh but we do our best!" Hannah put milk in her teacup and using the silver teaspoon delicately stirred the beverage front to back, slowly, and then took a sip.

Ella rolled her eyes as Alvah dug into his piece of cornbread ignoring Mrs. Durant. *As if he would know about what they served at a tea garden in London.* Ella examined Alvah's hands while he took a draw on his tea. They were the hands of a man that worked hard: calloused and stained black. He had taken the time to wash them she could tell, even cleaned under his fingernails. But the stains were so deeply embedded into his fingerprint they would not wash off.

"Back to the small infraction at Osprey," Mrs. Durant approached the subject now that Alvah had brought it up.

"Infraction ma'am?" Alvah took a slug of his tea and used the linen to wipe his mouth of the dribble of honey that clung to his beard.

"What I'm referring to is the altercation between you and my nephew Charles. I'm very sorry to hear about this. We consider you a good friend Alvah and we would hate to see this argument between you and Charles go any further."

"Well that would be easy then. You just tell that nephew of

yours that I'm not leavin' anytime soon. He thinks he can offer me a hundred dollars and I'll just vacate that land and set up camp somewheres else. Osprey's mine fair and square, Murray left it to me."

"We understand that, Alvah, don't we, Ella?"

Ella took a sip of her tea and set the cup down on its saucer. This was her cue; she had been given instructions as to what she had to say.

"Alvah, I know you're unhappy with the way things are changing here at Raquette," she said.

"You bet I am! Why these half-wits from New Yerk and especially Boston, they come up here with their new weaponry and thinks theys gonna shoot them a deer or a duck and they don't even know how to load a gun much less handle one. And I knows you can understand that Ella, cos from what I hear you know your way around a gun," he said.

Ella blushed at his compliment and continued with her prescribed script. "Well then, wouldn't you like to move to the interior, say near the chain of lakes, where it's more quiet? Your clients know how to find you. And the hotels are always looking for guides like you to lend themselves out to the clientele. You'll not lose business if you move."

"I personally believe Charles has not offered enough for what he wants from you Alvah," Mrs. Durant piped in. "How does three hundred sound? And William will offer some of our crew to help you move your belongings and build a new cabin in the woods wherever you land."

Ella shot her mother a look. *What was she doing?* That was not part of the deal they had arranged, and she knew her father would not like it either. William had told her that Papa had ordered him to New York City as soon as possible to sign papers to become President of the railroad company.

"Deal," Alvah said.

"Wonderful," said Hannah. She beamed at Ella.

"Make sure you put that money in the bank as soon as you get it, Alvah," Ella said to him.

"Never," he grunted. "I been to a bank before. I went up to the teller and gave him my twenty dollars and waited by the door to see what would happen to it. When all the sudden a man comes into the bank goes up to that very teller and takes out my twenty dollars!"

Ella waited to see what advice Hannah would offer to Alvah about banking etiquette, but Hannah looked confounded by the man.

He stood up from his chair. "Ladies, it was nice to have tea with you both. I must get goin' now. I have a client waitin' on me at Prospect House. I best get back to Osprey to pack up my things and when I get back from this excursion, you can tell Charles I'll be expecting payment and I'll talk to William about his assistance when I get back."

"I'm *so* glad we could come to an understanding, Alvah," Hannah purred as she lifted her hand in the air for Alvah to take into his own.

Alvah didn't take her hand in his own, just nodded at the ladies, put his hat back on his head and walked away.

William took the path he knew through the woods to the foxes' den he discovered last spring, wondering if a family was still there. It was under the roots of a large maple, a perfect spot to raise kits. The tree was perched precariously on the edge of the ravine. The roots, like gnarled hands, were grasping a large rock that was wedged underneath and protruding out of the stream bank.

The family of foxes had made their den between the roots and the rock. He sat down under a fir on the other side of the gorge and watched the entrance, a favorite pastime when he needed to think and reminisce. He was reminded of the Shanklin Chine on the Isle of Wight.

The chine was a deep gorge that ran to the sea. When he was young, his mother rented a cottage in Shanklin and every time he visited the chine he felt like he was entering a primeval forest, much as he felt now sitting by the stream. He and his friends used to wander along the trails, playing hide and seek in and out of the towering ferns and trees. There was an inn along the path and tourists from London would come and stay for a visit to take the restorative 'Victorian sea baths'.

Nestled in the hills overlooking the chine were bowers made of wood, the sides and railings decorated with tree limbs from the forest. He always admired those structures, small lookouts over the tumbling waters where he and his friends would picnic and listen to the roaring waterfalls.

A flash of red fur blazed through the green forest and caught William's attention. He turned toward the foxes' den just in time to catch the tail of a fox entering. Once again he observed the tangled mass of tree roots clinging to the rock and earth. How, William wondered, could he mimic this natural design on the buildings in Pine Knot? And then he thought about what Isaac had told him; that saplings were pliable and he used them to frame the arched roof of the longhouse.

William picked up a small branch. He could bend it to his liking, in any shape he wanted. It gave him the sense of control he had been longing for since he came to America.

"Will, mother wants to speak with you." William was startled to see Ella sitting next to him. He had fallen asleep under the tree. She was gently rubbing his shoulders.

"What's this about?" William was confused. What had he been doing before Ella came to get him? He was near the foxes' den. His favorite spot.

"Mother wants to speak with you." Ella stood up.

"What about?" He stood up and dusted the needles and duff off his trousers.

"She has come up with a way to get Alvah to vacate Osprey, making it free and clear for Charles to build," Ella said. "She needs you."

They walked side-by-side back to Pine Knot.

It was Ella that broke the awkward silence between them. "What does father know?" she finally asked.

"About you and Poultney you mean?" William replied.

"Yes."

"Nothing, I told him nothing. Poultney's a rake Ella, you know that, don't you?"

Ella shrugged. "It's an epidemic here in America. To hide the truth from others."

"Perhaps you're right. Although Poultney is not as conniving as some men I've met here in America, including our father. I see it all the time at the clubs in New York. Small white lies told constantly: stock tips to ensure one's investments don't go under; small transgressions sidestepped with a flimsy excuse; all for keeping on top of the game, as if the honor of one's family name is inconsequential. Only the gain matters and as long as that is for the benefit of the man or his fortune, then the end justifies the means," William said.

"I'm not aware of all the games that men play at the clubs you attend in New York. I'm aware of Poultney's tendency to flirt with the women," Ella said. "But he has been my only confidante here in America when no one else will do. Papa will never understand that. He has never tried to understand me."

"You're very good at playing the martyr, Ella. I hardly blame father for being upset with you. You have never followed his bidding on anything, including finding a suitable match for marriage."

"But I love *Poultney*! Oh I know he comes across as wily to you but I know him better. We share a passion for the written word and see the world as an endless opportunity to explore. Surely you of all people understand that? If only he would take me with him on his journey," she sighed. "I know I would make him a decent wife. And Will," she stopped to face him, "thank you. For not telling father what happened."

"I wouldn't risk it. He's ill. It might have made him worse. And besides, we look out for each other," William said. He refrained from telling her any more about Poultney's true intentions. Poor

Ella, would she ever find, let alone marry, a man capable of managing her passions?

"Speaking of which, what are you going to do about Louise?"

"What do you mean?"

"Don't be coy with me, you know what I mean. You are leading her on to think you might marry one day. You are just lucky she is not pregnant."

William let out a sigh. "I've thought it through. I've found a spot not too far from here where we can make a home together. Away from gossiping neighbors."

"You think you can marry Louise?"

"Why not? Louise has more integrity than anyone I know."

"Have you lost your mind? Father will never allow it."

"He doesn't have to know."

"How will you keep it from him then?"

"By the time I marry her father will be long gone and no one will care."

Ella shook her head. "You always were an idealist, William, but this, I don't know, this is different. This isn't like you trying to attract the attention of a courtier. This is keeping a secret that could ruin you if it became known."

"Enough ballyragging. Leave my life to me," William said.

Hannah was having tea with Margaret in her cabin when William and Ella arrived.

"Ella, Margaret, I want to speak with William in private," she said.

"Did Ella tell you what I negotiated with Alvah?" she asked him after they left.

"Some of it yes," William said.

"Did she tell you that I told him you would help him build a new cabin in the woods somewhere?"

"No, but have you told father this yet? He wants me to head to New York City as soon as possible."

"I will deal with your father. New York can wait. You have

greater concerns here, right now. You need to deal with Louise."

William was shocked his mother knew. And ashamed. What excuse could he offer to her? Not that she needed one.

"Don't look at me that way, William, I'm not an idiot."

"Mother, I can take care of Louise."

"No you can't. Not the way you need to anyway. You have your head in the clouds over that girl. You really think you can keep a mistress hidden away here at Pine Knot? Your father will be livid if he finds out she lives here now. He'll cut you off."

"It is not that strange to have a servant staying to watch over the camp, our neighbors do it as well," William said.

"That is where you are wrong dear boy. Most of our friends hire only married women to staff their kitchens. And don't think for one minute they are not talking about you behind your back! Mrs. Stott told me a few of their friends inquired about the 'lovely young Indian girl staying at the Durant hunting cabin'."

William cringed at his mother's mocking tone. "I think you are overreacting."

"And now that we have all of these tourists coming up from the city and staying at Under the Hemlocks and Antlers it only takes one glance through a spy glass for any of them to gather the gossip needed to scandalize the family name."

"I'm a gentleman, I will not abandon her, I plan to provide for her."

"No," Hannah said flatly. "That won't do. Louise needs to go back to her family and never set foot at Pine Knot again."

"But—"

"Listen to me." She leaned forward and put her hands on his. "No one can ever know you are having an affair with an Indian girl. You will do as I say. I've told Alvah you'll help him build a cabin in the woods. Take whatever workmen you need, and if you need finished lumber get it from Frederick's mill at Prospect House. He wants to build near Eighth Lake, I believe that is where Louise is from? Go with him, bring our workmen, and Louise and Ike. Build her a cabin near her family and say good-bye to her then. I can only give you a short period of time before your father will wonder what you're up to. Alvah's cabin is the only diversion I could think of. He'll get suspicious if you stay too long here after we leave. I can give you a month."

CAMP HUNTINGTON
AUGUST 2010

"When do you plan to pack it up?" Tom asked.

It was a simple question but it jolted Avery. She had been talking about that very thing with Jake while they were walking to Huntington and the conversation didn't go well. She put her cup of coffee down on the table and glanced over at Jake who was looking at her levelly over the brim of his own.

Avery took her eyes off Jake's and looked down. "I'm not sure yet, Tom. I'm still netting birds and I need to tie up some loose ends. Maybe by the end of the month I'll have an answer for you."

"Well you can take your time. Now that construction is done at Kirby we won't be disturbing your work and you can finish up what you started. Just let me know."

"Place looks great now," Frank chimed in.

Avery sat quietly eating her breakfast and recalled the unpleasant conversation with Jake. She had broached the subject of their relationship when it came time for her to leave.

"What're we going to do come September?" Avery said.

"What do you mean?"

"Well, I was thinking maybe you could come with me back to Vermont. Maybe sign up for a few classes at the University? Finish your degree?"

Jake was visibly annoyed. "Avery, we've been down this road before. You know school's not for me. I tried a semester at Paul Smith's College and got nowhere with it. It's just not my thing."

"Well what is your thing then Jake? What're you going to do with your life here in these woods?"

"Plenty."

"Plenty of what?"

"There's plenty to do here. I cut and deliver wood for people, maintain summer homes, work at the store in Raquette. There are folks that stay here all year you know. It's not that desolate. Me and my friends snowmobile all over the place and the winter ski resorts keep people employed."

"But what about me? What about us?" Avery stopped walking.

"What about us? Why does it have to end when you leave? We can still see each other. I'll come and visit you in Vermont. You can come stay with me anytime you like. I'm not going anywhere."

Avery stared at him. She was confused. This was not the proposal she wanted. "Forget it then." She stomped off ahead of him.

"Hey, what's with you?" Jake called after her. She took off in a jog down the path toward Huntington and snagged her foot on a protruding tree root, almost landing face-first into a tree. She caught herself in time, and bolted ahead of him.

Later that afternoon Avery sat alone in a big Adirondack chair on the front porch of Camp Kirby, with her laptop and Minnie's diary beside her.

Jake had not come back after breakfast. He and Frank had work to do on a cabin at Huntington. And he didn't say if or when he would see her back at Kirby. That was fine with her. She needed to think. She needed to get started on the methods section of her paper. Her abstract and introduction were complete. But the methods section was the most boring to write. It was just a tedious summary of all of the equipment, steps and measurements she took while netting owls in the woods. There was no poetry involved, no saga, and no emotion. Not like the emotions she was feeling right then.

A crackle of thunder brought her attention to the horizon just in time to see a dagger of lightning slash the distant sky. This was followed by a pick-up of the wind. The view across the lake was monochromatic. The cedar trees were clouded in a sheen of white mist. It slowly crept across the lake until it was upon her. A storm was coming. It started to rain, and a gray blanket descended over the lake blocking her view entirely.

The rain came in torrents, eating away at the soil around the roots of the hemlock tree in front of the porch. Avery thought darkly how the hemlock would eventually fall over, and could understand why the lake was dotted with so many upended trees. It would be difficult to be a tree along the shoreline of Raquette. It would be hard to take a stand.

She glanced at her keyboard, her notes, and then at Minnie's diary. Now that had emotion. Maybe Minnie would be a good diversion from her anger with Jake and his noncommittal attitude toward their relationship. She picked up the diary.

August 10, 1893

I have not seen William in days. His guests have kept him busy. Nate and I are reading "The Last of the Mohicans". Now I know why William has named our camp Uncas, after the main character in the book, and named the lake on which it sits Mohegan.

William loved this book when he was growing up. I can imagine him as a young boy in England, reading about the adventure of a war and the last Indian tribes that lived in the Adirondack wilderness. He must have had some romantic notions of what it was like to live here. Little does he understand how hard it can actually be when you don't have access to the money and labor he does. I don't think William understands this entirely although I know he is very loyal and generous to his workmen.

And as much as I love to read with Nate under our favorite tree, it is no replacement for my time with William. When will he come back? When will we move to Uncas? My father will start to wonder when I am coming home. I want to be able to tell him I've married. But William has made no commitment to me. I think I should go to Pine Knot and find him. But if I do that he will be very angry and it will only cause a scene.

Every night now when I go to sleep I imagine William beside me in bed, married, my husband. When will he leave Janet and come to me again?

Minnie

Avery finished the last line of the diary, watched the rain teeming down and thought about Minnie. The poor girl was trapped in her own ignorance. She sighed, went inside and tossed the diary on the couch. It teetered on the edge of the cushion for a brief moment then landed on the floor with a thud. She was too emotionally drained to care, she walked into her bedroom to type up her research methods on her laptop.

EIGHTH LAKE
FALL 1881

The day was ending. Fall came early in the north woods and didn't last long. Amongst the brooding Black spruce, the larch trees lit up the landscape like rays of sunshine, their yellow needles, waiting to drop. Red and orange maple leaves that had been whisked off the trees by the stiff afternoon breeze dappled the still lake waters in the eerie glow of the setting sun as if painted on a canvas.

William thought back on the first fall he had stayed in the Adirondacks with Louise by his side and was convinced that autumn was the most beautiful time of the year.

William was working side by side on the roof with Alvah and two other workmen in a location he had known would be perfect. He had scouted it out long before, in the days when he used to bring Louise and Ike back to see their family. And even better than the location, William had checked — the land was owned by the Adirondack Railroad Co. so if there were ever an issue with it, William could protect him from getting chased out of his home again.

So far Alvah wasn't showing much in the way of gratitude but at one point while they were pounding nails, William saw him sitting on his haunches, looking around him and smiling. Probably because he finally realized he was alone on a peninsula on Eighth Lake.

William also reveled in the quiet contemplation this time

afforded him as he knew within the month it would all be over. Soon he would have to go back to New York City, where he, along with all of the other harried men trying to climb their way or keep their place in the upper echelons of society, would be yearning for a respite such as these woods afforded.

William had other plans as well. Ever since the camping trip they had gone on with Ella and Poultney three years earlier, he had decided the small lake tucked away in the mountainsides would make a great site for a cabin. He envisioned building one there eventually for Louise and himself, as this banishment to the Lawrence household was, in his mind, only temporary.

Within days Alvah's cabin was complete and William turned his attention to Louise. He and his workmen left Alvah and pulled up to the longhouse in the woods. It seemed like eons ago when he had last visited the Lawrence household, now brimming with family. The longhouse had long since been upgraded to a post and beam building sided with wooden planks. There were windows with glass, and they had partitioned the interior with rooms.

When they arrived grandmother Lawrence was harvesting corn and the last of the tomatoes with Sarah, who had a babe strapped to her back in a papoose.

William found the contraption an ingenious piece of apparel. It had a long wooden board, handsomely decorated with red paint, and attached to a sling made of deerskin, with holes for the babe's legs to fit through. The board kept the child upright on Sarah's back while she walked around and tended to the garden, or cooked over the fire. The babe seemed completely content to spend his time there, strapped to his mother's back and taking in his surroundings. The whole time he was there, William never heard him cry unless he was hungry.

The rest of the family came out of the house en masse to welcome Louise, Ike and William.

Sarah had married a man named Jeff who worked with her brother Jake at a lumber camp. Although usually away working at the camp —a roving village of men that cut down trees in the wilderness and dragged them to the Raquette River for transport to the nearest mill — Sarah's husband Jeff and brother Jake came home for a short stay to help build the new cabin.

Jeff was glad to do it. The Lawrence house didn't leave much room for his growing family with Sarah.

Sarah and her children would use the cabin. And since Jeff's work with the lumber company kept him away most of the time, it would be good for her to have Louise as company.

Louise on the other hand didn't understand why this was not just a visit. She should be going back to Pine Knot with William, who had a hard time convincing her that staying in the new cabin he was building for her and her sister's family was for the best.

"I'll see you as much as possible," he said.

Louise was confused. "Will we live as a family here?" she asked.

William shook his head sadly. "No Louise. I can't live with you here. I will visit. I have to live in New York City. You know I do not live all year at Pine Knot either. I conduct my work in the cities and then when I can, I'll stay with you. Here."

"But why can't I stay at Pine Knot and wait for you there?"

"Louise, it's like this. Your sister stays here while Jeff works at the lumber camp right? Likewise I will be away at work. You're better off with your family while I'm away. Do you understand that now?"

"Yes," Louise said reluctantly. She couldn't help but feel that there was something more than what William was telling her, something he was hiding from her.

The new cabin was finished in days. There was no reason for William to linger any longer. It was time to say good-bye.

Isaac shook his hands. "Be well," he said.

Mémé came over to William and brought him a small leather pouch filled with cornbread and venison. She didn't say anything, she didn't have to; her deep, dark eyes spoke volumes as William locked in on them. He returned a look of guilt and remorse. He took the food from her and said, "Thank you." She nodded and walked away.

William held Louise as he said good-bye. She cried as he

murmured his promises to return. It started to rain as he mounted his horse for the ride back to Pine Knot. When he turned she was still standing in place, getting soaked by the rain. Sarah took her by the shoulders and gently guided her into their cabin. William pulled his collar up to protect his neck from the raw air, more determined than ever to build his own private compound in the woods.

CAMP KIRBY
AUGUST 2010

It was well past midnight and still raining hard when Avery finished writing her methods and analysis section. She stood up from her small desk, laced her fingers, stretched them above her head and swiveled her neck back and forth, up and down. She felt stiff and needed to rest. As she meandered into her bedroom and took off her clothes she couldn't help but notice how empty the bed was without Jake in it.

It was dark. She had forgotten how lonely it was here. Jake had been staying with her since June and she had gotten used to the way his warm body felt next to hers. She glanced over at the chair where his brown flannel shirt lay draped across one of the arms. She walked over to the side of the bed where Jake kept his books on a small table and picked up his book, *The Last of the Mohicans*.

Avery had never read it. Feeling sorry for herself, she slinked under the cool covers and opened the book. It was written in 1825. She remembered she had read somewhere that William West Durant used characters from this book to name his camps and buildings: Uncas, Sagamore and Chingachook.

She flipped the book open and started to read random passages, hoping to get the gist of the story. The last she read before she dozed off was about the massacre at Fort William.

Pages might yet be written to prove, from this illustrious example, the defects of human excellence; to show how easy it is for generous sentiments, high courtesy, and chivalrous courage to lose their influence beneath the chilling blight of selfishness, and to exhibit to the world a man who was great in all the minor attributes of character, but who was found wanting when it became necessary to prove how much principle is superior to policy. But the task would exceed our prerogatives; and, as history, like love, is so apt to surround her heroes with an atmosphere of imaginary brightness, it is probable that Louis de Saint Veran will be viewed by posterity only as the gallant defender of his country, while his cruel apathy on the shores of the Oswego and of the Horican will be forgotten.

There was a rapping sound like a tree branch hitting the rooftop. Avery bolted upright and glanced at *The Last of the Mohicans* resting on the bed where she must have left it when she dozed off. Maybe one day she'd find out what it was about in Sparknotes. Looking around her she tried to discern where the tapping sound was coming from. It was Jake. He was outside in the rain, soaking wet.

"What are you doing out there?" Avery opened the door a crack trying not to let the pelting rain enter the room.

"I just got back from the bar," Jake mumbled.

"Take your things off outside and come through the front then."

Jake walked to the front porch and sat on one of the Adirondack chairs. Avery went into the parlor and watched him from the window as he struggled to release one of his boots. He was obviously drunk. The boot gave out a loud clunk as it fell to the floor. He continued to work on the other. Then he slid off his socks, his pants and his shirt. It took twenty minutes.

"Look at you, you're soaked through to the bone!" Avery scolded and placed a blanket over his shoulders as he walked through the door. "Who were you with tonight?"

"Al. He called Anita, she drove me to Huntington. Tol' her I was gonna sleep it off in my truck, but decided to walk back here instea'." He flopped down in one of the chairs in the parlor and grinned.

"How much did you have to drink?"

"I dunno, five maybe six, or nine beers. I los' track."

"Good lord, let me get you something warm to drink." Avery left him dripping in the chair as she went to make coffee.

The last thing Jake heard was Avery clanging the tin percolator onto the stove. Then he was woken up by her hand shaking his shoulder.

"Here." She handed him a mug and sat down beside him.

"Thing is, Avery," Jake started to say, took a sip of his coffee and stopped. "Vermont sucks."

"What are you talking about?"

"Vermont, I hate that state. People there wear flannel."

"Jake, you wear flannel."

"Yes but my flannel is not plaid, like they wear in Vermon'. I mean who wears plaid flannel? And they wear those stupid boots."

"What boots?"

"Ya know, those L.L. Bean boots. They make 'em there. Like they invented boots or somethin'."

"I think you mean Maine."

"I'm talkin' 'bout Vermon'."

"I know, but they invented L.L. Bean boots in Maine."

Jake shrugged again and waved his hand in the air. "What ever."

He took another sip of the coffee. "Thanks for this." He raised the mug to her, then looked down at it. "The coffee is swirling with the room," he said. He looked up. "And they have the dumbest ice cream flavors, like Chunky Monkey – who would eat something called Chunky Monkey?"

"Are you talking about Ben and Jerry's ice cream?"

"Yeah – that." Jake gesticulated with his mug in the air, slopping coffee onto the floor. "And Burlington sucks."

"Ok, now you're really making no sense. You're being silly and spilling that coffee all over the place. Let's get you to bed."

"Avery, you shouldn't leave. You should stay here with me in the Adirondacks." Jake looked up at her with intensity.

Avery held her breath.

"Come on, let's go." She took the mug out of his hand before he dropped it on the floor, placed it on the side table, took hold of his arms and forced him out of the chair. He started for their bedroom.

"No way buster, not that way. I'm not sleeping with you when you're this drunk." She led him to the other bedroom and helped him slide under the covers of the bottom bunk bed.

"Burlington sucks. You should stay here with me. Keep me warm in the winter. It gets really cold here." Jake rolled over on his side and immediately started to snore.

"It gets cold in Vermont too, Jake," Avery whispered back.

The next morning Avery woke up early and groggy. Jake's snoring had rattled the foundations all night long. He had finally quieted down around four am. Figured. She checked to see that he was still breathing and gathered her mist net equipment. "One more time," she said to herself. "I'm going to catch the little bugger." And she took off for the White pine where she first found Minnie's diary.

EIGHTH LAKE
JANUARY 1882

Jeff was hammering the mark onto the ends and sides of the stacked logs while Jake measured and scaled them for market using his caliper. Once he had a reading for a log he would mark it on his tally board. On a good day the two of them could measure and mark at least forty of these logs and load them on sledges where they would be toted by horse to the banks of the Raquette River. Once there, they sat until spring thaw. Jeff didn't like the spring thaw. While some men reveled in it, he was more cautious. Maybe it was because he was a father now and had mouths to feed and a wife he loved.

When spring thaw came he was assigned the kedging process — that was less risky than being a river driver. At least with kedging he felt he had more control. Getting the logs into the sluiceways with a boom was the easy part. But once the logs started heading downstream all hell could break loose when the river currents took over. Some of the young men, and he had to admit he was once one of them, loved the thrill of tracking the logs and breaking up any jams.

He remembered those days; it was the life of a vagabond, following the logs downstream until they reached their destiny at a mill. It was how he met Jake, and in turn Sarah.

Jake had been a cook at his moveable camp that followed the logs downriver. Jeff smiled at Jake thinking about it. The boy had come a long way. It didn't take long before people realized Jake could read and write and the lumber camp needed him for more than cooking. He was an expert at measuring and scaling now. And he was young and had energy and skill like none of the others. In the summer months Jake could peel more hemlock bark with his spud in a day with dexterity and skill than any of them. Jeff could only imagine he learned it from Isaac and all the work they did over the years building canoes and packs.

Jeff had nothing but admiration for the Lawrence family. Was glad he married Sarah. It was love at first sight as far as he was concerned. It was two years ago, after a few of their men had died that day on the river, drowned. Jeff had witnessed it and was shaken up by the whole experience. The foreman suggested he and the rest of the crew take a day to recover from the shock. So Jake brought him to the Lawrence household for the night.

After a fine meal of potatoes, corn, fried onions and fish, they gathered around the fire with the others in the Lawrence family, including Sarah, and the old grandmother whom they all called Mémé. Isaac said to Jeff, "Tell me what happens when men drown in a river run."

Jeff was taken aback that Isaac had lived in the woods all these years and had never witnessed a river run before, but then Isaac was mostly a trapper. What business did he have watching the log drives that were destroying the woods he depended on?

"It started off clean enough," Jeff sighed and looked into the fire. "But there was still some ice on the river. The logs got jammed up in it. And the water was moving fast, all that snow melt, ya know?"

The family looked solemnly at Jeff and nodded to show they understood what he meant. It had been an unusually warm spring and the heavy accumulation of snow on the peaks was melting fast. The cold, crisp water came rushing down the mountaintops, sloughing off the debris, rocks, and stones in a mad rush to reach the nearest river. They knew not to go too close to the river when this happened, even for fishing.

"It isn't worth a fight with the fish, let him win," Isaac would warn when one of them was going to fish. "Don't go in the river

226

when the snow is still melting."

Jeff looked at his rapt audience and continued the sad story. "My crew was working their way to the jam but these young lumberjacks, it was their first time out and they just had to prove themselves; they rowed on ahead of us. We tried to get them to slow down and wait for us. But they wouldn't listen. There's nothing like the thrill of a river jam; it's hard to explain but the blood starts pumping through you as if it is gonna explode ya know, and you just have this feeling in your gut like no other in the world. There in front of you are these massive logs, the roar of the water and you and your pike and peavey ready to conquer it all. By the time we reached them in our boat they were in the thick of it. They was enjoyin' it too. Hoopin' and hollerin' as if it was all a game to them. We worked one end of the jam while they tried to dislodge the logs that had gotten clogged up with the chunk of ice. One of them was trying to push the ice out of the way while John was using his pike on the logs to get 'em back out into the current."

Jeff let out a long sigh and shivered. Sarah got up from her seat and placed a fur wrap around him. He looked on her kindly and started again.

"And that's when it happened. John wasn't payin' attention and once the ice was let loose all of the logs that had jammed up by it went flyin' downriver, including the one John was pikin' at. He fell overboard and the men in the boat tried their damndest to retrieve him but a log hit him in the head and he went under. And then all hell broke loose cause their boat upended from all their exertions and the men in the boat went under as well."

Mémé came up to Jeff from out of nowhere and gave him some tea in a tin cup. Jeff took it and thanked her. The group was quiet. Isaac never took his eyes off Jeff, but never spoke either. The long silence left Jeff with an eerie feeling, but the Lawrence family seemed to take it in stride. They knew if a person had a story to tell, it would eventually all come out. Jeff went on.

"We tried to reach them. We was rowin' and rowin' but the current was hard, fast. By the time we got to their boat they was gone under. Those logs were plowing right over them. A hit from one of them logs is all it takes to drown a man."

Jeff stayed the night with Jake's family and found comfort in the smells of body odor mixed with balsam. He was warm and snug under covers of fur, and for the first time since he could remember he slept like a baby. In the morning Sarah came to him while he was packing up and handed him a pouch filled with food and a trinket. It was a necklace made from leather with a small wood carving of a turtle. "The turtle can swim," she said to Jeff. "Can you swim?"

Jeff was surprised by her question. Of course he could swim, what boy brought up in these woods couldn't swim? "Yes," he said.

"Then you won't drown. And even if you fall in the river, you can do as the turtle does, and rest on top of the log." Sarah smiled as she put the leather necklace over his head.

Jeff blushed and held the small turtle carving in his hand. "Thank you." No girl had ever given him a gift before. And that sealed the deal for him. They were married within a year, a small celebration in the longhouse with her family.

Jeff's reminiscing was interrupted when the foreman showed up. "Jake, your brother Ike is here," he said.

Jake looked quizzically at Jeff, both men knew Ike should be trapping with Isaac. Jeff's hands were frozen stiff from the work and he flexed his fingers to bring the blood back to them. Then he cupped his hands and lifted them to his mouth to breathe warm air into his palms. It hurt when the blood finally started to come back. He stamped his feet, realizing they had gone numb as well. "I'll go talk to him. You finish marking," Jeff said.

He approached the logger's shanty with dread. He knew the only thing that would drag Ike away from his traps was a family emergency of some sort, and he prayed and hoped it wasn't Sarah or one of the children.

When he got inside though he knew it wasn't Sarah that brought Ike to the logger's camp. It was Louise. Ike was holding one of her shawls, it was covered in blood and he was crying.

Sarah's toddler was screaming. Louise was frazzled. She had hardly any sleep the night before. Sarah's baby, Nate, had a fever and the two of them were up all night trying to console him. Every hour they soaked a piece of linen with cold water and cooled his small body with it. Louise finally nodded off at the break of dawn only to be woken within the hour by Sarah's toddler who was hungry for her porridge. And the sliver of water left over from last night was frozen solid in the bucket.

"Shhhh," she tried to calm the girl. "Your mother and baby brother are sleeping." Where was Mémé? She needed her. No wonder she liked to stay in the other house, it was the only place to get sleep. As if on cue the old woman walked through the door.

"Fetch some water from the creek," she said to Louise.

Louise was glad for the reprieve. She pulled on her shawl, grabbed another bucket and headed for the door.

"Your gun," Mémé said. She picked up the screaming toddler and glanced at the rifle hanging above the door.

Louise took her gun down from the mount and made for the creek in the woods.

It was quiet. The falling snow muffled any sounds. It was a few minutes before she could hear the gurgling creek. Her thoughts turned to William, wondering when she would see him again. It had been three months since he had promised to come back. Now she wondered if he would. Her father suggested she find employment next Spring at one of the hotels with Emaline. But she stubbornly refused to believe the Durants wouldn't want her back. She and Ike had been very faithful to the family. It wasn't fair that her love for William would make her an outcast. What kind of family was it that didn't appreciate love?

She finally reached the creek and knelt down to collect water.

The sound of the creek was soothing. After her bucket was full she sat down on her shawl for a moment to enjoy the sound before heading back to the din at the cabin.

She was looking across the creek when she saw them: cat tracks in the snow. And blood. There was a kill here recently. Louise imagined that an unsuspecting deer was drinking from the creek when a wild cat came upon it and dragged it into the forest. They prowled these woods but were rarely seen. Louise shuddered and picked up the bucket to head back. She must tell Ike to set a trap for the beast.

As she was reaching for her shawl she heard a low growl. Startled, she looked up to find a cougar slinking along the other side of the creek. He had been stalking her. He bared his teeth and stopped once he was directly across from her. His large eyes turned to slits as they locked on hers.

What a fool she was for lingering. Every predator knows a creek is where to find unsuspecting prey.

Slowly, Louise reached for the rifle slung across her back and brought it in front of her.

The cat crouched low to the ground, ears pinned back on its head, ready to pounce.

Her heart was racing. She had moments to shoot before he lunged at her. The distance between them was less than a rod. He could easily reach her in one leap.

She aimed above his head figuring when he did spring it would hit him in the chest. A flicker of a thought passed through her mind that Ike would miss her singing.

The last thing she heard was the click of the trigger of her gun. It was this exact moment she realized in her haste to retreat from the cabin she had forgotten to load it.

Part Four

NEW YORK CITY
FEBRUARY 1882

It bothered William to have to wait in Sutphen's office. Secretly, William disdained the man. Trying to think of a word that described him, William realized what he disliked most was Sutphen's lack of what the Germans called, *einfühlen*. He had no idea why his father continued to employ him. Although maybe Sutphen's lack of empathy was what his father found most valuable.

William suspected the two of them were behind some shady dealings with the Adirondack Railroad investments. William had been appointed President of the corporation in January, and this was the third time he had been summoned from Saratoga to sign certificates of shares. Each time, the names on the shares were left blank and William was instructed by his father to sign, and not ask any questions. This time though, he had questions.

It was becoming readily apparent that his father was desperate for cash.

A telling sign all was not well was the delay, and in some cases, outright denial of orders he placed for materials and supplies to continue construction at Pine Knot. Just before coming to the Railroad offices he had checked on the shipment dates for furniture and was told by the New York merchant "Cash only, credit would not be extended."

And then last week, while visiting the Durant home in North Creek William was passing the library when he overheard his parents arguing about money.

His mother was crying, "Pet, I know some of the stock shares for the Railroad are in my name, can't we just sell them and raise money that way?"

"What do you think I am, Hannah? A magician? Do you think I can just snap my fingers and money will magically appear?" Dr. Durant bellowed.

"You know I've never asked you to do anything that you are not capable of. But Pet, be reasonable. There must be some investment we can access? What happened to your plans to sell the Adirondack Railroad land holdings?"

"I've had enough of this! You and William both need to stop meddling in my affairs!"

When he heard this last declaration William felt it was necessary to intercede, if for no other reason than to defend himself against his father's tirade. Just as he reached for the door handle, Margaret was standing next to him with a tray of tea. Although she must have heard everything, she appeared completely unruffled as she knocked on the door to the library.

"Who is it?" Dr. Durant yelled from within.

William opened the door for Margaret. She gave him a crooked smile and entered.

William was startled when Sutphen's clerk came out to the waiting room to retrieve him. "Mr. Durant, Mr. Sutphen will see you now."

William rose and followed him into the interior of Sutphen's spacious office. No wonder we're broke, William mused, the man has a bigger office than me.

"Mr. Durant." Sutphen looked up briefly from what he was doing, writing some last minute instructions. He handed the note to his clerk and gestured for William to take a seat at the large mahogany desk in the middle of the room. William sat down.

"Coffee or tea?" Sutphen inquired.

"No thank you, I just came from the Union Club."

"Very well. Let's get down to business then shall we?"

"Yes."

Sutphen rose from his desk chair and collected a large folder from his desktop. He placed it in front of William.

"This shouldn't take long. I just need you to sign off on these shares."

William opened the folder and shuffled through the twenty or so certificates — shares in the company stocks — the line bearing the holder's name left blank, to be filled in, when and to whom? after he signed them.

"I would like to know to whom exactly am I selling these shares?" William said as he closed the folder. He made no move to pick up the pen that had been placed next to his right hand.

Sutphen's brows flickered. "It is standard procedure for the company to obtain signed certificates in anticipation of future sales. I cannot be expected to draw these each and every time there is an inquiry for shares of stock. Signing these gives me the freedom to move expediently when the opportunity arises. This isn't the first time you have signed blank certificates, Mr. Durant. Is there a reason you need to know now?" His eyes locked on William's.

William shifted uncomfortably in his seat. *What did this man know about his family's finances?* He cleared his throat. "I think I would enjoy a cup of tea after all," he said.

"Very well then." Sutphen opened the door to his office to find his clerk. "Jones, bring us a tray of tea." He came back and took his seat across from William at the table. "Your father expects you to sign these. He left me no further instructions."

"Yes, I see. But then, for whom do you work? Me and the Adirondack Railroad Company, or my father?"

Sutphen's lips curled into a slight smile, which did nothing to improve his sinister appearance. "Mr. Durant, rest assured that as the lawyer for the Adirondack Railroad Company I represent the interests of your father, a stockholder, and by default, the Durant family. Selling these stock shares is imperative to the solvency of the Railroad. As President of the corporation you should be aware of the gravity of the situation at hand."

William had no idea what the situation at hand really was; he just knew his company was insolvent and his parents were once again on the brink of financial ruin. It was a replay of the Panic of 1873. How naïve he was to think that by becoming the official owner of the company, whatever economic quagmire the family was in would be fixed. William realized he was President in name only.

"Just do what I tell you," his father would say whenever William tried to prise more information out of him about company strategy. He was perplexed about why he was being left in the dark. And at this moment, staring back at Sutphen, his anger got the best of him. *To hell with his father and his games.*

"I'm the President now, not my father. And as such I have every right to know who exactly is purchasing these shares," William practically spit out the last sentence as he glared into Sutphen's eyes.

"I see. Maybe then you should take this up with Dr. Durant? These certificates can wait," Sutphen said and in one smooth motion made a move to reach for the folder. William put his hand over it to prevent him from taking it away.

"I will. And I'll take these with me." William picked them off the table and put them in his leather satchel.

Sutphen gave off a heavy sigh as his clerk came in with a tray of tea. William watched as the clerk served the tea, appearing out of sorts about the whole affair, flustered and nervous — like he didn't know what he was doing. His long neck and blushing skin reminded William of the flamingoes he shot while hunting in Egypt. He gave himself a moment to reminisce about his adventures there, a reprieve from this awful encounter with Sutphen. The clerk finished serving and left them.

"That would be impossible I'm afraid. I cannot have these certificates leave the office. It would be a disaster if they were somehow lost and not in my care." He gestured toward the tray between them, "Do you take milk or sugar with your tea?"

William shook his head no. Sutphen was stonewalling him and

he was running out of options. He knew if he didn't sign these certificates his father would be enraged and threaten to cut off his allowance, or worse have him fired as President of the company. Meager as the pay was, it was all William had and his membership to the Union Club was coming due, so was the rent for his flat in Saratoga.

He took a sip and held back a look of disgust over the tepid liquid, realizing he had yet to meet an American who knew how to properly brew tea. Avoiding Sutphen's sneer, it took all of his effort to reach for the documents in his satchel where he had just placed them.

"I'll sign these then if that is what is necessary to keep the Railroad Company solvent." He tried to keep his hand steady as he picked up the pen to sign.

"It is indeed," Sutphen said, pretending not to notice William's obvious discomfort.

The cold air slapped William in the face when he finally got outside Sutphen's building and into the New York streets. He lifted the collar of his wool coat up as far as it would reach on his neck and shuddered at the image of Sutphen hovering over the documents he had just signed. He couldn't shake the feeling that he had just signed away his life. He walked briskly toward his office and wondered how Louise was faring. He had told Ike in case of an emergency to send news by way of telegraph. Cousin Frederick had one installed at Prospect House. When he had the opportunity, William planned to get a telegraph line set up at Pine Knot so they could communicate.

When he arrived at his office there was a telegram from Ella. She was in New York City, had a suite of rooms at the Sherwood House and wanted him to stay with her. Her message concluded with: *"I'm attending the Trinity Church charity ball. Would you be willing to accompany me?"*

So their father was letting her travel to New York City without a chaperone. Given the arguments at North Creek about finances,

William was surprised she could book a suite anywhere.

William looked over the rest of the mail and messages on his desk. Along with Ella's telegram there was also one from his father that read:

"Mother is frantic over Ella's whereabouts. If you receive word from her, tell her to contact home immediately."

He shuffled a few papers around. His family's affairs, the events at the furniture merchant's store, and then the indignity of signing blank certificates while drinking stale tea with the insipid Sutphen had left him spent. He looked up at the clock and wondered how to reply to Ella and his father. He was in no mood for Ella's antics. And he was sure she planned a clandestine meeting with Poultney. He had no intention of getting in the middle of the two of them ever again. Nor did he want to act as peacekeeper between Ella and his father.

He let out a sigh, took a watch out of his vest pocket and looked at the time. If he could find a cab quickly he had time to see Ella before his appointment at Delmonicos.

Ella rearranged her boudoir to make room for her dresses. *Maybe she had brought too many?* She knew she was just filling in time, waiting to hear from William. She had checked in earlier that morning after a fretful train ride from North Creek and was hoping they would connect and he would escort her to dinner.

She hung the last of her tea dresses in the wardrobe, sat down on the bed and stared at the door. If William wasn't going to call on her maybe she would call on Martha. The events of the last twenty-four hours had shaken her and she needed to talk to somebody.

It started when meddlesome Margaret came into her bedroom while she was folding her clothes and packing her trunk. Still acting as though she was her governess, Margaret immediately demanded of Ella where she thought she was going without an escort. This interrogation led the two to argue and eventually her mother overheard the commotion. She ascended the stairs, entered Ella's room and inquired where she was heading.

"I accepted the invitation from Reverend Dix to attend the Trinity Church charity ball," Ella took a moment from packing to address her mother. Margaret stood across the bed from Ella like a vulture waiting for a wounded animal to die so it could feast.

Ella continued packing as Margaret clucked her disapproval. Ella glared at her and unfurled a petticoat in the direction of her face, hoping it would snap on her mouth, taking the place of her own hand.

"You can't go gallivanting off to New York City unescorted to a charity event Ella. I have already responded to Morgan that we are unable to attend," Hannah said.

"Well good for you, Mother. I know how much you tire of traveling back and forth to New York City. But I'm still young and would like to socialize with people who are not only my own age, but also have better manners and a larger vocabulary than the farmers and miners in North Creek."

"Humph," Margaret said.

Ella turned to her. "Would you kindly leave this matter to my mother and me?"

Hannah gestured for Margaret to leave.

"Ella." Hannah kept her voice low as she took hold of her daughter's arm and held it tight. "I'm not sure if you are quite aware of our family's financial predicament."

"What are you talking about?" Ella wrested her arm away and went to her dresser to pick out jewels to pack.

Hannah started wringing her hands and pacing the floor.

"To put it simply, the railroad has run out of track, your father has come up short with investments to carry the railroad to Canada and in case you haven't been reading the news lately, the Adirondack Railroad Company is bankrupt."

Ella tittered nervously. "As I recall we have been in this situation before and Father has always found a way out of it."

Hannah shook her head. "It's such a disgrace, I know!"

Ella noticed she was on the verge of tears.

"Mother, what's wrong?" She went over to her mother and put

her hand on her arm gently guiding her to sit on the bed.

Hannah's eyes welled up with tears. "I have nothing left to sell. He has spent all of the money we acquired from my father's property in Brooklyn, and I sold all of my jewels when we left England during the last crisis. I have nothing left to give." Hannah started to sob. "There is no one to borrow from, there is nowhere to turn."

Ella held her close and looked out at the dreary streets of North Creek. A thought occurred to her.

"All the more reason for me to go," Ella said, determined. If she had learned anything from her time in England and the plight of the landed gentry who found themselves titled but penniless, it was that maintaining an air of prosperity while suffering penury left the door open to opportunity. She still needed a publisher for her book of poetry, and Morgan Dix had assured her that George Putnam from Putnam and Sons Publishing House was coming to the ball.

"Mother, listen. Don't fret. I'll represent the family in a dignified manner. Can you imagine if none of us attend? After all that the Dix family has done for us and General Dix, rest his soul, did for father and the Union Pacific? The least I can do is attend in honor of him. They would be very disappointed in us otherwise."

Hannah sat up and sighed. She patted her daughter's hand. "You do know how to charm don't you?"

"It's settled then, I'm taking a train in the morning. Jem is driving me to the station."

"But where will you stay dear? William no longer has his apartment and I don't think you'll be allowed to stay with him at the hotel."

"Don't worry about that. I have it all figured out. I'm staying with Martha Parker."

Hannah stood up. "Heavens no. Your father will already be upset with me for allowing you to go unaccompanied to New York, you mustn't stay with that woman!"

"Where would you have me stay then? The Dix's have company coming in for the ball and you said yourself I can't stay with William."

"I don't know Ella, but we can hardly pay the servants much less pay for a fancy hotel." She sat back down on the bed and pondered for a moment. "Don't tell me you're chasing after that Bigelow fellow!" she said.

"Of course not, don't be absurd," Ella said as she stayed focused on her packing so she would not have to meet her mother's eyes.

"I know how much you adore him dear but he is not right for you," Hannah said.

"Oh he's not is he?"

"No, he is much too, what's the word I am searching for? Cocky. Yes, much too sure of himself that one. And for no good reason either."

"Well I assure you, I am not going to New York City in pursuit of Poultney." Ella failed to mention the real reason for her journey — to meet Putnam.

"As much as I'd like to believe you, I know you better. Ella, swear to me you will not make a fool of yourself for him! I know how much you long to return to London but he is not your savior. Besides, your father has never approved of him. And call it mother's intuition but the two of you would make a horrible match. You are both too much alike — head-strong." She shook her head.

"You have to admit Mother, he is much more appealing than some of the dolts trying to court me here in North Creek."

Hannah did not disagree. "But still there are other prospective men your father has suggested you consider."

"Hah! Wealthy industrialists twenty years my senior. I'd rather stay a spinster than marry someone like Papa."

"Hold your tongue Ella. He has his faults but he has provided for us."

Ella was tired of arguing with her misguided mother. She went back to her dresser to collect the jewelry she intended to take. Looking up at her mother from the mirrored reflection she said, "Don't worry, Mother. I'll stay with Estelle."

Ella had no intention of staying with Estelle; it would be no better for her under Uncle Charles' roof than here in North Creek. The domineering tyrant would be telling her and Estelle where and when they could go out and about in the city and with whom. But Ella wasn't about to let her mother or father know the truth. She had been squirreling away the money she was making selling poems and short stories to *The Queen* and other ladies magazines. She knew where she could board without anyone taking notice: the Sherwood House, although risqué, was cheap. And nobody, including her mother, was going to stop her from meeting the publisher George Putnam.

The next morning Ella watched from the front entrance as Jem Stone put her overflowing trunk of gowns in the carriage. She was putting on her gloves when Margaret slinked up close and said, "I suggest you take meals in. The servants are resentful that the mistress of the house is dallying in New York City while their pay is delinquent."

Once again, Ella found herself staring down into the pinched face of her mother's companion. Memories of Margaret's terrifying predictions of her downfall when she misbehaved as a girl came flooding back. How she loathed the woman.

"I hardly think one delay in payment will cause my parents' faithful servants to abandon their station. Nor is my social life any of their business."

Margaret managed a sinister smile that made Ella uneasy. She leaned into Ella and said in a hushed tone, "Maybe not. But be careful, Ella, or you may end up becoming the very woman you vilify. An old maid like me, whose only available occupation is a governess of spoiled children and companion for a tired old dame who thinks she still deserves the respect that wealth brings."

"You're an evil woman Margaret," Ella hissed back. "Why my mother has allowed you to stay with us all of these years is beyond me. But I will not have you talk about her that way."

Margaret shrugged. "I'm still here because she has no choice now does she? I have always been there for her and know more about this family's secrets than you or your brother. What would happen to the family's reputation if I were to be cast out on the street as you so desire?"

It took only a second for the familiar rush of blood to reach Ella's head, bringing with it the heat and oxygen she needed to lift her hand and bring it across Margaret's smirking face. The sound startled them both. Jem Stone saw it all from the carriage, although he did not know the cause.

"Is everything alright Miss Durant?" He came up the porch steps to find Ella looking bewildered and Miss Molineaux, her complexion a crimson red, gawking and holding one hand to the cheek Ella had struck. Neither was speaking.

Ella started to tremble. "Take me to the station now. I have had enough of this household." She fastened her cloak around her neck and fled out the door.

"Why is father asking me where you're staying in New York?" William demanded to know as Ella opened the door to her room at the Sherwood House, hoping he was coming to take her to dinner.

"Good evening, William, so nice of you to stop by." Ella swept her hands in toward the room to allow him entrance. "Not exactly the Astor House, but then you get that privilege, not me."

"This place is a disgrace," William said as he looked around, afraid to sit on the divan for fear it might host fleas.

"This suite of rooms is all father can afford from what I understand," she said, not wanting to tell him she was paying for the rooms herself. "Besides, the keeper is being kind to let you stay here with me. She doesn't approve of male guests and rarely takes them in. She is only allowing you to stay with me because I convinced her you were my brother."

"Well I am after all aren't I?" William looked around at the shabby surroundings. "Father doesn't know you're here and if he did he wouldn't approve. Wherever did you find this place?" William lifted one of Ella's shawls off the arm of a chair and placed it on the cushion before he sat down.

Ella frowned and walked toward him. "Get off that, it is one of my better shawls," she said as she pulled at the corner of the shawl that was sticking out from under his trousers.

William lifted himself off the chair and handed her the shawl. She wrapped herself in it.

"I can't stay anyway." He skimmed his pointer finger along the table to see how much dust it would pick up and then rubbed it off with his thumb.

"I'm meeting Malcolm Forbes in about a half hour. I just wanted to stop in and check on you before I telegraph father. He asked me to look out for you."

"You're meeting Forbes, the financier? What for?"

"He's an avid yachtsman, like me. Don't worry your pretty little head about it." William nicked her on the chin and went to the door.

"Please don't tell Father I'm staying here."

"Why not stay with Martha Parker?"

"Both mother and father disapprove of her. The least I could do was find an alternative accommodation. Besides, Martha has a new beau. I'm not sure who it is yet, but she's been alluding to it in her letters lately. I didn't want to intrude, if you understand my meaning."

William rolled his eyes. "Only too well."

"Aren't you a bit quick to judge?"

Out of the corner of his eye William caught a glimpse of the dim yellow carpeting and the worn-out pattern of green tendrils and thistle. The white spray of thread along the edges was frayed and dusty looking. For some reason the thistle reminded him of the cabin he had built for Louise and the thick bear rug that Ike draped on the plank floors for Sarah's baby to crawl on.

"How is Louise faring by the way?" Ella knew him so well.

William was quickly brought back to the squalid conditions of the suite and the pathetic attempt by his sister to behave like a socialite.

"I'll stay in the other room tonight Ella, but tomorrow you need to call on Estelle and stay with Uncle Charles. Father would be livid if he knew you were here." He changed the subject.

"That is impossible." Ella bristled at the suggestion. "I won't stay with Uncle Charles, he's worse than father."

"Then your visit to New York ends after the ball. I will not allow you to stay here any longer than you have to and I don't want to either."

When William left, Ella looked around her and tried to ward off a wave of depression by opening up the latest letter she had received from Poultney. She thought it might lift her spirits, until she read it:

Dearest Ella:

I hope you are well. I am bravely working my way through the last semesters of law school, knowing full well I have no intention of becoming a lawyer for anyone. But alas, it was what my father wanted of me and I feel obligated to abide by his wishes.

I received your last poem – 'Friends' – I assume it was aimed at me?

Ella I apologize for misleading you in any way. We are both adults and are free to do as we choose. You however are bound by your family's dictates of propriety and social status that I am not sure I can ever fulfill. I will always be a parvenu in your mother's eyes, and I unfortunately lack the industriousness your father demands of his offspring and their suitors. I am but a poor writer, making his mark by his pen. It is not an illustrious career choice, nor will it bring your family's fortunes any higher than they already are. (Ella found that comment especially ironic given her family's current financial predicament).

And my life would be so very boring to you my dear as I travel the world seeking out stories of government corruption and reform in far off places in squalid conditions – no place for a lady of your upbringing.

I do hope you forgive me and do not fret over this too much. We can, although I sense the sarcasm in your poem, remain friends. For a lifetime.

Yours affectionately,
Poultney Bigelow

Ella stared at the letter one more time before putting it down and picking up her journal. She flipped to the poem 'Friends' she had indeed written for him.

No, let us part, we ne'er can be
Mere friends, since liking has grown such
It needs but word, or look, or touch
To change it to love's ecstasy.
Mere friends? why dost thou when alone seem moved, and speak in accents low.
And let gaze, voice soft, tender grow till all my firm resolves are gone
When thou couldst ask, nor be denied
Mere friends? Why does the warm blood creep into my cheeks when thou art near;

For friend to thee I cannot be.
If through the years some strength I gain,
Then can my soul with struggle o'er,
Know friendship's pleasure as of yore
Without this passion and this pain.
But now, O! deem me not unkind. That I fain banish from mine eyes
Thine image I too dearly prize;
We part — since thou as friend art blind.

Ella shut her journal and stared at her bleak surroundings.

William and Ella descended from the carriage to find their cousin Howard waiting for them at the entrance to the downtown hotel that was hosting the charity ball for the Trinity Church committee on social welfare. The committee was made up of the wives of industrialists who were eager to show they cared about the plight of child laborers and unwed mothers.

As they entered the enormous ballroom the threesome heard the clinking of glasses echoing throughout the two-story room. William and Ella held back as Howard went headlong into the crowd once he recognized a client from his family's refinery business.

They looked around for their friend Morgan Dix and spotted him chatting with a small group of women around a bowl of punch. Ella wandered over to the group, leaving William to fend off an eager investor who had skirted past several couples to introduce himself, and without further inquiry as to their well-being, launched into a slew of questions for William about the Adirondack Railroad Company.

"What we need is a decent place for these mothers to bring their children for health services, education, and once in awhile, a decent meal." A rotund woman was pressing her point to a rapt audience of ladies holding crystal punch glasses that held some type of pink-tinted liquid.

"Ella, my dear, so glad you could come." The Reverend looked up from the discerning group of women to acknowledge Ella standing at the edge waiting for an opportunity to say hello. He reached for her hand and brought her into the fold.

"Ladies, may I introduce you to a dear family friend, Heloise Durant."

The women nodded politely.

"Please call me Ella." Ella shook hands with the four women as Morgan introduced them by name.

"We were just discussing the need for a shelter for the influx of laborers and their families coming to the city and faced with very unsanitary conditions," explained one of the women.

"I'm sure Ella would love to hear more, but I might steal her away for a minute so I can let my wife know she is here. We were worried about your arrival." Morgan looked over at Ella. She blushed, wondering if her father had contacted him.

"Oh, yes, the roads this time of year are just awful aren't they? And the railroads are no better — ice on the rails will stop a train in its tracks!" One of the ladies provided an excuse for Ella to keep quiet.

Ella said good bye to the drab-looking group of women, momentarily sensing she was over-coiffed. She realized her corset was tied too tight, her bosom heaved a bit too high, and her neckline plunged a little too low for this crowd. Perhaps she had misunderstood the purpose of the ball? She had been under the impression from the invitation that there would be dancing and gaiety, but the mood was rather somber.

Morgan gently glided Ella through the room until they landed next to his wife Emily. She was close in age to Ella and he knew they enjoyed each other's company.

"Ella, so nice to see you dear." Emily Dix held Ella in her arms and brushed both her cheeks with a kiss. "Tell me how are your mother and father? Well I hope?"

"Oh yes, they send their love," Ella responded. She looked over Emily's gown: a simple white waist-dress, feminine and refined with small pink bows tying each sleeve delicately around her petite arms. "Emily that gown you have on is absolutely lovely. I wish I was wearing something like it," Ella said.

"Why thank you Ella," Emily said.

"Ella, I wonder if you recall the short verse my father wrote you on your birthday celebration in Paris years ago?" Morgan said.

Ella nodded.

"As I am writing his memoir and would like to include it. Maybe you would write it down and send it to me?"

"Of course, Morgan," Ella said.

"Tell me," Emily said, taking hold of Ella's right arm. "I saw Howard, is your cousin Estelle coming as well?"

Ella looked around a bit bewildered. She hadn't even had a

chance to ask Howard if Estelle was coming. She just assumed she would, given that most of New York's social elite were her friends.

"I forgot to ask. Quite frankly it has been a bit of a whirlwind since I arrived. Both Howard and William started right into business conversations."

"Well I do miss her and our outings together. Perhaps we could call on her while you're here and do some shopping together?"

"There are the stars of the ball," William said as he walked up to them.

"William!" Emily extended her hand. "So nice of you to come and support my husband's charity work."

"My pleasure." William bowed as he took her hand and kissed it solemnly. "Morgan, so good to see you again."

"Good to see you as well William, how is your dear mother?"

"Fine, fine."

"Oh, William, before I lose sight of you, I wanted to introduce you to Andrew Carnegie." Morgan took William in hand and escorted him to meet the Scotsman.

Emily pulled Ella aside and said, "I do hope they get moving on with the night's activities. After Morgan's speech there should be music."

Ella scanned the crowd wondering who among them was George Putnam. It was just like William to get to meet the men he needed to fulfill his destiny while she waited on the sidelines. She decided to take a chance and ask Emily if she knew which of the men milling about was Putnam.

"Yes. In fact, there he is." She used her small pink Asian fan hanging from her wrist to point out Putnam. "Come, I'll introduce you both."

And they proceeded toward the man that Ella hoped would be her future ticket into a life as an independent woman and writer.

After her discussion with Putnam and the go ahead to send her collection of poems, Ella found herself increasingly bored. The tea-totallers orchestrating the event had no intention of allowing the guests to revel in the libations that were at the root of so many of the societal ills befalling the very poor of New York City. Besides, they were too busy making speeches. Reverend Dix made a somewhat monotone plea for support of the work of the Trinity Church charities. And the ladies who had been conferring over the punch bowl made their way to the podium to lament the sinful state of affairs of the poor immigrant families that were flocking to the city and swelling the tenements.

Ella stifled a yawn and looked for William. Last time she'd seen him, he was flirting with a young woman Howard had introduced him to — Miss Stewart, a socialite that hailed from a wealthy Chicago family. She finally spotted her brother alone in the corner watching over the crowd, looking bored as well. She walked over to stand by his side while the speeches were being made.

"Keeping yourself busy Ella?" William said.

"You noticed? I hardly thought you were paying attention to anything but Miss Stewart."

"Oh, I can take in a lot at once." William smiled. He watched Ella's eyes dart about the room. "You won't see him here. This isn't his type of gathering."

"Whoever do you mean?" Ella flicked open her fan and waved it over her face to hide her wandering eyes.

"I mean Poultney. He won't show up here."

"Pfft," Ella said. "I don't care. Men have been fawning over me all night."

William let out a short laugh and the people around them glared.

"Hmmm, I guess you're right to be cynical. This affair isn't quite as gay as the balls at Binstead we used to attend is it?" Ella smiled under her fan.

"There you are, I've been looking all over for the two of you," Howard said and pulled out a small flask from the interior of his waistcoat. "Would you like to liven up that punch?" He gestured at William's glass. William extended it.

Howard leaned in toward his cousins. "Let's get out of here," he said so that others would not overhear him. "They have my check and I don't think I can stand another lecture about the working poor. Besides, I told Estelle I would meet up with her and her new beau at Sherry's. Miss Stewart and her cousin may be interested as well." He looked over at the two young women stoically listening to the endless speeches. Without asking if his cousins agreed, Howard walked over to the ladies to invite them to come to Sherry's.

Ella, Howard and William took Howard's carriage while Miss Stewart's driver escorted the ladies to Sherry's to meet them. Ella looked out the carriage window at the streetscapes of New York City as Howard rambled on about the refinery business. The freshly fallen snow made everything sparkle. As the driver took them through the theater district on Broadway, Ella longed to be amongst the bustle of crowds exiting the shows. She watched as people poured out of the theaters and climbed over the mounds of snow that had been plowed from the streets and piled up along the sidewalks to make room for the carriages and trolleys. And then she saw them: Poultney and Martha – coming out of the Star Theater just as the driver turned their carriage onto 13th Street.

"Isn't that your friend Poultney Bigelow?" Howard asked Ella when he noticed her gazing at the pair. The carriage had stopped at the intersection and she hoped they did not see her gaping at them from the window. She quickly leaned back in her seat so she wouldn't be detected. How absurd, she thought. It was not as if she didn't know them to be friends. She peered out the window once again.

Martha was leaning on Poultney's arm. Ella watched as she turned her head toward his ear and said something that caused him to laugh. Ella sensed Poultney's pleasure to be arm and arm with Martha, who looked striking in a seal-skin coat that showed off her slim figure. Suddenly, Ella's stomach started to knot.

"I hear those two are quite the pair these days," Howard said.

"How do you mean?" Ella said.

"I mean, they're seen all over town socializing together and I hear Poultney's father is not too happy about him courting a divorcee, especially one that is almost ten years his senior. But then I say, good for him, why not? Enjoy it while you're young."

William said nothing.

"Didn't he have an eye for you at one time, Ella? As I recall he was quite smitten that summer we came up to visit your family at Pine Knot a few years ago." Howard looked directly at her.

Ella wished she could climb into her skin. She slunk down further in the carriage seat and by the time they got to Sherry's she was in no mood to socialize. "William, please take me back," she said weakly.

"What's wrong, Ella? Not feeling well?" Howard asked.

"It has been a long journey," Ella replied.

William got out with Howard and gave the driver instructions to take Ella back to the Sherwood House. "I'm staying with Howard. I'll be back later this evening," he said through the carriage window.

"You're leaving me?"

"I'll return later tonight. You should make plans to return home." He left her stewing in her seat.

Ella didn't sleep well. By four am William hadn't arrived back from Sherry's, and she tossed and turned in her bed. It was six am when he finally knocked on the door to the suite. His coat and top hat were dusted with snow and he shook them both at the entrance, allowing the snow to cascade to the floor forming a small puddle of water as it melted. He placed them on the coatrack before stepping onto the carpeting.

"Where have you been? You reek of alcohol and cigars." Ella pounced on him the moment he entered.

William swayed over to the divan and held his head in his hands. "I stayed at Howard's last night. Don't scold me, Ella, my head hurts."

"Why on earth didn't you return? I was worried sick about you."

"We stayed up late playing cards at the club. And I didn't want to wake you when I came in so I stayed at Howard's."

"Howard's indeed. You and Howard were out carousing with those young women, I'm sure of it." Ella's voice rose an octave. "I was just the fifth wheel in your plans." Her nerves were on edge from waiting anxiously for William to return. William had never abandoned her before, not even for a young lady. Their loyalties always resided with each other, and she was in desperate need of comfort after seeing that traitor Martha on the arm of Poultney.

"Stop behaving like a harpy." William looked up from his seat. "Do you want to embarrass us both by waking up the rest of the tenants with your ranting? And don't put yourself on high moral ground when you practically threw your virginity at Poultney."

Ella turned on him. "How dare you of all people say that! You hypocrite! You, who led that poor girl Louise on to think you could marry her when you have known all the while it would be absolutely impossible."

"So *you* say, Ella, but that doesn't make it true."

"Pfft." She flicked her hand in the air. "Of course I state the truth William. You know very well that Papa would never allow such a union. And to think, here you are in New York City flirting with that Miss Stewart." She walked over to the chair, picked up her shawl and draped it over her shoulders. *"T'es devenu quoi alors?"* she said under her breath.

Stung by her last remark, William stood up to leave. "Don't you dare question my integrity. I've had enough of your childish antics Ella. No wonder Poultney won't have anything to do with you. All my life I have had to safeguard you from people who wouldn't put up with your tempestuous behavior."

He retrieved his coat and hat and glared at her from the door. "Well no more. I'll have nothing more to do with you while you're here in New York City." And he walked out the door.

The door clicked shut behind him and Ella started to cry.

William hailed a carriage to take him back to his hotel. He did not appreciate Ella's accusations. Miss Stewart was an attractive young lady, charming, and a perfect match for him actually. Her family had money and was well-connected to the railroad industry — her father had business in steel. His father would be thrilled with his choice if William ever planned to marry.

Besides, last night was a pleasant diversion from the stress of everything he had been subjected to lately: the Adirondack Company's bankruptcy, his father's failing health, and lack of communication from Louise.

Failing to secure a carriage, he walked the lonely path back to his hotel room to take a nap before heading into his office.

Ella did not leave New York City right away. Damn the whole lot of them, she thought, including her brother and Poultney. She decided to take miserable Margaret's advice after all and dined in so that her small savings would last her long enough to gain another audience with George Putnam's publishing house. As directed by Mr. Putnam she had sent him a copy of her collection of poems. She titled the work *Pine Needles or Sonnets and Songs* — and was waiting for a message of encouragement.

In the meantime she had downgraded her suite of two rooms to a room with one bed, one chair and a table. She shared a toilet closet with four other women. She came to realize that the Sherwood House was a way stop for many women first coming to the city to find work. They were from small rural towns or foreign countries and left their homes either out of desperation or hope. They had a cursory education and took jobs as secretaries, clerks, housemaids or laborers in the factories.

The boardinghouse was a replacement for the family life they left behind, even if it was less than ideal. Ella was intrigued by their diverse vocabulary and unending optimism. Many were either hoping to land a husband, were giving up on ever finding one, (Ella put herself in this camp) or like her friend Mary, were avoiding one. Ella was especially fond of Mary.

She was from some small farm town in the midwest. She told Ella her story one night while sitting on Ella's trunk drinking lukewarm tea that Ella had managed to scrounge up from the cook after dinner one evening.

"He was a terrible man, my husband. I had to run away."

"But why not go back to your family then?" Ella asked.

"They wouldn't take me. They said I had made my bed I had to lie in it." Mary took a sip of her tea. "My father was a mean one as well. Thought he could solve every problem with us children with the back of his hand. I went from the frying pan into the fire for sure."

Ella loved these colloquial sayings. She overheard so many while dining with the ladies of the household. They would gossip at the table about the latest job prospects, a surly boss, or floor manager at a factory and say things like "He was fair to middlin' — meaning about average. Or her favorite when they were in a hurry to get somewhere — lickety split. She had lived in America now for more than five years and couldn't recall ever hearing these phrases from the company she kept. Or maybe she just never noticed. She was ashamed to think of how she had always shunned people like Mary.

"He would come home drunk," Mary continued, "and start fights with me all of the time over simple things like the bacon being under-cooked. Sometimes he would hit me." She looked down at her hands and wrung them together for a moment before picking up her teacup again.

"I started to save money from the allowance he gave me for food and hide it in the floorboards of the bedroom. I did this for over a year. Then one day he came home — drunk again — and he started to rave at me about the meal I had cooked. He said some terrible things to me that night, said I was worthless and barren." Mary put her hand to her womb out of habit. She looked up at Ella, pained. "I couldn't take it anymore. I told him he was a no good drunk. And that is when all hell broke loose."

Ella was gripped by the story. She imagined her own father, stewing in his anger. The one positive thing she could say about him was he controlled his temper, usually. Her mother knew how to prevent an outburst. He had never been violent with his children or his wife. "What happened?" she asked.

"He started fumbling for his belt. I knew he was going to try and use it on me. He had threatened before. I just couldn't take it!" Mary choked back tears. "I picked up the milk jug and swung it down on his head and he fell over. And then I ran into the bedroom, grabbed the money I had been stowing away under the floorboards, took a small bag of clothes I kept packed in the back of the closet, and ran to the train station. I was so lucky a train was leaving fifteen minutes after I arrived. If he had come after me I don't know what I would have done. Then I got to New York City and looked up my school friend Velvet here at the Sherwood House."

Ella knew Velvet, she worked as a clerk in a milliner shop nearby and wore the smartest hats when the girls all went for their weekly Sunday stroll in Central Park.

They sat in silence. "What do you plan to do next?"

Mary shrugged. "I've been looking for work, and I have an interview tomorrow."

"Wonderful! Where?" Ella said.

"One minute." Mary got up to go to her own room to find the newspaper advertisement for the job.

"See here? It says secretary needed." She retrieved the newspaper and pointed excitedly at the ad. "And I can read and write as good as anybody, I made it all the way through the eighth grade."

Ella looked over the advertisement. "Why, I know this man. His company does business with my father. Let me write you a recommendation letter."

"You would do that for me? How grand you are!"

"And what do you plan to wear to the interview tomorrow?" Ella asked as she glanced at Mary's attire. Mary's wardrobe left much to be desired, she feared she would make a fool of herself in an uptown office; one look at her shoes and they would show her the exit.

"I don't know." Mary looked down at her worn-out waist coat and fiddled with a loose string hanging from the hem.

"Well I think I have just the outfit for you." Ella brightened.

"Let's look through my trunks shall we?"

Mary was offered the position, and the ladies all celebrated the next night with a bottle of champagne that Ella had splurged on when she heard the news.

"Ella, what do you do for work?" One of the girls asked after they had clinked their glasses in a toast.

All eyes turned to Ella.

"Well I, uh, I write." Ella stumbled for words. "Yes, that's right, I'm a writer." Saying so felt good to her own ears.

"Really? What kinds of things do you write?"

"Well I'm working on a book of poetry." The ladies murmured approval.

"And a play on the life of Dante." She received blank stares.

"Who's Dante?"

Ella looked around the table at the eager faces. "Well, he was, oh well, never mind. I also write short stories for magazines."

"Oh gee! What kind of short stories? What magazines?"

"Oh you know, silly love stories for magazines like *Godey's*, *The Queen*, that sort of thing."

"Ooooh." The ladies gave off a collective gasp of approval.

"I see the Missus reading those while I'm working. When nobody's looking I look inside at the pretty pictures," one girl whom Ella hadn't met yet told the group.

"We have a real live writer in our company!" the brown-haired girl named Shelly said. "Tell us about your latest story," she added.

"Well," Ella started nervously, then found encouragement as she looked around at her rapt audience. "It is about a young maiden who is in love with a Lord."

"Set in England then? Are you from there? Is that why you speak with an accent?" Shelly asked.

"Yes, I lived there awhile," Ella responded. "As I was saying, the fair maiden is in love with a Lord but she can't marry him."

"Why not if she's in love?" Mary said.

"Well, he is too far above her station you see. But he is in love with her as well." The ladies all nodded in sympathy.

Ella went on with the love story she had been cooking up in her head over the past few weeks. She had jotted down a few notes and struck out a lot. However, once she wrote them, these short stories seemed trite. To make them marketable she had to use a simple formula she read in all of the other works like them: man meets woman and they fall in love; something, whether it be their station, their health, or an evil family secret, kept them apart. They miraculously overcome the odds and end up married, the end.

It had to have a happy ending otherwise it wouldn't sell. It was not as if the American audience was looking for a Shakespeare tragedy. Especially if, as she observed, most of her reading audience was in any way like these ladies, fleeing to New York to seek their fortunes. Who was she to deny them?

She finished her story to a hushed silence. The ladies were enraptured.

"Tell us another one then!" said the brunette from a small town in Pennsylvania.

Ella knew she was onto something when she told them another tale about a Duke and Duchess who learn they have an illegitimate grandchild when their son dies after being thrown from a horse while fox hunting. They clamored for more. That night she got busy writing down her stories. She posted them in the mail at the end of the week to the ladies magazines to see who would offer her the most. At least these stories could keep her 'in clover' as she often heard the girls say over dinner, while she waited on Putnam to decide about her book of poetry.

A few weeks later Ella saw her father on the street. It was a wet, cold, February day. She was coming out of Neamanns' Jewelry Store where she knew her father's credit was still good, after purchasing a baby's silver cup — a christening gift for one of the Dix's grandchildren. She was lost in thought about whether the magazines would accept her short stories when she saw him. He was weaving in and out of the crowds without looking up to see where he was going, or if he was in anybody's way, a man on a mission; no doubt to attend some business meeting or gathering at his yacht club.

"Father," Ella called to him. He looked peaked, had lost some weight, and he was coughing when she stopped him.

Dr. Durant looked up to see who was interrupting his token apology to the man he had bumped into. It took a moment to realize it was his daughter. He hadn't seen her in weeks.

"Fine to see you here in the streets of New York City," he said between fits of coughing.

"Where have you been and who are you staying with these days? Your mother is worried sick, asking about you all of the time, as if I would know where you are. I readily admit I am inept when it comes to your governance," he said sarcastically.

Ella, who had reached to kiss his cheek was taken aback by his animosity and poor appearance. "I've been staying with friends," she shivered as she lied. "I wrote mother last week. And I'm doing fine, Papa, if that's what worries you."

Dr. Durant brushed that notion off like dust from his lapel. "What worries me, Ella, is that you left our household in a rage, accosted your mother's faithful companion Margaret, and are now spending your time at clubs and the theater with divorcees and actors. It is no company for a young lady." He raised his voice. "Especially one that is *unmarried*."

Ella instinctively held her package a bit closer to her chest as curious bystanders stopped to witness the scene that was unfolding in front of Neamanns.

She had slapped Margaret, it was true, but the woman deserved it for practically threatening to expose the Durant family skeletons. It was so long ago she had forgotten. If he only knew how ludicrous the rest of his accusations were he would not be accusing her of being a spendthrift. Ella barely had any of her small savings left, and what little she had wasn't even enough to attend the theater. Besides, as much as she would've liked to, there was no one to accompany her anyway. Martha had proved an unworthy friend, Poultney and William had abandoned her, and her cousins were too busy with their own beaux. None of the girls at the Sherwood House could afford it.

No one was concerned about Ella's social life, no one that is, but Ella.

She moved closer to her father and said, "This is not the place to discuss my personal life or marital state."

"Maybe you should consider where the right place is then because you have outlived your welcome in our home. It might be time to consider your alternatives as a spinster."

"Excuse me, Miss, is this man bothering you?" A young gentleman had overheard Dr. Durant berating Ella and felt compelled to stop when he saw how distressed she looked. Ella looked from the kind stranger to her father. How odd this must seem to the gawkers on the street. Her father looked wild, his hair was unkempt and straggling out of his top-hat. His ruddy cheeks were aflame. His eyes looked manic. It was as if he was another man, not her real father. He started to cough uncontrollably.

"Sir, do you know this young lady?" The gentleman inquired when the doctor had stopped coughing long enough to hear him.

"Of course I do you idiot! She's my daughter. Now leave us alone."

The startled man hurried away and the others who had stopped to see what would happen put their heads back down to the cold drafty wind and followed his cue, moving along to their destinations.

Dr. Durant tipped his hat in a gesture of courtesy and kept walking. Ella could not recall a time he had ever been so cruel.

"Are you quite sure? This doesn't sound like your father." Morgan Dix consoled Ella.

She had found her way through blinding tears to the Trinity Rectory to talk to the Reverend. He was the only one she could think to turn to after the public berating.

"It is exactly as he said it," Ella said. She knew she sounded like a dribbling fool but one look at the Reverend's calm face and she was reminded of all the kindness his family had bestowed on her and her mother and brother over the years. It was a stark contrast to how unkind her own father could be.

"Come now, chin up young lady," he said as he guided her to a chair in front of the fireplace. "Mrs. Daly is getting us some tea. The world's problems can be solved over a strong cup of tea." He patted her shoulder.

Ella smiled at him. "You're so good to me. I am sorry to be burdening you with my problems. But I have nowhere to turn."

Although just hours ago she had been confident that she could sell her stories and make a living as a writer in New York City, the confrontation with her father left her feeling insecure. If her own family would not support her, who would?

"I must confess my savings are almost exhausted and I cannot stay any longer in the city. But after that public rebuke there is no possibility of me going back to my home in North Creek, even if I did choose to grovel."

"I'm sure your mother would take you back?" Morgan said.

"I can't go back there! I was a prisoner in my own home. Is there no way for me to stay here? Could I help by cooking or cleaning at the rectory in some way?"

Mrs. Daly came in and put a tray of tea between them and Morgan poured them both a cup.

Morgan shook his head. "Menial labor is not your type of work I'm afraid. No need to stoop so low. No, I have a better plan for you. Why not enter our convent and do the good work of the Sisters as they help the poor and destitute?"

Ella lifted her head up from the scalding hot teacup in her hand. She put the cup down on the saucer and considered her prospects. The convent might be just the answer to her public humiliation, both from her father and Poultney. However.

"Don't women that enter the convent tend to, um." Ella stopped to think of how to say what she was thinking tactfully. "Aren't they considered fallen women?"

Morgan scoffed, "Fallen from what? The sky? No, the sisters you'll meet are no more fallen than the rest of the poor lonely creatures that inhabit this bagnio we call New York City. You will find Ella, there are quite a few young women such as yourself, looking for a chance to meditate and assist those in need."

Or run away from their problems in a reputable manner. "I accept your offer," she said.

When she got back to the Sherwood House she made arrangements to have all correspondence sent to the Sisters of St. Mary's Mother House. She packed her bags, said her goodbyes and never looked back when she entered the convent doors the next day.

William was sitting in his office in New York City, staring at the calling card he had received that morning from Miss Stewart; it read:

Another lovely evening at Sherry's. Thank you.

He guiltily put it away in the drawer of his desk, thinking how he too enjoyed his second date with the young lady. If only he could hold Louise in his arms, he might be able to stave off this craving for human bonding. If he didn't hear soon he would find a way to head up there, some excuse, any excuse to go. He knew he could come up with something his father would not argue about.

William was worried about his father. It had been over a month now since Ella had entered the convent, and he was forlorn and confused about why Ella had chosen this path.

Earlier in the week he had met his father at the yacht club for dinner and his father expressed his concern. In hushed tones he said, "Our family has never been over-zealous when it comes to religion. I can't think of any reason she would enter the convent except because she is a fallen woman."

"From what Morgan has told me she is not becoming a nun, father. She is assisting the poor. It is noble work." William tried to sound encouraging.

His father had looked ill. He had been coughing more than usual and recently was diagnosed with emphysema. William had suggested to him that he travel with Hannah south, to warmer climates, both to improve his father's health and to keep him out of the Adirondack Railroad business. He refused of course.

When William finally gathered the courage to ask him about the family finances, his father brushed him off, saying, "The creditors think they can take the Adirondack Railroad away from me. Well that will never happen as long as I am alive!"

"Maybe we should consider selling some of our land as you suggested? I have some plans drawn up for a development near Eagle Lake—"

His father waved him off. "It was a good plan at one time. But not now. The vultures are circling, William," Dr. Durant said.

It was a difficult discussion to have at the club with all of their friends sitting at nearby tables. Eavesdropping was not just a custom for ladies in tea parlors. Leaning in towards his father , William was about to inquire further when cousin Howard came up to greet them, ending any chance for William to pursue it.

A sharp rap on the door to his office brought William to the present.

"Mr. Durant?" It was his clerk.

"Yes? Did I forget an appointment?"

"No sir." His clerk entered with a telegram in his hand. "This came for you, sir."

"Thank you," William said as he eagerly opened it and waved him away. It was from his cousin Frederick at Prospect House on Blue Mountain Lake. It read:

Ike arrived after walking for days in a snow storm. Louise is dead.

Part Five

CAMP KIRBY
AUGUST 2010

"Avery, I'm glad I found you here." Avery was looking through her backpack to find Minnie's diary when Tom came upon her at the White pine where she was setting up her net.

"Tom, goodness you startled me!" Avery gave up looking. It occurred to her she had left it under the couch.

"So sorry. There are a few fellows here from Paul Smith's College wanting to talk to you about your research. They came with your professor, Dr. Martins."

"Dr. Martins?" Avery was puzzled he had not told her he was visiting. Was he checking up on her progress? She had to admit yesterday was the first time in awhile she had taken the time to write. Between spending her time netting, with Jake, or reading Minnie's diary, she hadn't been very communicative this summer.

"Yes, sorry for the short notice, is it possible for you to follow me back to Huntington? They're waiting for you."

"Can I stop and get my laptop?" Avery wanted to show Dr. Martins she had indeed been working. All of her data was on the laptop.

"Sure, I'll walk with you."

Avery started to protest, "It's ok, Tom, I can meet you there." *If Jake were still sleeping it would be awkward.*

But Tom insisted. "No worries, I want to see how the loft renovations came out anyway." And he stayed with her.

Avery's spirits were raised when she noticed Jake had not only left but made his bed beforehand, and then in turn sunk when she went to retrieve her laptop only to find that Minnie's diary was no longer under the couch where she had cast it in disgust the night before. *Did he find it?* She didn't have time to think about it because Tom was coming back down from the loft and hurrying her along.

"Of course there is a theoretical basis for your research?" One of the researchers from Paul Smith's asked Avery in between bites of macaroni and cheese in the dining hall at Huntington.

Avery loved the macaroni and cheese they served here but today she had no appetite. It took her a minute to decipher the meaning of his question. Dr. Martins rescued her. "He means Avery, what is your hypothesis?" He raised an eyebrow at her as if to say, come on, get with it!

"Umm, well you might say I'm trying to discover why males of the species are so hard to track."

"Meaning?" The man would not take that as an answer. Avery could see she had to offer her entire dissertation on the subject.

"Well, as you know from your own banding program, it is more common to find females in the nets during migration. I'm trying to discover if males are staying put in their nesting territory. There could be a myriad reasons they're able to survive the winters here in the North Country: body fat, food supplies, metabolism..." Avery went on to tell them her discoveries so far.

Dr. Martins was pleased and asked her to show them her makeshift banding station at the *Barque of the Pine*. It was almost dinner time when she left to head back to Camp Kirby. She found Jake sitting on the front porch reading Minnie's diary in the dim evening light.

He looked up as she approached the porch steps. "How long have you had this?" he asked her. Relief washed over her as she sat down next to him to confess how she discovered the diary.

EIGHTH LAKE
MARCH 1882

Nothing mattered to William now but seeing where Louise was laid to rest in the woods. He had had enough of New York City. Besides the humiliating meetings with Sutphen that had become more frequent lately, he also had to contend with the smug looks he received from those he had considered his friends at the social clubs since the announcement of the Adirondack Railroad Co. bankruptcy. He gladly packed his things, made excuses to Sutphen and others in the company that he had some business to attend to in the Adirondacks and left the city behind.

It took him ten days from the day he left New York City to reach the Lawrence compound on Eighth Lake. He took the train to North Creek, borrowed a family horse and sleigh and drove with Jem Stone to Pine Knot. He planned to stick around until spring, as long as he could before his father summoned him back to the City. He hoped their impending departure to Florida would keep his parents preoccupied and not fretting about his whereabouts.

He had lied to his parents, telling them he had word from Frederick someone had broken into the kitchen at Pine Knot and was stealing household items. Whether they believed a native would actually need crystal glassware or plan to hawk it, he didn't care. He needed to go to the woods.

After arriving at Pine Knot, he left Jem Stone behind while he traveled by sleigh over the ice to Eighth Lake and the Lawrence household. When he entered the cabin he had built for Louise and her sister he was confronted with the reality she was no longer alive.

Sarah, who looked so like her, was sitting in a rocking chair, nursing her baby Nathaniel. Her toddler, a girl, was tottering around at her feet playing with corn husk dolls Mémé had made.

William looked around for the old woman, she wasn't there. Neither was Ike or his father Isaac.

"Where is everyone?" he asked.

Sarah looked up from the baby's face to William and asked him to sit down.

"Ike is trapping with my father and the rest are napping. Can I get you some tea?" she asked him as she lifted the sleeping babe off her breast.

William shook his head.

"Louise? How did it happen?"

Sarah looked away, her eyes welled with tears. She remembered that day vividly. Mémé was worried when she didn't come back with the water and sent Ike to find her. He followed a bloody trail leading into the woods away from the creek. He discovered her body, ripped apart by the wild cat, and her shawl soaked in blood.

William looked around the cabin and when he saw the bed from the open doorway into the room he had shared briefly with Louise he was grief stricken to realize he would never again feel her warm body next to his. He watched Sarah prepare their tea.

"Anything you need, Sarah, anything, you must tell me and I will provide it for you and your family."

Sarah nodded. She already knew that. After he had drunk his tea she led him out to a clearing in the woods where they had buried Louise. Just a mound in the woods William thought, nothing but a dirt mound with a small wooden cross to mark the grave. Ironic, his love was buried under a small pile of dirt in the Adirondack forest while his own father, bankrupt as he was, had just commissioned a Durant mausoleum in a Brooklyn cemetery. He had to look away. The mound was a cruel reminder to him of what he had lost with Louise.

William ignored the nagging voice in the back of his head telling him he should return to New York City. He was paralyzed by grief. And the hum of activity in the Lawrence household, the way Sarah and Emaline managed the children, the daily chores, reminded him of Louise and he wanted to let the feeling linger. He stayed in the second bedroom of the cabin while Sarah went about her tasks, which were endless with a baby, toddler and an extended family to feed. Emaline was often in the cabin as well, assisting with the children and chores.

During the night he would hear Sarah cooing softly in the next room when her son Nate woke up hungry. Once he knew the babe was not stressed he let her soft voice lull him back to sleep.

One morning after rising from bed to the sound of the children, William put on some clothes to go outside and use the outhouse. It was a clear crisp morning. On his way back from the outhouse to the cabin he stopped to admire his surroundings. The sun was climbing over the tops of the evergreens, casting a warm glow on the hoar frost that was clinging to the needles of the trees like petite crystal pendeloques dangling from a chandelier.

A doe came bounding out of the row of spruce, stopped and looked straight at him. He reached behind for the rifle he had strapped to his back. He brought it to his front, took aim and pulled the trigger. He could hear the echo of the shot ricochet against the mountainsides.

For a brief moment the doe's startled eyes bore into his before her legs buckled, and she crumbled to the ground. A dark pool of blood was forming in the snow as William walked up to her. Her eyes were still wide open. He knelt beside the animal and a flood of remorse struck him. Like this doe that had just lost its life, he had lost something he would never get back.

While William stayed on at the Lawrence household Ike and Isaac took the opportunity to teach him about trapping. William especially loved this time. He learned a lot from both men about the habits of the woodland creatures they trapped.

They would strap on snowshoes and enter the deep woods. Ike would spend the morning checking his traps, or setting them up. Either way it was a long day of hiking. William found it invigorating. The city life was a distant memory for him. One day they went out to set up marten traps. The marten, a member of the weasel family had a yellowish brown coat that was in demand. Ike brought along some dried fish. He showed William how to look for the marten tracks in the snow, small footprints, and the back paw a little larger than the front. "Otherwise they're not easily found," Ike said. "They hunt at night. Look." He pointed to tracks in the snow that appeared like canines, a slight claw print above each toe.

When they came across an area with tracks, Ike looked for rotting trees with caverns or caves and proceeded to set up a small teepee of branches. In the center of that he laid down the bait, and then placed the steel-jawed trap over it. He covered the tee-pee with boughs of pine.

"He'll go after the fish and when he enters the trap it will clamp down on his head," Ike said.

Ike's trapping business was doing quite well. One night over dinner he had explained to William how he had brought a sled full of mink, marten, and otter with him to the Prospect House and he received $750 for the pelts from a local trader. William knew Ike could make even more if he delivered them to a New York furrier himself. And he could easily convert one of the smaller cabins at Pine Knot into a trapper's cabin for Ike to store his pelts and equipment.

"I'll collect your next batch of pelts and get you a better price for them." They made a deal. Ike could set up operations at Pine Knot and William would get them to market in New York City, removing any middlemen. "By Spring I should have twice the number of skins," Ike said.

William might have stayed on longer but one night Jeff arrived home unexpectedly from the lumber camp. That night, William could hear the bedposts softly banging against the wall in the bedroom Jeff and Sarah shared with the baby. He had lingered long enough. It was time to move on.

With assurances of visiting as long as the weather permitted, he left the Lawrence family waving from the door of the cabin with little Nathaniel strapped to a papoose on Sarah's back.

His mind was on trapping when he wondered how Alvah was faring. On his way back to Pine Knot he decided to stop at Alvah's cabin to see. He pulled up to the little cabin set back off a logging trail in the woods and was alarmed to find there was no smoke coming out of the chimney. Even if Alvah had gone off to hunt he would have kept coals burning. William got out of the sleigh and walked with trepidation to the front door.

"Alvah?" he called as he knocked.

There was no answer from inside. William walked around to look through the windows. He could see someone lying on the small bed. It had to be Alvah. He knocked as hard as he could on the glass without breaking it. An old man turned over in bed. It looked like Alvah, but it was hard to be sure through the thick glass.

"Alvah! It's William Durant. Open the door."

Alvah slowly crawled out of his bed and tottered to the door. He threw it open and staggered backwards at the force of the cold air.

"Whatdoya want from me?" he hollered. He looked ghastly. He was wrapped in a bearskin, yet visibly shivering. William entered the cabin. The air inside was so cold, he could see his breath. Coals were glowing in the hearth but there was no wood left to burn.

"I planned to get out today to chop some," Alvah said to him when he saw him looking at the empty hearth. "I aint lazy ya know, just durned tired is all. I can't hardly move." Alvah started coughing and sank back down on his bed. William walked about the cabin looking for wood to light the stove and make some tea. He found however that the cupboards were bare.

"How long have you been sick?" William asked the wheezing wreck of a man sitting down on the bed. This was not the stalwart Alvah he knew so well.

Alvah flopped back down in his bed and refused to answer, grumbling something about being left alone and for William to mind his own business.

It took all of the cajoling William could muster to heave Alvah out of his bed, out of the cabin, and into the sleigh. When they arrived at Pine Knot Jem Stone greeted them and helped Alvah down.

"He's burning up with a fever. You take care of the horse and I'll get him to my cabin," William instructed Stone.

William gently guided Alvah into his cabin where there was a fire burning and a bed made. "You're staying here until you feel better Alvah. You could have died out there in that cabin of yours. There are disadvantages to being a hermit you know," William chided as he went to the fireplace to boil water for tea. Luckily, Mémé had given him a few tinctures, including a dark broth made with balsam pitch.

"Good for coughs," she said.

For two weeks Alvah stayed on at Pine Knot, falling in and out of fitful sleeping bouts while William and Stone stayed in Dr. Durant's cabin. Everyday William would come to make sure he drank some tea or broth. And everyday Alvah complained that he was being kidnapped.

But he never asked to return to his cabin until one day William came in from hunting rabbit and saw Alvah, fully dressed, looking more flush than he had in two weeks. "I want to go home now."

It was the last chance to go before the ice broke up on the lake. William insisted they take Alvah back, not allowing him to walk in snowshoes.

"I just spent two weeks holed up in your durned cabin escaping death's door, why'd I want to take a risk of fallin' through the ice on that fancy cutter?" Alvah said when William told him of the plans.

William was losing patience with the man. "I'm going that way to collect a load of furs from Ike. I just took this route last week. I have it all mapped out in my head where the ice was thinning. Trust me. Let's move on before it gets too late to reach the Lawrence place."

They got a late start due to Alvah's grumbling. Jem Stone drove reluctantly. He knew Alvah was right about the risk, even the horse appeared hesitant. The past few days the lake had been popping and pinging as it expanded and contracted between warm days and cold nights.

"Mr. Durant." Stone stopped the horse when they reached a juncture where he could see a small fissure in the ice ahead. "Maybe we should go through the woods?"

"Not yet, it will take us all day to reach Alvah's cabin. Look over there," William pointed toward the shoreline, "there's a small spring outlet — watch for the current under the ice. That's where it will be weak.

"Steer the horse to where the ice is black," Alvah hollered from his seat in the back of the sled.

Stone drove the cutter in a meandering route, avoiding mottled- looking ice. Although it was only a seven mile trip it was slow going, and before long dusk started to set in, making it harder to see clearly. *Was that black ice ahead of him or the shadow of a tree?* He was fatigued by the effort of concentrating and a small nagging ache started to work its way from the back of his head toward his temples. His eyes started to throb.

He was in a daze when he heard it, a sickening, creaking sound, and then a CRACK!

The back end of the cutter's rails caved through the ice. The horse heaved in a panic at the sound. The men jumped from their seats.

"Bloody hell! We have to undo the harness or he'll drown with the sleigh!" William shouted, frantically trying to cut the harness loose from the desperate animal.

Stone's head was pounding. His eyes, blinded by the glare of the afternoon sun all day, were blurry, and he was unsure what was happening. He had no idea where the shore was, he couldn't see it, so he staggered away from all the noise.

Alvah took hold of William's coat sleeve and started to pull him from the edge of the cracking ice as he tried in vain to undo the harness from the horse. William fought him off, screaming, "Let me go, I have to save the horse!" He struggled to free himself and they fell down hard.

"Damn it, William!" Alvah cursed, picked himself up, took hold of William's sleeve once more, and scuttled along the ice, dragging William along with him. He managed to get him to a safe distance from the gaping hole before they both slipped and landed on the ice next to Jem Stone.

William watched, helpless and horrified, as the hole doubled in size.

The water, black as night, churned, engulfing the rails, then the carriage. The horse, still tethered, kept kicking at the lip of the ice, attempting to get out of the hole and back on top of it. He put all of his strength into counteracting the weight of the sled, but his efforts were fruitless. The sled sank deeper, dragging the horse with it until both were consumed by the watery grave.

The last thing the men saw was the look of terror in the pupils of the horse's eyes.

Alvah stood up and spat on the ice. "That's a damned waste of a good animal," he said.

William turned over on his side and vomited.

NORTH CREEK
SUMMER 1883

"What are you doing here?"

Ella lifted her skirts off the porch floor, brushed past Margaret and waved at Jem Stone to bring her trunk into the parlor. "Good to see you as well Margaret. I've missed your prudish pout. Where's my mother?"

"Ella, oh dear Ella. Your father is so sick!" Hannah Durant came tumbling down the stairs at the sound of her daughter's voice. "Please, we mustn't cause a stir today. Margaret, go fetch Ella some tea will you dear?"

Margaret was indignant. "Humph," she said as she walked away from the reunion of mother and daughter.

If he had all of his wits about him Dr. Durant would be rebuking his prodigal daughter, as she stood there at the door, calling her all kinds of nasty names. Margaret was sure of it. More than once Margaret had overheard Dr. Durant tell Hannah he thought Ella had become a harlot, one of the theater girls, a disgrace.

Although Margaret and Hannah were getting on in age—both in their mid-fifties, and the care of Dr. Durant was taking its toll, asking Ella to help was not a good idea. But it didn't matter what she thought. Hannah always had a soft spot for that spoiled brat of a girl, now disgraced woman, Ella Durant.

She knew that it was only out of desperation that Hannah had summoned Ella from New York City.

For the past three days, since he had taken ill with pleurisy, they had been spending day and night attending to Dr. Durant's needs, trying to take the pain away with the medicine the doctor had left, and keeping him comfortable when he went into sweats. Even the butler was asked to assist.

It was no use as far as Margaret could tell. He was going to die. She was sure of it. It was just a matter of when. She wished William would get here to straighten out matters and take things into his own hands. It was time for Dr. Durant to cede control to William.

Dr. Durant was racked by a coughing fit when William entered his room. Ella was calmly helping him out of a nightshirt that was soaked in sweat. William was taken aback by his father's appearance. He looked gray. The man who had driven his laborers on the transcontinental line to mutiny because of his harsh tactics and relentless drive, was no longer present. His father was as vulnerable to death as the rest of humanity.

William stood at the door and watched Ella comfort their father. She gave him a spoonful of liquid medicine and his cough started to subside. She gently made him lie back on the pillows, and then sat next to him to wait until he fell asleep. William waited by the doorway, not wanting to disturb the scene. Ella had changed as well. Her composure was more mature. Was it because of her recent experience with the Sisters? He wasn't sure what Ella had been doing this past year. His mother never revealed anything to him, and he never asked.

Ella gathered the spoon off the bedside table and strode over toward William, motioning him to follow her out the door.

"He'll sleep now for awhile. The medicine the doctor left him is very strong," she said in the hallway.

William could hear the grandfather clock ticking in the entranceway at the foot of the staircase, the sound filling the space between them. He was reluctant to speak to Ella, believing deep down that this short burst of compassion for their father wouldn't last. How much, he wondered, was this an act of contrition she had learned from her time spent at the convent? And how much was a façade she was putting on for her mother to see, ensuring she wouldn't be left out when their father's will was made known and all the land holdings in the Adirondacks were at their disposal?

He finally broke his silence. "Estelle told me that Putnam has agreed to publish your book of poetry." It was the only thing he could think to say that would not end up in an argument.

"Yes."

"Very good."

"Thank you."

"Is he dying?"

"Yes. But he's fighting it."

"It's just like him to do so."

"Yes, it is." Ella looked back at the door to their father's room. A look of disgust fell over her.

She turned to William. "I'm here because of mother."

William smiled momentarily. So he was right about her act of contrition. "Of course, why else?"

"He treated me very poorly the last time I saw him. I will never forgive him. And I intend to take control of my own life once he is no longer with us." She said this with such venom it took William by surprise.

He did not want to start a fight with her in front of their father's bedroom door and he knew Ella enough to know that she would try to drag him into one.

"I'd better go speak with mother now." William left his sister and headed down the hall toward his mother's bedroom.

He didn't tell Ella that the family lawyer, John Barbour was on his way. William had telegraphed him from New York City. He needed to find out if father had a will.

"Ella is attending him. He's sleeping soundly," William said once he entered Hannah's bedchamber and sat down.

"Tell me, Mother, where has Ella been staying when she is not at the convent assisting the Sisters?"

"She stays with the Dix's. She seems to get about fairly easily for herself now. She does look happy, I must admit."

"I see," William said. He wondered what she would do once their father died and she no longer had to repent behind the convent walls.

He looked at his mother sitting at her vanity table, attending to her hair.

"I've asked John Barbour to come," he said finally.

Hannah looked up from her brushing. "Heavens, what for?"

"Mother, we need to find out what father's intentions are. He has obviously been planning for this, this situation." He tried to stay delicate with her. "He has commissioned a mausoleum at the Green Wood cemetery in Brooklyn, and—"

"You think I don't know? We planned that after we sold the property for Prospect Park. We both decided to rest where we had first lived."

"The most practical thing is to find out what else he has planned for when he dies." There, he'd said it.

There was a knock on the door.

"Come in," Hannah called.

The butler opened it to announce that Mr. Barbour had arrived. William looked over at his mother. Her brows were knit together in concern.

William met Barbour in the hallway entrance. "John, thank you for meeting us at such late notice but my father is very ill."

"I know all about it, William. I received word from Sutphen."

William wondered how Sutphen knew; he certainly hadn't told him anything.

"William." Barbour pulled him aside toward the door to his father's library. "We need to talk. Before your mother comes down."

The men went into the library.

"Can I get you a drink?" William said as he poured himself a glass of whiskey.

"Yes, that would be wonderful." Barbour settled himself into one of the comfortable chairs that faced the garden. "I have drawn up some papers that I think you should read. One is assigning the deed to this house in your mother's name, the other is a document that was forced on me quite frankly. Some of the stockholders in the Adirondack Railroad Company want your father to sign over his shares. Sutphen sent me these papers weeks ago. I just haven't found a good moment to show them to your father."

Interesting, William mused, that Barbour chose the most opportune time, when his father was at his weakest, to present him these papers. As for signing the deed to the North Creek house over to his mother, he wondered why that was necessary.

"Why does my mother need to be brought into my father's messy business affairs all of the time?"

"Signing over the deed to her protects her and the rest of the family, William, it will save the house from creditors."

William realized Barbour was right. The last thing he wanted was to see his mother cast out of her own house. "My father is resting now John. We'll have our dinner and see how he's feeling tomorrow. I assume you brought luggage so that you could stay the night?"

Barbour nodded.

"Fine then. Let's not say anything about these documents to my mother just yet."

"But she has to sign this. You know as well as I do, William, that your father is obstinate to the point of being irrational." Barbour started to lift legal papers from his satchel just as Hannah entered the room.

"Good evening John." She met him as he stood to greet her. They embraced. "William," she turned to her son, "I've sent word to your Uncle Charles."

The men looked at her solemnly. So she finally accepted this was going to be the end.

However, it wasn't. Two days went by and then one bright sunny morning Dr. Durant woke and asked for his breakfast in bed. By then the house had been deeded over to Hannah, but there was still the matter of the stocks. Barbour decided to bring him the documents and explained his reasoning for changing the title to the house.

"We put it in Hannah's name, Thomas," he said. "It was a precautionary measure. In case you, well, let's face it, we don't want Hannah to lose the house when you're gone." He felt he need not explain any further. His client would know that the creditors were waiting for any assets they could take from Thomas Durant. "And then there is this." Barbour put the papers from Sutphen on his lap.

Dr. Durant picked them up and examined the contents.

William had never seen his father look so angry.

"I think I've heard enough John, leave me with William," Dr. Durant said. He was seething when John Barbour left them to speak privately.

"Why the hell did you put the house in your mother's name? And what's the meaning of this document." He waved it in William's face.

William looked down at his father by the side of the bed. How could this man, who was almost dead, suddenly become so enraged?

"Why don't you ask Sutphen about that document? It was his doing, John was only a messenger."

"To hell with Sutphen, they're paying him off to do their bidding. He goes to the highest taker. If you haven't figured that out yet you're more of an idiot that I thought."

William was stunned. He knew the man was sick but his father had never insulted him this way. Is this what his father truly thought of him? Would he ever then, be in charge of the Adirondack Railroad Company as his title implied? He took the document from his father's hand and stood up to leave.

"Where are you going son? Stay here. We need to talk about a few things."

William kept walking. He opened the door to the bedroom and there in the hall stood Ella's friend Fran Murphy. William had forgotten Ella called on her to help out. She had a tray of coffee.

"Oh William," she said, embarrassed for him, as she had heard the whole exchange while she waited by the door to enter, "I'm sorry, you startled me."

William looked down at Fran in a daze, his mind reeling. *No doubt Ella will hear what their father had said to him as soon as Fran had the chance to tell her.*

He felt faint. He knew his father was calling to him, telling him to stay, but he needed to get out of the stifling room. He swung the door open wider for Fran to enter and said nothing as he shut the door firmly behind him. He took a deep breath before walking to his room to collect his luggage.

CAMP KIRBY
AUGUST 2010

"I can't understand why you kept it from me all this time," Jake said.

Avery plopped down in the seat next to him on the porch. "I know, I'm not sure either. Don't be cross with me, Jake. At first I just wanted to keep the diary to myself. But then after I saw how excited your mother was about finding that book in the loft, I thought I'd better tell you. And then every time I started to say something, we were interrupted. I began to feel that destiny didn't want me to reveal the secret. After awhile, I knew you would be sore because I hadn't said anything. So it was a vicious circle for me — one part of me felt guilty and the other part felt that maybe Minnie's diary was meant to stay hidden."

Jake sat thinking. After a moment he said, "Have you finished it?"

"The diary? No."

"Well, you might want to, and then decide what to do with it. I'll be back tomorrow and we'll talk more about it." He put the book down on the table between them and walked off the porch to the trail leading to Camp Huntington. Avery picked up the diary where she had left off.

August 15, 1893

I am desperate. I can't stand it any longer here. My father will be expecting me back to school in a few weeks. I need to know from William what he expects from me. He has not come to see me in days. So I sent Nate to Pine Knot to deliver a note. I told him to meet me.

He finally came last night and looked so very, very tired. He said his sister had served him notice she was planning to sue. I'm not sure why. But I had enough of his troubles. I told him how I am feeling. As much as I love Nate, why does he have me secreted away in this cabin with the boy? Is he ashamed of me? Couldn't we admit our love for each other? After all he is planning to divorce Janet, isn't he?

That is when he confessed a very dark secret, one that only a few families in the area know and no one would ever reveal. He was once in love with Nate's aunt. She died and he has never gotten over her. He used to stay with her here, in this cabin. That's why he feels such an obligation to Nate and his family.

I asked him, will you ever tell Nate the truth. He shook his head, sadly. He said no. He couldn't. Only Ike knows the truth.

Minnie

August 20, 1893

A terrible thing has happened to me, to William, and it has all come to an end. I woke this morning in the early hours, before the sun had even risen in the sky, to find William asleep, next to me in bed. His breath smelled of smoke and liquor, he had been up all night playing cards with his gentlemen guests.

"William," I cried, "What are you doing here?'

He didn't talk, he reached for me and I was so terribly frightened. I have never seen that look before, his eyes were dark, distant, he was not my William but some stranger. "What are you doing here!" I cried again.

But I was fooling myself, we have been fooling ourselves all summer. Why did I think this was not how it would end? And then, I heard Nate, he must have heard my cries.

"Get out of here sir," he said. Suddenly, it was as if William woke up out of a bad dream. He looked confused, he looked crestfallen. "Oh, my Louise!" he cried as he leapt off the bed and stood helpless in the middle of the room. I climbed out of the bed as fast as I could and ran out the door and into the woods. The sun was just rising and I found the tree that Nate and I visit to look for the saw-whet owl.

And I sat there in shock, as I am still in shock, until Nate came for me. He put his small hand out for mine and said, "It's ok now, you can come back, he's gone."

Oh, I know as I write this I should be so glad that William is gone, but alas, I am not. Nate is loading the boat with my things and he is going to take me to town so I can catch the train home. I have to go home now. My magical summer with William is over. It was all just a game, a dream that was never to be.

I do not know what to do with this diary. I cannot burn it because there is no fire and no time to make one. I am going to hide it in canvas and put it in the cavity of the tree. There, I hope, it will rot away into the ground, to be forgotten, just as I hope I will forget my love for William.

Minnie

Avery slammed the little book shut. It had been an exhausting two days and this last revelation put her over the edge. She needed a drink. She scrounged around the kitchen and found a beer in the refrigerator, took it to the front porch and listened to the sounds of the birds calling to each other before bedding down for the night.

The next morning Jake showed up early. Avery heard him in the kitchen banging around in the cupboards for the coffee and then the friendly sound of the percolator. He brought in a hot mug of coffee and she sat up in bed to drink it.

"What should we do with it?" she asked as she blew over her coffee to cool it down.

"Bury it," Jake said.

Avery's eyes flickered surprise. "You want to hide it from your mother? What about the rest of the people at the College that have been searching for the truth about Minnie?"

"Some things are best left unknown," Jake said.

She got dressed and followed Jake to the White pine. Once there he got down on his hands and knees and dug out some of the earth that was at the base of the rotting trunk, put Minnie's diary, wrapped in canvas, in the earthen hole and covered it. They held hands as they walked back to Camp Kirby.

EPILOGUE

December 1883

He waited patiently for his mother to tell him why she asked to meet at Prospect Park in Brooklyn. He wondered if his father's health was failing again.

They were in a tea house at the park. It was very festive. The centerpiece on their table was decorated with holly and evergreen boughs and small glass ornaments. The place was full of tourists visiting New York City to conduct their shopping for the holidays. A waiter came up and left them with their order. William took up his coffee and a biscuit.

Hannah let him know her intentions as soon as her tea was poured in the cup. "I called you away from business to talk about your marriage prospects."

William gagged on his coffee.

Hannah raised her hand in the air to stop him from unleashing any protestations. "Hear me out," she said.

"You've been carousing around New York City with Miss Stewart long enough. You may not realize that her father is going to pay for a peerage and ship her off to England to become a Baroness."

"How convenient for him," William said.

"Pfft," Hannah replied.

William snapped his head up at that sound, it reminded him so of Ella.

"Considering that you spend most of your time in North Creek I'm surprised you are able to keep up with New York City social affairs," he said.

"Oh I keep my ears open to the tea parlor gossip. One visit with my friends here and I learn all the news that will be splashed across the pages of the society section of the *New York Times* the following Sunday." Hannah took a biscuit from the tray. "Gossip is a public sport here in America."

"You're being a bit judgmental aren't you, Mother? I recall you imbibed the tea parlor gossip in London as well."

"That may be, but at least in London we had good sense to keep it amongst ourselves."

William chuckled at his mother's hypocrisy.

A smile crossed Hannah's face. "It's so good to see you merry again. You've been brooding too long over the death of that Lawrence girl."

William frowned. "I'd rather not discuss it, Mother."

She patted his hand. "As I was saying, I'd like to see the Durant name in a headline story that contains good news for once. That is why I've suggested to your father, and he agrees, that Janet Stott would make a suitable match for you."

William set down his coffee cup. He wasn't surprised by the suggestion as much as he thought he should be. His mother was smart, and unlike his father, practical. However. "Isn't she a bit young?"

"Hardly, she's eighteen. Just the right age to marry before she becomes, well, like Ella, and too old to marry."

"Janet's a lovely girl but I think I can find my own match for marriage. Thank you anyway," William said. He thought about Janet Stott, Jennie they called her. Although they were family friends with the Stotts, he never had occasion to visit with Jennie, until last summer when he stopped by their family camp on Bluff Point at Raquette Lake.

He had been standing on the front porch speaking with Francis Stott, inquiring about construction progress of the Episcopal church on St. Hubert's Isle on Raquette when he heard the sounds of laughing and looked out at the lake to see a boat full of young girls screaming and splashing each other, trying to tip the boat over. After a lot of tumbling about, they succeeded, and the exertions sent them into hysterics.

How innocent it all seemed, and charming.

"Your father has already written Francis Stott, and I have offered $3,000 for Jennie's trousseau."

"Is that necessary? It sounds like a bribe. And where are *you* getting the money?" William said.

"Don't worry about where the money is coming from. You forget that I once owned all of this." She gestured with her hands to encompass the land her father once owned and that Dr. Durant had sold to the City for $200,000. "And I too hold meetings in Sutphen's office." She raised her brows at William.

William recalled the blank certificates he had signed over the past two years since becoming President. How many, he now wondered, were in his mother's name?

Hannah continued to press her point. "The Stotts are a respectable family, and their business connections have always been helpful to your father. You should be thankful Jennie will have you. You have quite the reputation with the ladies I understand, and the Durant family name is not exactly nectar to the bees these days," Hannah said.

"And you forget, I've been through this before with my own father. When he went bankrupt in England it broke my mother's heart. I cannot stand the idea of being tarnished by bankruptcy again."

"But that's one reason father put the company in my name and put me in charge. You need to have more confidence in me." William tried to reassure his mother although he himself was not convinced by his words.

"The steamboat line is profiting handsomely. And I have word from the Hewitt Company that the iron ore sample I sent is good quality," he added with optimism.

"Is it enough though?" Hannah said. "And as much as I have confidence in you, son, I also know your father better than anyone. You'll never really be fully in charge of the Adirondack Company and all of the land holdings as long as he is dangling William Sutphen from strings like a puppeteer."

William knew she was right.

"It's settled then?" he said.

"Yes," Hannah said as she set down her teacup. She and William sat quietly looking at the people idly strolling by. How many of them the mother and son wondered, were as worried about the future, and their station in it, as they were?

AUTHOR'S NOTE

In 1948 two professors from the State University of New York College at Cortland were canoeing along Raquette Lake looking for a site for an outdoor education center when they came upon Pine Knot/Camp Huntington. After inquiring about the site with the locals, they discovered that it was owned by the Huntington family, descendants of the railroad tycoon Collis P. Huntington. They also found out that the family had not visited or used the camp since he died there in 1900. The Huntingtons gifted the land and camp to Cortland College and it has been under their care ever since.

I was first introduced to the architecture of William West Durant while taking part in a field experience at Huntington. But it was years later while staying at Camp Kirby with other fellow Alum of Cortland College that I became intrigued with the story about Minnie. After finding her obituary (with the help of a librarian) I was hooked. The staff at Huntington also provided me with some research files that were put together by sorority sisters that visit Huntington every year. So began my research journey which is chronicled on my website: http://www.wwdurantstory.com

This is a work of fiction. Although I have tried to stay true to the timeline of events, I invented many elements of the story.

Many of the characters are historical figures that were servants, friends or family of the Durants. These include in order of appearance: Margaret Molineaux, the Napier brothers, Charles Locock, Charles Arkwright, Charlie Bennett, Alvah Dunning, Jerome Wood; Howard, Frederick, Charles, Elizabeth and Estelle Durant; Francis, Elizabeth and Janet Stott, W. H. Murray, Poultney Bigelow, Anna Leonowens, Fran Murphy, the Dix Family members, Cornelia Kirby, William Sutphen and John Barbour.

Minnie Kirby is also a true historical figure, although the evidence of her affair with William consists of a silver candy tray with her calling card left behind at Camp Kirby. Camp Kirby was never listed on the inventory of Camp Huntington when the college acquired the property. I conjecture it was a hunting cabin built by Charlie Bennett as he once claimed the land on Long Point and did some land swapping with Dr. Durant.

Although I wrote the letters of correspondence between Ella and Poultney the tone of them convey feelings that were portrayed in original letters I poured over in the libraries and museums I visited. They maintained a friendship well into their 80s.

The story of Nala – as written in Sanskrit and left behind by Anna Leonowens at Pine Knot – is real. The Adirondack Museum has the original which is found in the Pine Knot guest book and dated 1878. It was transcribed in 1968 by Professor Clifford Wright from the School of Oriental Studies, University of London.

William's love affairs are all fictional. His eventual marriage to Janet Stott is not. The Lawrence family is fictional. However, I base their presence as inhabitants of the Adirondacks on fact. One of my sources, a book written by George Washington Sears (1880), chronicles traveling and hunting with a Mohawk chief, William Bero of the St. Regis Tribe. He describes the Chief's wife with a child strapped to a papoose on her back. And one of the more famous guides in the region from that time, Mitchell Sabbattis was an Abenaki.

The source of William's preservative – betulin – is also fictional, although I found evidence of its use as a coating compound that was patented in 1912 by a Swedish inventor.

The Swiss cottage music box mentioned in the story did exist. One of Durant's biographies mentions he used the music box as a model for building a cottage on Eagle Lake. There is a picture of the music box in one of the old photos taken by Ray Stoddard at Camp Sagamore in 1899.

I found no evidence that William Durant visited Switzerland. He did however spend time in Dorf Gastein (Bavaria). He also spent a considerable amount of time on the Isle of Wight, England. Queen Victoria's husband, Prince Albert, had a Swiss Cottage built on the grounds of their summer home at Osborne House on the Isle of Wight in 1856 as a playhouse for their children. There are various theories as to why, some say it reminded him of the architecture in his native Bavaria, and there is also a reference that Queen Victoria's half-sister Princess Feodore had constructed a similar cottage for her children in Baden-Baden. According to my sources, the Swiss chalet style was in vogue in Germany, France and Britain in the early nineteenth century. William could have easily seen this style in any of his travels.

Poetry featured in the story is from *Pine Needles or Sonnets and Songs* by Heloise (Ella) Durant (1885).

Quotes mentioned in Minnie's diary are taken directly from the book *Adventures in the Wilderness* by W.H. Murray.

Tenting in the Old Camp Ground was written by Walter Kittredge in 1863.

ACKNOWLEDGEMENTS

Numerous archivists and library staff assisted me with my research. These include the staff at Cayuga Community College , Onondaga County Library, United States Library of Congress, Bird Library at Syracuse University, Adirondack Museum, and the New York Public Library.

I accessed the following manuscripts for my research:

Heloise Durant Rose Letters, Special Collections Research Center, Syracuse University Libraries.

Poultney Bigelow papers. Manuscripts and Archives Division. The New York Public Library. Astor, Lenox, and Tilden Foundations.

William West Durant Papers: Adirondack Museum.

William West Durant correspondence. Library of Congress.

Other sources for my research can be found on my website: http://www.wwdurantstory.com/

I would also like to thank Harvey Kaiser for his consultation on the history of Adirondack architecture; Craig Gilborn for his insight on the biography of William West Durant; Jerry Pepper at the Adirondack Museum; Scott Weidensaul from Audubon for his knowledge about saw-whet owls; Alex Beldon, who has assisted me throughout my research and writing journey; Jeni Chapelle for her editing assistance, Brendan Cox Design Studio for the cover art and promotional material and Martha Clement Rochford from Highland Words for promoting the book.

Finally, I need to thank my family and friends for their encouragement.

'15 melissa johnson

Made in the USA
Middletown, DE
21 June 2015